HEAVEN SENT

A CHRISTMAS ROMANCE

SHERRI SCHOENBORN MURRAY

CHRISTIAN ROMANCES

SHERRI'S CHRISTIAN ROMANCES:

Christian Romances
Fried Chicken and Gravy
Sticky Notes
The Sticky Buns Challenge
A Wife and a River
Heaven Sent – A Christmas Romance

Counterfeit Princess Series
For ages 10 to 100
The Piano Girl
The Viola Girl

All of Sherri's books
are available in audio
on Audible.com

INTRODUCTION

For those of you who've read *A Wife and a River*, you may recognize Wilhoit and a handful of characters. I was hesitant to label this a sequel as there is no fishing in this particular love story, so I kept it as a standalone.

This is a work of fiction. All characters, places and incidents are used fictitiously. Any resemblance to actual persons, either living or dead is completely coincidental.

Heaven Sent – A Christmas Romance
Christian Romances
Copyright © 2017 All rights reserved.
Cover photo by Clari Noel Photography
Cover art by Steve Novak Illustrations
Printed in the U.S.A.

*To my dear friend,
Annette Bartausky,
whose friendship
and encouragement
has been such
a blessing to me.*

* * *

*The Christmas Chapter
Luke 2:1-20*

CHAPTER 1

Willamette Valley, Oregon, 1965

While they drove north on Wilhoit Road in her sister's Model A Ford pickup, Isabelle pulled her aunt's gift out of her coat pocket. *Autographs* was scored across the avocado green cover; a darker green ribbon bound the side.

"What's that?" Mae glanced over at her.

"Aunt Elsie got me an autograph book and had everybody sign it." Her pulse picked up a little as she turned to the first page.

Isabelle,

I hope this little book captures a lot of memories for you of your trip. Remember us at Wilhoit and those that love you best.

Aunt Elsie

Was Albert's next? Did she even want to know what he'd written? He'd been so moody as of late. He'd left this morning without saying much of a goodbye—like it was just a regular old day.

Isabelle,
You're going to miss me and my cooking.
Don't you fret none.
We're going to miss you, too.
Fletcher.

She wasn't fretting. Didn't they know? She was on pins and needles; she was so excited. Then, she turned to Al's loopy handwriting, and, for a second, her heart forgot to beat.

Izz,

Sure hope you enjoy the Christmas choir. It's going to be mighty quiet around here without you. It ain't gonna be as pretty sounding either.

—Albert

That was all? She was going to be gone for five weeks, and that's all he'd written? Closing the book, she stared at the dash. That couldn't be all. She read it through a second time looking for hidden meanings.

There was nothing to read into. All those years of wondering how he truly felt about her and now she knew. Not all that much.

"What'd Al write?" Mae asked.

"Nothing much." She stared at the Douglas fir trees lining her side of the road. What was the good of getting a fellow's autograph if he was going to write something so utterly unromantic? She should just throw the little book out the window now before it ruined her trip.

Mae shifted into a lower gear, giggling for some reason. "Looks like he has something to tell you in person."

"What are you talking about?" Isabelle followed her sister's gaze to Albert's black Ford truck parked sideways in the middle of the two-lane country road.

She sucked in her cheeks, curbing a smile. He might not

have said much on paper, but he'd come back on his lunch hour to tell her goodbye.

Mae brought the old Ford to a jerky stop.

Thirty feet away, Al was just sitting in his truck. Fortunately, the old dead-end road leading to the resort didn't get much traffic this time of year.

"What's he thinking?" Isabelle leaned toward the dash.

"I don't know."

Albert's door swung open, and he got out—all six-feet and four-inches of him.

"Prepare your heart, Izz."

Her stomach dropped. "Do you know something I don't?"

"No. But, he parked across the road, didn't he?"

Arms tingling, she lowered one high heel to the paved road and then the other before closing the old truck door behind her.

In his dark blue coveralls with his name embroidered below the square *Molalla Ford* logo, Al stood waiting halfway between the two vehicles. He riffled a hand through his dark hair. He was better looking than Clark Gable and James Dean, with John Wayne charisma.

She wasn't exaggerating.

"Hey, Al." She halted a few feet away. "Kind of makes it feel all serious, you parked across the road like that." Her gaze traveled from his truck to his darkly lashed blue eyes. They'd grown up together out at Wilhoit Mineral Springs Resort. And, even though they'd been sort-of-sweethearts off and on through the years, things had never gotten all that serious between them. Maybe on account of Uncle Donald's lectures.

Kissing is reserved for courtship. And, courtship is reserved for marriage.

Up close, he was pale-faced and wide eyed—nervous looking for Al.

His silence made her uneasy, chatty. "What do you think?" In her three-inch high heels, she turned to show him the tailored lines of her new tweed coat. "Ruby helped me pick it out." Al's sister-in-law had an eye for fashion. "It even has silk pockets." It was by far the nicest coat she'd ever owned.

"Sure fits ya." The corner of his mouth twitched.

"What kind of compliment is that?"

Albert bent one knee to the paved road and his somber gaze locked on hers.

"What are you doing?" The knot in her gut cinched tighter before she lifted her gaze to the road behind him. Twenty-some miles away in Silverton, there'd be restaurants, a theatre, and maybe even viewpoints where she'd be able to watch the sunset. The anticipation of performing with an all girls Christmas choir made it difficult for her to tell, but the glassy sheen in Albert's eyes almost looked like misery.

Was he in love with her? All these years of living out at Wilhoit together—is that what he was saying? Or not saying?

"I'll be home in ten days—for Thanksgiving."

He shrugged like things could change.

"What are you doing, Al?" It was pretty hard to propose if he didn't even open his mouth.

"Stay." His chest expanded as his lungs filled with air.

"Sta-ay?" Did he mean *no Silverton*?

He nodded. "Stay," he repeated the one-word command like he was talking to his hunting dog, Max.

"I'm only going to be gone for five weeks." She'd already spoken with her host family—the Coopers—on the phone; not to mention Mr. Hoffmeister, the choir director. And, besides, she'd never been anywhere all by herself.

Al had always had dreams—his shiny black Ford truck being one of them. And, she finally had a dream of her own, and she was going to follow it.

Al peered up at her, now, his gaze steady—his old confidence returning.

Had he even said *hello*?

If it was a ring in his pocket, he'd forgotten to take it out.

"Don't go." His Adam's apple bobbed.

"Don't go?" No Christmas choir. That is what he was saying.

She slid her hands inside the silk-lined pockets of her coat. If she wasn't careful, she'd wake up one morning with five kids, piles of laundry, and a voice that might have made it on the Lawrence Welk Show.

"I'm going. I haven't *ever* been anywhere." Not that she was going far. Silverton was only twenty miles away. But this was her chance.

She glanced back at her ride. Mae sat wide-eyed in the cab of her truck, holding a tissue to her cheek like she was at a drive-in picture show. All she needed was a tub of popcorn.

"If you leave . . ."

What did he mean *if you leave*? Her gaze locked on his. She *was* leaving.

"Your voice is going to bring you a slew of proposals."

Was he afraid she wasn't coming back? That she'd marry someone else? For her, there'd only ever been Al.

Al and Izz.

Her gaze lowered to where the coverall fabric stretched tight across his hip pocket, outlining what was too square to be a pack of gum.

"If you leave, Izz, you won't be coming back. Not with a voice like yours."

When Al got to talking, he could talk a goat out of a briar patch.

Not that she'd stay. Her heart was set on Silverton and the all girls choir, but it would be nice if he said something sweet.

Try, Albert. Please, try.

"Izz . . ." The old, familiar softness entered his gaze.

She had to be careful and not say *yes*. "What, Al?"

He swallowed and blinked. Whatever sweet things he'd been about to say, something had changed his mind. It was the mule in him. His father was stubborn. His brother was stubborn. And Al was just like them: a Gleinbroch to the core.

"Stay." Was that his confession of love? He'd left Molalla on his lunch hour, maybe even bought a ring, and blocked the road so he could say *stay*?

He wrestled what was indeed a little black velvet box out of his pocket and held it toward her.

"Al . . ." Tears rimmed her gaze. "You know, I can't."

"Then . . ." Eyes steady, he sucked in a breath. "Another girl will be wearing this ring by the time you get back." He rose to his feet.

"What?" She could barely get out the word.

"You heard me." He started for his truck.

"I don't think I did." He didn't mean it. Did he? She picked up a baseball-sized rock from alongside the road and thought of throwing it at him.

He turned and, folding his arms in front of him, grinned like a donkey. "I said: the ring will be on another girl's hand by the time you get back."

Her grip on the rock tightened. With her aim, she'd miss and hit his beloved Ford. Maybe she should. Then he'd have something to remember her by.

He climbed inside his cab.

"Albert Gleinbroch! That must be the most romantic proposal ever spoken! Ever said." As he was pulling closed his door, she wound up and chucked the rock.

It hit the rear fender instead.

His door swung open. "What in the world?" he yelled, poking his head out of the cab.

She stormed back to Mae's truck.

"Don't call home. I don't want to hear your voice!" he shouted.

Her voice? She sunk her teeth hard into her lower lip. Is that all he loved about her?

"You're not the only one who lives there." She swung open her door, fumbled her way inside, and slouched down in the seat so he couldn't see her.

"There's a dent. I can see it from here." Mae covered her mouth with one hand and stared.

Isabelle reached up, locking her door.

"He's starting his truck." Mae turned the key in her ignition, too. "He's looking over here. Now, he's driving out."

Isabelle sat up in time to see his tailgate disappear around the tree-lined bend.

"Did you tell him *no*?" Mae shifted into first.

"Didn't you hear?" They'd pert near been yelling at each other.

"No, and I can't read lips."

"It was the most awful proposal in the history of humanity." Her voice quaked as she stared at the empty road. "Just like his autograph."

CHAPTER 2

While her husband watched television in the front room, Nettie Cooper tucked herself away in her kitchen nook and dialed her good friend's number. She couldn't wait to tell Opal the news.

"Hargetts' residence, this is Opal speaking." Opal, a retired schoolteacher, had a no-nonsense way about her.

"Opal, it's Nettie. Is now a good time to talk?"

"Yes, it is. Is your new choir girl there?"

"Yes, Isabelle's upstairs with Carolyn, unpacking their things."

"My girl's here, too. What do you think of Isabelle?"

"She seems sweet." Nettie kept an eye on the doorway into the living room.

"That's good. What does she look like?"

"She's cute. She has dark hair that's half pinned up and half down. Oh, what's that style called that the young girls are wearing nowadays?"

"A bouffant?"

"That's it! She's cute."

"Cute can mean a great many things. Name an actress that she looks like."

Nettie stared at her nook area's wallpaper. "I guess she looks a bit like Audrey Hepburn. She's petite and has dark hair and eyes just like Audrey. Except, she's a tiny bit shorter. Otherwise, they could be sisters."

"Well . . . between you and me and the fencepost, I don't think my choir girl's the one we've been praying for."

"Oh, why do you say that?" Had Opal's choir girl even been there ten minutes?

"She had Wesley carry in her *three* suitcases from the car. She might have an hour-glass figure, but he was not impressed. Said she's bossy."

"Bossy?"

"Yes, *bossy*. Thank heaven my Wesley is a good judge of character."

Nettie couldn't agree more. The last thing Opal needed was a bossy daughter-in-law.

"Grandma?" Carolyn, her twenty-year-old granddaughter, stepped into the kitchen.

Nettie covered the receiver. "Yes?"

"We're leaving. Mr. Hoffmeister said that practice will end today about four thirty." Carolyn blew her a kiss.

"Bye, honey." Nettie fluttered the fingers of her free hand. She glanced at her tea kettle clock on the nearby wall. It was already one o'clock. "The girls are just leaving. They're walking to church," she told Opal.

"I called the church earlier and left a message for John to call me. I'm hoping he can give Darlene a ride to practice."

"What about Wesley?"

"He just left for his afternoon shift."

"Well, he should have taken her!" The Union 76 gas station that Wesley worked at was only a few blocks from the church.

"I think it best that he's not alone with Darlene too much. Picture Marilyn Monroe as a brunette."

"Really? Are you joshing?"

"I wish I were. Too much time alone together might make my poor Wesley forget his first impression of her if you know what I mean."

"Well, John shouldn't be driving her either then!" Nettie said. "Heaven forbid! We don't want a bossy pastor's wife!"

"He'll have to take what he can get."

* * *

Two strides past his door, John Hugg followed the bend to the right in the wood-paneled hallway. "Any messages?" he asked his elderly secretary.

"Just one." Virginia kept her head of silvery curls bent as she made an entry in the payables ledger. Without lifting her gaze, she scanned the next check and made a second entry. She'd always treated him this way, ever since her Sunday school class twenty years ago when he'd put a garden slug in her pocket and wiped his hands on her skirt.

"Did you know that Velveeta started out as cheese in a tin?"

"No." The corner of her mouth twitched.

He nodded. "It was a type of military food invention. I read an interesting article about it in the paper this morning. So were M & Ms."

"Oh." Peering over the top of her eyeglasses, she handed him a slip of paper.

The message read: Opal Hargett called at 12:25 p.m.

"Did she say why?"

"No."

John eyed the elderly woman through narrow slits. "The Hargetts don't happen to be hosting a choir girl?"

"They are. Why?"

He tapped his fingers on top of her desk. "Did you know that the Carlsons invited me to dinner last night?"

"No." Virginia's slow smile was building.

"Their choir girl just happened to show up an *entire* day early."

Virginia's cheeks inverted ever so slightly. "What was she like?"

"Well, Evelyn Pickett is painfully quiet. Over the course of three hours, she said a total of eight words: *hello, nice to meet you, thank you,* and *goodbye*." He tallied on both hands.

Gazing up at him, Virginia blinked.

"First Rose and now Opal. What do you suppose she's plotting?"

"Plotting is a strong word, John. Try and take it as a compliment. You're young, moderately good looking—and a bachelor."

"Moderately?" He suppressed a grin.

"And ever so humble."

"I'll call Opal and get it over with." He turned the black rotary dial phone around to face him and picked up the receiver. Before Sunday, he hoped to thwart any other matchmaking the host mothers might be dreaming up.

Opal answered after two rings.

"Opal, it's John Hugg."

"I am so glad you called. Arnie's fishing, Wesley's at work, and my car's making an awful racket." Opal paused long enough to take a breath.

"Uh-huh."

"I need to get Darlene—the choir girl we're hosting—to the church by two o'clock for their first practice."

Bingo.

The Hargetts lived three miles out of town. Though the elders would undoubtedly frown upon him spending time alone with any of the choir girls, John appreciated the fact that this introduction would be brief—a ten-minute car ride—not an entire evening spent in awkward conversation.

"I'll leave here shortly. Will that work for you, Opal?"

"Yes, that's wonderful, John. Thank you."

He hung up the receiver and slapped the top of his knees. "Opal's car's making an awful racket and Arnie's fishing. She wants me to drive Darlene, choir girl number two, here for practice."

"Opal's needed a new muffler for months." Virginia swiveled her chair half a turn and pulled open a drawer in the tall, oak filing cabinet behind her.

"Should I address bearing false witness this Sunday?"

"Perhaps. But . . . be gentle about it." She turned to peer over the top of her glasses at him. "Their motive is *love*."

John chuckled.

After this drive, he'd only have two choir girls to go. Carolyn Cooper—choir girl number three—regularly attended service here with her grandparents, Russell and Nettie Cooper. Besides, she was engaged.

"Who is choir girl number four staying with?" he asked.

"The Coopers. They thought it would be fun for Carolyn to room with one of the girls."

"Hmmm . . ." He was surprised that Nettie Cooper hadn't been the first to scheme something. "I see. Well, if for some odd reason Nettie should call, tell her that I'd like to have all of the matchmaking over by Sunday."

"Sunday?" Virginia chuckled softly. "This will go on until Christmas."

"Don't tell me that." He should never have agreed to host a Christmas choir.

"You're going to have to learn to say *no*."

He wondered if his grandmother had anything to do with

the outcome—four young ladies, all unmarried and in their early twenties.

"Do you know something I don't?"

Virginia peered at him over the top of her glasses. "I know a lot of things you don't."

He should have been more specific.

* * *

Darlene, the attractive young woman seated across the cab, had shoulder-length auburn hair and a figure that screamed Jane Russell. John kept his gaze fixed on the road and told himself to only pay attention to her words. Elm and maple trees lined the curvy section of road into town.

"Mrs. Hargett said that the first Mrs. Hugg did not have a very good singing voice," Darlene said.

Opal Hargett needed a lecture.

"Have you been married before?" Darlene asked, leaning a little toward him.

"Opal's referring to my grandmother. My grandfather used to pastor Calvary Christian. He had a stroke last December."

"For some reason, Mrs. Hargett was surprised that I don't have a boyfriend."

John kept his eyes on the road. "Where are you from, Darlene?"

"Molalla. I was almost valleyvictorian of my senior class."

"I see." He bit down on the insides of his cheeks to keep from laughing. "Are you going to college?"

"No. But, if I ever do, I'd major in . . ." she paused, probably waiting for him to look over at her, but he didn't, "Home Ec."

His stomach churned.

He drove south on Water Street past the Union 76 Gas

Station on his right before entering the heart of downtown. Storefronts dating back to the 1880's lined the road, and traffic slowed near the historic Palace Theatre. At the intersection of Main and Water Street, he rolled to a stop. His was the fourth car in line, which was odd for so early in the day.

Up ahead, the town fire truck blocked both lanes of traffic, its ladder extended to the second floor of the old L. Ames Building. A fireman was hanging an evergreen wreath with a large, red velvet bow in the center of the window.

John tried not to feel like a humbug. Did they really have to do this already—ten days before Thanksgiving? He patted a hand to the steering wheel and recalled what a member of the Chamber of Commerce had told him only yesterday. *Decorations are important for the town's after-Thanksgiving Day sales.*

Across the street, Bill Roluff, the owner of the 99-Cents Store—and church elder, stood outside his store and eyed the cab of John's truck.

His stomach knotted.

"I just love Christmas—the lights, and all the pretty, little things." Fluttering an empty left hand, Darlene smiled over at him.

John glanced at his wristwatch. Their ten-minute car ride had already been fourteen.

"I just love Christmas," the girl breathed.

Any minute she'd break out in song.

Not knowing what else to say, he quoted Luke 2. "For unto us is born this day in the city of David a Savior, which is Christ the Lord."

"Don't forget the star, the shepherds, and the sheep," she said.

"Yes, you're right. God thought of everything."

Finally, the wreath was centered, and the ladder lowered. Traffic continued south, and he waved briefly at Bill as they drove past. After two blocks, John took a left on Jersey Street. Calvary Christian, a white clapboard-sided church with a pinnacle bell tower, sat in the middle of the residential area. He slowed to a stop alongside the curb.

"It was nice to meet you, Darlene."

"You, too, John." With a soft, chin-bobbing smile, choir girl number two got out, flung her plaid scarf over her shoulder, and closed the door behind her. In her spiked high heel shoes, she strolled toward the concrete flight of steps and the main double doors.

He parked across the street in the church's gravel lot. To avoid running into any more choir girls today, he'd write his sermon at home in the small parsonage house on the west side of the church. And, in the future, he wouldn't be so quick to drive choir girls *alone* around town.

CHAPTER 3

*A*fternoon sunlight streamed through the tall arched windows on each side of the cathedral-ceilinged room. Eight solid oak pews lined both sides of the main aisle. Isabelle sat in the front between two girls, Carolyn Cooper, her new roommate, and a soft-spoken brunette named Evelyn.

Ted Hoffmeister, the girls' choir leader—a lean, elderly man—stood up front holding a clipboard. "In the order you're now in, beginning with Darlene," he pointed to a brunette on the right side of the pew, "I'd like you to walk up front, tell us a little bit about yourself, and then sing the first stanza of *Amazing Grace*."

The girl's auburn, shoulder-length curls bounced as she walked up to the podium. Then, she turned to face them.

"Hi, I'm Darlene Berry. I'm from Molalla, Oregon, home of the Buckeroo." Her lime green dress was tight at the bodice, fitted at the waist, with a knee-length skirt. She smiled brightly. "I'm twenty-one, and if anyone should ask, I *don't* have a boyfriend, presently…" She winked.

The girls all had a good laugh.

And then, with impressive poise, Darlene belted out the lyrics in a rich alto voice.

Isabelle was glad she wasn't next.

Carolyn strode toward the front. Her roommate was short, five one at best, buxom with short, blonde pin curls. "I'm Carolyn Cooper." Her voice reminded Isabelle of Ethel Mertz's on the *Lucille Ball-Desi Arnaz Show*. "I'm from Canby, but my grandparents live here in Silverton. Since I was about this tall," she held a hand low near her side, "I've attended this church every Sunday. When I was six, I was saying my prayers, and my Grandma Nettie told me it was time to ask Jesus into my heart... and I did."

Isabelle's gaze lowered to the wooden floor. If only her own testimony were as easy to share.

Carolyn's soprano voice was sweet just like her personality.

Isabelle's turn was next. She walked up the steps of the stage, turned to face Mr. Hoffmeister and the three young ladies, and gripped her hands tightly behind her.

She'd looked forward to Silverton and the Christmas choir for months, and now that she was finally here, Albert's awful proposal took away a little glitter from the day.

He'd always been her biggest fan. If he wasn't beside her playing his guitar and beaming, he'd been in the crowd, beaming. Not only was Al not here, he didn't even want to hear from her.

At the Wilhoit gatherings, she usually found her father's wheelchair and focused on him—her pillar of strength. Now, she didn't know where to look. Her gaze drifted to the arched windows and the gray sky outside, before returning to the girls.

"I'm Isabelle Bucknell. I'm from Wilhoit, which is an old mineral springs resort seven miles south of Molalla. About twenty miles from here." Might as well have been a thousand, for as far away as it felt.

She took a deep breath and began singing the beautiful old hymn.

"Amazing grace! How sweet the sound
That saved a wretch like me!"

Her soprano voice filled the cavernous room. The lyrics, only four lines in all, were still long enough for her to tear up.

"I once was lost, but now am found;
Was blind, but now I see."

Eyes glassy, she descended the stage. Why couldn't Al have just been happy for her?

"Very nice," Mr. Hoffmeister said.

"Thank you." She returned to sit beside Carolyn and tried to collect herself.

The gal seated to her left walked up next. Her dark hair was cut fashionably short and teased at the crown. She wore a white, long-sleeved shirt with a corduroy jumper.

"I'm uh . . . Evelyn . . . Pickett. I'm from Mt. Angel. It's about four miles that way." She swished her wrist forward at the hip. Then, clutching her hands in front of her, she closed her eyes and started to sing. Her voice trembled like an earthquake was happening in her throat.

Isabelle knew just how she felt.

Near the end, Evelyn's alto voice finally settled.

"Thank you." Mr. Hoffmeister walked up front. "Coffee break for everyone except Isabelle…" he glanced at his clipboard, "Bucknell. Carolyn, can you show the girls downstairs? My wife made coffee and cookies."

While the girls exited, Isabelle remained seated and crossed her saddle shoes beneath the pew. Mr. Hoffmeister had heard her sing once before on Easter Sunday at the community church in Molalla. After the service, he'd asked her to join the choir. Maybe he regretted it now?

"Let's have you sing another piece." He carried his guitar over to her side of the aisle and sat down in the pew about three hymnals away. "What do you know?"

"Mockin' Bird Hill?" The hit song was one of Aunt Elsie's favorites. While her elderly aunt played the piano, Isabelle would sing in the great room of the old hotel.

"Do you know 'The Old Rugged Cross?'"

"Yes." But she didn't want to sing a sad song right now, not when she was feeling as weepy as the old cherry tree back home.

Mr. Hoffmeister strummed through the first stanza, and then, starting over, nodded for her to join in.

"On *a hill far a-way stood an old rug-ged cross.*" She remained seated and kept her gaze on the rough-hewn cross on the wall behind the podium.

At the end of the verse, he stilled the guitar strings. "People will like seeing your emotion, especially with this song. Plan on singing it this Sunday, and we'll see how you fare."

She nodding, curbing a smile.

"And, try and hold your hands in front of you in the future."

"Yes, sir." She liked her hands behind her—where she could fidget and fiddle with them when she was holding and hitting high notes. She sure hoped he didn't expect her to waltz around like Darlene.

She didn't have it in her.

* * *

PORCH LIGHTS OUTLINED THE COOPERS' sage green bungalow

on Center Street and the gnarly oak tree in the front yard. Isabelle followed Carolyn up the brick pathway.

"Yes or no, do you have a boyfriend?" Carolyn had been prying for their entire half-mile walk home.

"Sort of." With a knot in her chest, she got out the next words. "To be honest, I'm not sure."

"And your sort-of-boyfriend's name is . . . ?"

She inhaled past the knot in her chest. "Al-bert."

"Okay." Carolyn laughed softly and headed inside.

The ding of an oven timer echoed through the main floor, greeting them at the door.

"Carolyn, get that for me," Nettie said loudly.

"Yes, Grandma." Carolyn tossed her wool scarf and coat over Isabelle like she was a coat tree.

After Isabelle hung their things in the entry closet, she made her way through the front room. A tropical design of palm branches and hibiscus was woven into the short, pale gray carpeting. Russell and Nettie, the elderly host couple she'd met earlier in the day, sat in the La-Z-Boy recliners that separated the living room from the formal dining table.

"Isabelle, are you a fan of chicken pot pie?" asked Nettie. The wiry, elderly woman's short, white hair was tucked behind her ears, and she wore a red cardigan sweater over a blue plaid cotton dress.

"Yes."

"Then, you're going to love what I made for dinner."

Russell swished his hand for Isabelle to move.

"I'm sorry." Unknowingly, she'd been blocking the television screen. Stepping aside, she continued into the galley kitchen.

With her back to the room, Carolyn used hot pads to transfer individual-sized, golden-brown pies from the oven onto Corelle dinner plates.

"Wow! Your grandmother's been busy."

"Not really." Carolyn closed the oven door. "Don't tell her that I told you, but . . ." She opened up the cabinet beneath the sink and pulled one of the red boxes out of the garbage. Swanson Chicken Pot Pie was on the cover.

"Oh!" She'd heard of them. Now she'd finally get to try one.

"Hurry, girls! Lawrence Welk is on," Nettie called from the other room.

While the girls delivered dinner to the elderly couple, orchestra music filled the air and champagne bubbles floated on the black-and-white screen. Carolyn and Isabelle sat down on the couch and carefully tunneled their knees beneath the skinny legs of the metal TV trays. The camera panned to the Champagne Lady, Norma Zimmer, a blonde with shoulder-length curls, singing "He Walks with Me in the Garden."

"Grandma, someday we might see Isabelle on this show," Carolyn said.

One could dream.

"Nawh." Nettie flicked her wrist.

"You'll see. She has a solo this Sunday."

"Shhh!" Nettie raised a finger to her lips. "Norma's singing." On the footrest, her sock-clad feet bobbed at the ankle to the old-time hymn.

Isabelle took her first bite of pot pie and chewed. The sauce was surprisingly good, and the pie had a delicate crust.

Onscreen, Norma appeared as comfortable in front of the live audience as if she were standing in the Coopers' living room. With outstretched arms, she smiled, embracing all of America. She almost looked like she'd taken lessons from Darlene Berry. *And the joy we share as we tarry there, None other has ever known.* She caressed the last note as the show went to a commercial break.

"So you can sing like Norma?" Nettie's sparse brows

disappeared behind the hexagon-shaped frames of her glasses. There was a hint of an accent in her voice, maybe Missouri.

"I don't think I'll ever be as comfortable onstage as her." She could barely sing and smile at the same time.

"What does Albert think about your voice?" Carolyn asked.

Nettie's head swiveled. "Is Albert your boyfriend?"

Isabelle slowly lowered her fork to her plate and, with a slight shake of her head, swallowed. Maybe she shouldn't have shared what she had with Carolyn. She'd kept it secret for all of five minutes.

"He's her *sort-of-boyfriend*, Grandma."

"Oh, what does *sort-of-boyfriend* mean?" Nettie peered over at her.

Mrs. Cooper was just like her granddaughter—zeroing in on questions about her love life. "He didn't want me to do the choir." Isabelle shrugged, trying to make light of Albert's one-word proposal.

"What'd ya think of my pot pie?"

"It was good. Thank you."

"You're gonna learn how to make your hubby happy when you're here." The elderly woman beamed.

"You mean her *future* husband, Grandma."

"What's fer dessert, Nettie Bug?" Mr. Cooper asked.

"Nothing."

The wrinkle lines on his forehead deepened. "I was hoping you made some of that chocolate pudding."

"You never told me you wanted some."

"Roth's doesn't close 'til eight, girls." He leaned forward in the recliner and fished his wallet out of his back pocket. "Buy a box of that chocolate pudding for dessert," he eyed Carolyn. "How we doing on milk, Ma?"

"Get some milk, and Velveeta, too. We'll have macaroni and cheese tomorrow night."

Isabelle wondered if Mrs. Cooper made macaroni and cheese the same way as Fletcher, the cook back home, or if her version would come out of a box.

CHAPTER 4

"John, remember you're driving me home." His elderly secretary poked her head inside his office. At least once a week, he drove Virginia home when her husband took their car to go fishing. "And, I almost forgot…"

The woman rarely forgot a thing.

"Lilly called earlier and wanted you to call her back."

"Did she say why?"

"No."

He flipped through the Cs in the Rolodex on his desk, found the card titled Thomas and Lilly Crawl—in his grandfather's handwriting—and dialed the young widow's number.

"Hello, this is the Crawls' residence."

"Lilly, it's John Hugg returning your call. Is everything okay?"

Virginia paused in the doorway, her dark coat on, the handle of her purse in the V of her arm.

"Took you long enough," Lilly said.

"What can I do for you, Lilly?"

"My truck's out of gas, and I need to go grocery shopping. The Goffs have my gas can and promised to fill it for me the next time they're in town."

"Can it wait until morning?" He wasn't particularly fond of driving young widows around after dark.

"I s'pose. I'll just eat stewed tomatoes for supper and breakfast."

"That isn't all you have."

"No. I can season them with salt, pepper, and the last drop of Worcestershire sauce."

"Lilly." He rolled a kink out of his neck. "How in the world did you get down to just stewed tomatoes?" His gaze locked on Virginia's and he nodded.

The elderly woman disappeared from the doorway.

"It's bad enough that my boss has to drive me to work. I can't expect Mr. Schoenberger to take me grocery shopping, too."

Taking Lilly Crawl grocery shopping, alone after dark, might even be more frowned upon by the elders than driving an unchaperoned choir girl to practice. But, he wouldn't let her starve.

"I'll leave shortly." John hung up the phone and rolled a kink out of his neck. "Lilly's truck's out of gas and, she needs groceries," he said loudly, informing Virginia.

"Oh, the poor girl!" The elderly woman strode into his office and, near the corner of his desk, shook open a brown paper bag. "I've told her firsthand about the closet." Virginia set a can of tuna, a can of pork and beans, and a box of Kraft Macaroni and Cheese inside the bag.

"I told her that I'd take her to Roth's."

"Just the two of you"—Virginia peered over at him "—alone?"

"I'm not going to tell her *no*."

Her mouth pursed thoughtfully. "I'll go, too, then."

He was hoping she'd say that.

* * *

IN THE HEADLIGHTS of John's '54 Chevy pickup, Lilly's large, galvanized mailbox—the landmark for her property—came into view. He slowed and made a right-hand turn into her narrow, gravel drive. While he neared the cabin, the headlights shone on her three-year supply of firewood, which Tommy had split, stacked, and covered in a lean-to shed. Tommy, her late husband, had been a logger, a faller for the mill. In February, a tree had kick backed over the stump, taking his life.

"How well do you know Lilly?" John glanced across the cab at Virginia.

"I know she's a hurting young woman who needs our prayers." Virginia sighed. "Nettie Cooper told me about a gathering when Lilly smelled like alcohol, and you took her home early."

"Nettie!" He'd have to speak to her *again*. "Did she tell you that Russell was with us?"

"Yes. And I told Nettie, we're here to love, not gossip. In the meantime, Lilly's been in our prayers."

John knew by *in our prayers*, Virginia meant in the prayers of the Seven Blocks of Granite. Years ago, his grandfather, a devout Packers fan, had nicknamed the group of elderly women during a sermon, confirming the rumor of their existence. He'd said, "Very few needs in this church slip past the Seven Blocks of Granite."

"How many are there in the group—the Granite Girls?" He glanced over at her.

"I'm not at liberty to say." She cleared her throat. "There are still seven."

"That's what I thought." Then, leaving the warmth of the

cab, he strode across the gravel to rap on the front door of the cabin.

"I'm coming!" Lilly bellowed from inside. She'd sounded fine enough on the phone, but the grieving process had made her unpredictable. A minute or two passed before she pulled back the curtain covering the door's upper glass to frown at him. Hopefully, in jest. Sometimes it was difficult to tell with Lilly.

The door swung inward, and he saw her agile, lean frame wrestling on Tommy's old red and black mackinaw which was several sizes too big.

"I'd almost given up on you." Maybe it was her tomato diet, but she was too thin, her complexion too pale. Her long, wavy, red hair was pulled back into a tight knot at the nape of her neck.

"Virginia decided to tag along, too. She's in the truck."

"Oh. Taking the widow grocery shopping, you both should earn a badge or something."

Ignoring her remark, he said, "I can always pick up a few things." Then, he led the way to his truck.

Lilly rounded the tailgate and climbed in the passenger side. Virginia scooted to the middle, and the two women exchanged hellos.

Except for the hum of the heater, the cab was quiet as he drove the curvy wooded road toward town.

At Roth's FoodLiner—Silverton's newest and largest grocery store—John steered the shopping cart for the two women. In the produce area, Virginia was torn between Newton Pippin apples or Gravensteins for her Thanksgiving pie.

"I use both for my pies," Lilly said.

John didn't know enough about apples to help in her decision making.

Virginia flicked a hand at him. "Go on ahead. I'll be a while."

"I don't mind waiting," he said.

She flicked her hand again.

"Okay, we'll wait for you in the next aisle."

In aisle two, Lilly pulled down a box of Quaker oatmeal and, pausing near their cart, studied the side panel.

"What are you reading?" John leaned his forearms on the long, cart handle.

"A recipe for meatloaf."

At this rate, he'd never get home in time to wrap up his sermon. Good thing he still had Saturday.

"Velveeta," mumbled a dark-haired, young woman as she scanned the nearby shelves.

"Velveeta's about eight feet . . . north," John said.

When she glanced over at him, he pointed further down the aisle.

"Thank you." She cast him a smile.

Only that morning, he'd read a fascinating article about the history of military food—Velveeta being one of them. In his profession, he knew not to take such coincidences lightly.

Am I to witness to her, Lord?

Lilly's continued pause felt like a parting of the Red Sea.

Boxes of Velveeta sat two shelves above the young woman's gaze.

"Bright yellow box," he said. He rounded the side of the cart and walked toward her.

She turned slightly. "I thought it was cheese, but it's not in the refrigerated section."

"No, it was a military food invention for World War I. It started out as cheese in a tin." He paused beside her.

"Oh . . . canned cheese."

"Yes." Their gazes locked.

Dark hair, ebony eyes . . . a vision.

"You, uh . . . don't want to eat it plain." His pulse noticeably picked up before he pulled down a box, handing it to her. "You melt it and uh, put it in things. Then it's great."

She curved her wrist around the box and tucked it against her like a football. "Thank you."

Both his tongue and shoelaces felt like they were tied together. He stepped back, giving her a little space. "Do you ... uh, have a home church?"

"Yes." The blush in her profile deepened. "Thank you, again." She turned and before he could warn her, plowed into the hip-high display of Maxwell House Coffee, sending light-blue tins clattering to the floor.

"You must be new in town." He chuckled. Then, crouching, he picked up several cans.

The hem of her tweed wool coat touched the speckled floor as she retrieved nearby strays. "Why? Does this happen a lot here?"

"Yes." He chuckled. "Roth's is famous for stacking coffee in awkward places."

While he stacked, the girl went quiet on him.

He glanced over his shoulder and then did a double-take. Virginia had joined Lilly, and, with furrowed brows, the two women stood behind the cart, watching.

The young woman set the last of the tins on top of the display.

Now was his chance.

"I'm John," he said, meeting her gaze.

"I'm . . . I'm, uh, in a hurry." Turning, she strode empty-handed toward the front of the store.

"Miss . . ." He grabbed the box of Velveeta from a nearby shelf. "Miss! You forgot your . . ." He held it up.

She turned and, shoulders stiff, started back toward him.

The attraction was not mutual. But, she was definitely flustered.

He met her halfway.

"Thank you, again." Not quite meeting his gaze, she took the box from his outstretched hand.

"You're welcome." Though he wanted to, he knew better than to ask for her name a second time.

* * *

"What apples did you get?" Lilly asked.

"I decided on the Pippins. I've always liked them best for my pies."

John kept his eyes on the road and waited for one of the women to address what had happened in aisle two.

"John . . ." Lilly leaned forward to peer past Virginia, "when you said that you needed to pick up a few things, I didn't think it would be a young woman."

Virginia pressed a hand to her mouth.

Driving south on Water Street, he passed the A & W Drive-In, the library, and the police department on their way out of town.

"Have either of you ever seen her before?" he asked.

"I haven't," Virginia said.

"Nope, not me. Have you ever heard the old saying *'Don't judge a book by its cover?'*" Lilly asked. "Men seem to forget that when they're around a beautiful woman."

"Do you think I was too forward—helping her like I did?"

"After a while, I couldn't watch. It was painful." Lilly was her diplomatic best. "But you know, people who talk to themselves are only asking for trouble."

"I just saw the tail end of it," Virginia said. "She looked like a sweet, young woman. Maybe a little shy. Nervous."

"Awkward," Lilly added.

"What do you mean, *painful*?" He glanced at Lilly.

"She was trying to be courteous, but she had *escape* written all over her."

"Thank you for the encouragement."

"She was skittish, in case you didn't notice."

He had.

"You're a man, John. God made you a man."

He nodded. It was good to hear Lilly talk about God.

"And it was entertaining to see you behave like one."

Virginia's nearest shoulder shook against his own.

Maybe it was good he hadn't seen the young woman again in the store when he'd searched. If he had, he probably would only have made a fool out of himself—a second time.

CHAPTER 5

Sunday morning, Isabelle knotted the belt of her wool coat and glanced at the tea kettle clock in the nook area.

9:50!

Her heart leaped to her throat. They were already late.

Nearby, in the reflection of the back door's half window, Mr. Cooper wrapped his skinny black tie around his neck and slowly began to tie it.

"Granddad, we need to hurry." Carolyn strode into the kitchen. "Mr. Hoffmeister wants us to be at church ten minutes before it starts."

Behind her, Nettie wobbled through the living room. "Russell, did you take my shoe?" she yelled.

"What shoe?"

"My black left pump."

"No, Nettie. I have my own shoes."

"Did you take my right—"

"Grandma, we need to hurry! Mr. Hoffmeister wants all the choir girls to be up front early for the opening song."

"Why didn't you say something?" Nettie entered the

kitchen. "Do you think anyone will notice?" She pointed down at her shoes. Beneath her knee-length dress, she wore one black pump and one dark blue pump.

"No. Get in the car," Russell said, holding open the back door.

"Just hide them beneath the pew, Grandma. No one will notice."

Isabelle followed Carolyn through the door. Overgrown rhododendron bushes lined the mossy brick path from the house to the detached garage. The cloudless blue sky was deceiving. The temperature felt like a walk-in freezer.

Inside the garage sat a maroon and cream sedan with flared tailfins. Isabelle climbed in the back seat and pulled the door closed behind her.

"Brr!" In front, Nettie rounded her narrow shoulders. "Too bad you didn't preheat the car. It's cold."

"Twenty degrees colder than yesterday." Russell turned the key in the ignition, and a high-pitched grinding noise followed. "Maybe we will get snow."

"Nawh! It's not even Thanksgiving." Nettie waved a hand.

Isabelle glanced at her wristwatch, her stomach a bundle of knots.

"Come on, Hilda." Russell turned the key.

The grinding noise followed.

Patting at her hair in the rearview mirror, Carolyn appeared calm enough.

Russell turned the key again, pumping the gas pedal. If he weren't careful, he'd flood the engine.

How would the choir sound with only two alto girls and no sopranos? Darlene would manage somehow.

"Did you ever tell Grandma about the guy at Roth's?" Carolyn asked her.

"No." He was the last thing she wanted to think about right now.

"Oh, who was he?" Nettie half turned in her seat.

"He told me his name, but I can't remember it." Isabelle shrugged.

"He flirted with Isabelle right in front of his wife. Got her so flustered that she walked right into a display of coffee," Carolyn added.

"You're kidding!" Nettie giggled.

Isabelle glanced over at Carolyn. "Should we walk?" she whispered.

"Nawh. It just takes a while to warm up."

"Is it the battery again?" Nettie clicked open her purse.

"Nope. Say a prayer, girls." Russell patted the maroon-colored dash with one hand and turned the key with the other. "Come on, baby doll. Come on, Hil-da."

A metal on metal sound followed.

Isabelle leaned toward the front. "Maybe it's the starter." Albert worked on vehicles all the time in the back garage at Wilhoit, and she'd hand him tools.

"Today's not a good day to be late, Granddad."

Please, Lord, get us there on time. Isabelle's lashes fluttered against her cheeks.

"Come on, sweet sugar pie pumpkin." Russell turned the key.

"With whipped cream on top," Nettie added.

For some reason, maybe prayer or because Nettie spoke so sweetly, the engine sputtered to life.

Isabelle glanced at her wristwatch. The choir had started singing four minutes ago. Would Mr. Hoffmeister understand? Thank heaven her solo wasn't until the end of service.

Humming the melody to "Taps," Russell drove down the hill and over the bridge, crossing Silver Creek into the downtown area.

"Peppermints?" Nettie turned in the front seat and held out the red-and-white striped candies. "When Pastor Hugg tells us to look in our Bibles, that's when I twist open the wrapper. With all the pages flipping, no one can hear a thing. I hurry and pop the peppermint in my mouth before he sees me."

"Thank you, Nettie." Isabelle slid a peppermint into the silk-lined pocket of her wool skirt and tried to slow her pounding heart. In front of the entire congregation, she and Carolyn would have to walk up the center aisle and join the choir.

Carolyn leaned forward and patted Russell's shoulder. "Granddad, drop us off by the back door."

He nodded and, took a right on a narrow gravel road right in front of Calvary Christian. If Carolyn rolled down her window, she'd be able to touch the church's white clapboard siding. Near the far corner of the building, Mr. Cooper brought the old Bel Air to a jerky stop.

"I'll work on getting the car started earlier next Sunday, while you girls are getting ready."

"I'll try and remember to remind you." Nettie clicked closed her purse.

In the back entry, the girls hung up their coats on mounted pegs. Then, Carolyn nudged open the rear sanctuary door. Over Carolyn's shoulder, Isabelle could see the packed little sanctuary. The choir was mid-song, and half the melody to "I'll Go Where You Want Me to Go" was missing, although Darlene was trying to make up for it.

Carolyn slipped through the half-open door. Then, heart pounding in her ears, Isabelle quietly clicked closed the door behind them. Angel that she was, Carolyn had waited for her. In single file, they made a beeline across the stage to their places in the front row. She and Carolyn, the first and second sopranos—the melody—joined in. *"I'll go where you want me to go, dear Lord. O'er mountain, or plain, or sea."*

Mr. Hoffmeister's tall and wiry frame was easy to spot in

the front pew on their left. With a slow blink, he nodded their direction. He didn't appear mad. If anything, he looked relieved.

They were here. They'd made it. Feeling the weight of the world slip off of her shoulders, Isabelle focused on the lyrics with new conviction. *"I'll say what you want me to say, dear Lord, I'll be what you want me to be."*

Carolyn squirmed a bit beside her.

Then, someone pinched the back of Isabelle's arm. And, it hurt!

There was only one person behind her who would do such a thing.

Darlene!

* * *

JOHN WAS SURPRISED to see Russell and Nettie Cooper hurry up the front steps. With their new role of hosting choir girls, he would have thought they'd be on time, if not early. He swung the door open for them.

"Hi, John." Nettie patted at her heart. "I hope Ted's not mad about the girls running late."

"A little car trouble this morning." Russell jangled his keys in one hand as he stepped past.

"Sounds like the choir's all here now," John pressed a finger to his lips.

"Ahhh!" Nettie neared the open sanctuary door. "Look, Carolyn's standing in front," she whispered, wrapping her arm in Russell's. "First time she ever sang a solo was here, for this church. She was only seven. Do you remember?"

"Sure do."

John thought he did, too. "Go find a seat." He motioned them forward. The Coopers were usually the last to arrive. Too bad it had been the same way this morning. He picked up his Bible from the entry table, and then closed the sanctuary doors quietly behind him.

The choir was mid-chorus when he made his way up the center aisle.

Seated in the third pew from the front, Lilly peered over her shoulder at him, and, eyes bulging, mouthed his name.

Lilly! Such antics before his sermon would only serve as a distraction.

He sat down in his usual place, the middle of the front pew in which the Waggoners—Charlie, his wife Beth, their daughter, and son—were also seated. Robby, the six-year-old, shimmied across the pew toward him and didn't stop until he nestled in the curve of John's arm, draped along the top of the wooden bench.

John had just been to their home last week for dinner, and the boy felt more at home with him than usual.

Now that the girls were all here, the acapella choir sounded great. He glanced at the young women. In the back row, Darlene was the tallest. As he'd feared, their eyes met.

Robby tapped his shoulder. "We saw a white-tailed buck in the bakyard this morning," he whispered a little too loud.

Nodding, John pressed a finger to his lips to hush the youngster. Then he turned a bit in the pew and, hopefully without drawing too much attention to either of them, he glanced at Lilly.

She darted her gaze to the choir and then back.

What was she going on about?

He paused for a moment and looked toward the rough-hewn cross hung high on the wall behind the pulpit.

"My dad went and got his shotgun," Robby whispered. "And Mom ran outside in her pink fluffy slippers to shoo it off."

"Shhh!" John tapped a finger against his lips.

"Emily screamed. She was afraid Dad wouldn't see Mom."

Robby scrunched up his lean, freckled face. "But... how couldn't he? She was wearing her bright-pink bathrobe."

John suppressed a chuckle. Then, his gaze drifted toward the choir.

Standing next to Carolyn in the front row stood a dark-haired, young woman.

It couldn't be.

He blinked and found himself staring.

"Dad said it was a six-point, biggest buck he's ever seen. Maybe a Boone and Crockett record," Robby's voice lilted.

John forced his gaze to the cross. The beautiful, young woman who wouldn't tell him her name in Roth's grocery was one of Ted's choir girls.

Choir girl number four.

* * *

THE GIRLS DISPERSED to sit amongst the congregation. In the third row from the front, Isabelle sat next to Carolyn and stared at the back of the oak pew in front of her.

The Velveeta Man was here! *Out of all the churches in Silverton, Lord, why does he have to go here?* She'd simply avoid him. Pretend Roth's grocery had never happened.

An elderly man with a loud, clear voice stood behind the pulpit and announced the birth of a baby girl. He asked for prayers for Ralph Ferguson to find employment.

Isabelle repeated to herself. *Pray for Ralph and his family.*

After the announcements, Darlene sang "Tell me the Old, Old Story" with Mr. Hoffmeister accompanying her on guitar. She held out her arms, embracing the audience. She looked so at home like she'd grown up in this church and knew everyone by name.

Isabelle scanned the nearby pews, looking for the red-headed woman she'd seen at Roth's with the Velveeta Man.

For some reason, the woman was seated two rows behind him. Why weren't they sitting together?

After Mr. Hoffmeister and Darlene descended the stage, the Velveeta Man rose to his feet.

He carried a Bible as he walked up the steps.

Please, no. He can't possibly be.

Maybe he was simply going to read a verse.

He perched the large, black book on the pulpit and cleared his throat. Then he smiled, and, with one hand, made sure both sides of his dark tie were uniform.

He'd told her his name was . . . John. That was it! . . . John.

He couldn't be John Hugg, this little church's pastor.

She stared at the hymnals stored in the back of the pew in front of her. *Do you have a home church?* His steady hazel eyes and soft, tugging smile had flustered her, maybe even more than the gal standing behind the cart... Isabelle's gaze shifted to the red-haired woman.

"It's not every day that you wake up to such a beautiful, late November morning," John said. "After I saw the cloudless blue sky, I was tempted to take a walk. The problem was, I hadn't planned my morning right—and many of you may have found it odd to see your pastor out taking a Sunday morning stroll while you were driving to church." He paused to let them chuckle.

The man from Roth's was this church's pastor—Pastor John Hugg. And, right in front of his wife, or his sister, or whoever the red-haired woman was, he'd flirted with her.

No. *Flirted* is the wrong word. He was a pastor. Reaching out to strangers extended beyond these walls. He'd simply been thinking of her as a soul to be saved, not as a woman.

She'd imagined it all.

"People new to this church often ask what style of windows these are." John's gaze shifted to the west-facing windows on the Coopers' side of the sanctuary. "This is a

Carpenter Gothic-style church, and the windows with their peak at the top are called lancet-style. But I prefer what I overheard ten-year-old Samuel Waggoner tell his younger brother this week.

"According to Samuel, 'The windows are shaped like the bow of a boat, like the boat Jesus' disciples were in.'" He smiled.

The congregation peered with interest at the windows lining both sides of the high-ceilinged room. In the upper arches of the clear leaded glass, Isabelle saw it too—the bow of a boat.

"Turn with me in your Bibles to Matthew, chapter 14."

She reached for a Bible in the rack in front of her.

"Hurry!" Nettie whispered, shaking her peppermint.

Isabelle had forgotten her host mother's little tradition. Leaning back, she fished the candy out of her pocket. While thin, silky pages of the Holy Book were being turned, she, like the other Coopers in their row, twisted the crinkly cellophane wrapper and popped the peppermint into her mouth.

It almost felt sinful.

As John Hugg narrated the familiar story of Jesus walking on water, Isabelle found herself only half listening.

"I see myself in Peter." John stepped away from the pulpit. "In the middle of a boisterous sea, he got out of the boat and with his eyes on Jesus, took several faith-driven steps toward Him. And then Peter took his eyes off Jesus, looked around him at his circumstances," John's gaze scanned the congregation, "and began to sink."

His speaking abilities made everyone attentive and comfortable—except for her. She cringed, closing her eyes. Why did she have to have a solo?

If she went to the restroom, would anyone notice if she never came back? She could thumb a ride home.

Carolyn nudged her. "Stop fretting; you'll do great."

Isabelle inhaled deeply.

"Keep your eyes on Jesus." Pastor Hugg's gaze swept the congregation. "And, have a Happy Thanksgiving with your families. Ted Hoffmeister, our choir director, has one last solo. Oh, and don't forget, our monthly church potluck is right after service today. Don't know how that worked out, but we're blessed with two feasts in one week." He grinned. "Make sure you introduce yourselves to our new choir girls. They'll be with us now through December nineteenth."

"We're staying for the potluck," Nettie said, and reaching across Carolyn, patted Isabelle's arm.

She nodded.

Guitar in hand, Mr. Hoffmeister started for the front.

Isabelle was supposed to head up there, too. Gripping the curve of the pew in front of her, she almost felt sea sick.

"Go." Carolyn nudged her. "You're on."

Albert wasn't here to pick her up and cart her, limbs flailing, to the stage. Six years ago that's exactly what he'd done. Now, she had to be a big girl all by herself. Arms tingly and vision swimmy, she made her way toward the front.

Seated on his stool to the right of the pulpit, Mr. Hoffmeister tuned his guitar, waiting for her. She ascended the three steps, stopped beside him, and turned to face the congregation. Her cheeks already felt warm. The elderly man strummed the first few chords. Her heart thumped around like a fish out of water while she scanned the sea of faces. Albert's wasn't among them. Not that she'd expected him to be, but he'd always been there for her before.

Don't call home. I don't want to hear your voice.

She gripped her hands behind her back and tried to think about God and not Albert.

From the third row, Nettie and Russell smiled broadly at her. Carolyn winked. And then there was Mr. Hoffmeister's pause, his cue.

Isabelle peered up at the tall, bow-of-the-boat-shaped windows which cast thin fingers of light over the ocean of unfamiliar faces. Breathing in through her nose, she felt her abdomen expand and then her gaze drifted once more toward the back of the sanctuary. *"On a hill far a-way stood an old rugged cross . . ."*

People often told her father that they loved how distinct her voice was and how they could discern every word. *"The em-blem of suff'ring and shame."* Albert used to call the stillness that settled at the Wilhoit gatherings *a hushing silence.* It had already settled here, as well.

She squeezed her hands behind her as she held the high notes. Tears ebbed. And, mid-song, she felt herself relax in the sea of melody and purpose. Then, remembering her audience, she looked straight at the red-haired woman, her eyes dark and unreadable.

Not wanting any more surprises, she lifted her gaze to the peak of the windows. *"I will cling to the old rugged cross, and exchange it someday for a crown."*

After she caressed the last note, the room was completely still.

Nettie Cooper sat frozen—her hands inches apart.

An elderly man sniffled.

And, there was the click of a purse.

Isabelle took a half step closer to Mr. Hoffmeister.

"Thank you, everyone." He stood up, holding the neck of his guitar. "Don't forget the potluck downstairs and keep the first Sunday in December open for our Christmas Choir's first performance."

People rose to their feet, turning toward the aisle.

"People don't always clap when they're in the House of the Lord. Don't worry about it." Mr. Hoffmeister eyed her over his shoulder. "You sounded great."

"Thank you."

She retrieved her coat from the back room and, carrying it in front of her, returned to the half-empty sanctuary.

The young pastor stood near the doorway to the foyer, smiling and shaking hands with each person who passed. To get to the potluck downstairs, she'd have to pass him.

She inhaled, trying to be brave.

This time, she'd tell him her name.

CHAPTER 6

Isabelle stood at the back of the line to greet the pastor. The line moved forward, and so did she. Three people dwindled to two. John Hugg shook hands with an elderly man in front of her.

He's a pastor. Not someone to worry about, she reminded herself.

"You're getting so much better. *So* much better," the man said with a chuckle.

"Thank you, Cecil. That means a lot hearing it from you."

She took a step forward.

Mr. Hoffmeister emerged from the foyer and, stopping beside John, grinned at her. "You did great. We'll continue to work on your presentation a little."

"Thank you—"

The pastor stuck out his hand. "John Hugg."

"Isabelle Bucknell." She slid her hand into his firm grip.

"That was an *incredibly* moving song."

"Thank you." She inhaled.

"And, Isabelle, before I forget . . ." Mr. Hoffmeister peered over the top of his dark frames at her. "I want you girls here ten minutes before church starts not—"

She stopped breathing. Did he think she was the reason the Coopers were late?

"Hey, Ted," John chuckled under his breath. "It's Russell that you need to speak to about timeliness. They've had car problems for months."

"Oh, I see." Mr. Hoffmeister's expression softened. "I'll speak to him about it."

"He's staying for the potluck."

Mr. Hoffmeister nodded.

She sighed. *Saved by the pastor*.

"So, what do you think about our finale girl?" Mr. Hoffmeister grinned. "She can hit anything."

Any note, maybe, but she didn't have a very good aim. She thought about Albert's truck.

John Hugg smiled at her.

She let her gaze drift ever so subtly to John's left hand.

There wasn't a ring.

Heat crept up her neck, and she wobbled on one heel.

"Where'd you find her?" John asked.

"She's the girl from Wilhoit Mineral Springs that Pastor Cordill said I needed to hear."

"Wilhoit?" John's voice lilted.

"Yes." Isabelle nodded.

"I used to go there as a boy. We'd stay in the cabins and fish the creek. Never cared for the water, though."

"It's an acquired taste. One of the pumps is sulfur. Smells like rotten eggs."

"That's the one I remember. You live there all of your life?"

"Pretty much—since I was eight."

"I recall an old-timer with a cane and a tin can." His slow grin revealed a dimple in his broad, handsome face.

"Uncle Donald. He always makes sure folks pay their entrance fee. Every two bits counts." She had to leave now before he delved any deeper. "Excuse me; I'll go join the others." She stepped around Mr. Hoffmeister and made her way through the empty foyer. When she was halfway down the dimly lit stairwell, she covered her mouth with one hand, stifling a nervous giggle.

What was this little church thinking – hosting an all-girls choir? Their young pastor wasn't even married!

* * *

AFTER BEING ROPED into dishwashing help, Isabelle left the church kitchen. Across the room, she spotted a vacant seat next to Nettie. She made her way between the long dessert tables and sat down between her host mother and another elderly woman.

"Isabelle, have you met Harriett?" Nettie gestured to the woman on Isabelle's left.

"No, I haven't." The woman's short, white curls framed her powdered round face.

"You've been blessed with a lovely voice, dear." Harriett patted Isabelle's hand in hers. "This is my husband, Frank." She nodded to the gentleman beside her.

"You're Isabelle; I take it." He reached across his wife to shake her hand. "Your name sounds familiar. Are you from around here?"

"Yes, Wilhoit."

Frank's hair was thick and white. Behind his black-framed glasses, his eyes were sharp and keen. "So, you're going to spend the next couple of weeks here in Silverton, singing with Ted Hoffmeister's group?"

"Yes."

"Look . . ." Harriett patted her husband's arm. "John's

trying to make his way over to us, but every other step someone nabs him."

Isabelle followed their gaze to John Hugg, where he stood conversing with a sturdy-looking fellow.

"He's still trying." Harriett nudged her husband.

"Victor just nabbed him. It's over." Frank stood up and ambled over to the dessert table where he picked up a plate.

"He's going to get some pie." Harriett patted Isabelle's arm. "The men in my family like pie."

"How's his hand?" Nettie asked.

"The same. He's tired of everyone asking." Harriet lowered her voice. "He tries to hide it."

"What's wrong?" Isabelle watched Frank slide his left hand into the pocket of his suit coat. Then he set his paper plate down on the table.

"Last year, shortly after Christmas, he had a stroke," Harriet whispered. "At first, it affected his entire left side; but now it's only his hand. All in the Lord's timing."

They watched Frank scoop a piece of mincemeat pie onto a plate and add a dollop of whipped cream. After he sat down, Harriett rose. Taking short steps, the elderly woman walked over to the dessert table and set two cookies on her plate.

"So you're from Wilhoit?" Frank glanced over at her.

"Yes. Wilhoit Mineral Springs." The answer alone usually didn't satisfy people, so she added, "My great-uncle and aunt have owned the resort since 1935."

He nodded. "If I remember correctly, the park used to get more visitors in a day than Crater Lake," he said.

"It did. At the 1908 World's Fair in Spokane, the mineral water won second-best to Ragoozi Springs in Germany." She repeated what Uncle Donald told everyone. "But... the resort's never been the same since the first hotel burned down."

"I thought they rebuilt it."

"On a much smaller scale. We call it the retired hotel now. People still come out—mainly in the summer months. Sometimes they'll camp or stay a night in the cabins."

"I haven't been out there for years. Kind of a magical place." Frank stretched his long legs out in front of him.

A nip of homesickness settled on her. In her mind, she walked the wooded grounds of the park by lantern light, listened to the ramblings of the little creek that flowed through the property, and held Albert's hand in hers.

She lifted her gaze.

John was looking right at her.

Catching her breath, she looked away.

"Your turn, Isabelle." Harriett returned to her chair and sat down. "I'll save your seat."

John and a tall, wiry-built man were conversing in the middle aisle. She walked to the table on the left side of the room. There were two slices of mincemeat pie and iced apple bars. Cookies with a walnut filling caught her eye. She set one on her plate. Her gaze drew her further down the table to a plate of icebox cookies. She lightly bumped elbows with someone. "Sorry, I'm all elbows."

She glanced up to see the pale face of the red-haired woman.

"And lungs," the woman said, flatly.

Heat climbed Isabelle's cheeks.

The woman reached for a walnut cookie. A wedding ring shone on her slim hand.

They were married!

And, for some reason, he wasn't wearing a ring.

Isabelle's cookie almost slid off her plate before she righted it. Feeling sick to her stomach, she returned and sat down between Nettie and Harriet.

She was just about to take a bite of her cookie when

Harriet leaned toward her. "Did Lilly say something to upset you, dear?"

"Lilly? You mean . . . Mrs. Hugg?" Isabelle glanced toward the red-haired woman.

"Yes, Lilly. You were fine, and now you're not."

Isabelle's hand dropped to the plate in her lap. They were married. In Roth's grocery, John Hugg had flirted with her right in front of his wife.

"Our dear Lilly needs your prayers," Harriet said.

Isabelle gazed into her tranquil blue eyes. The sweet elderly woman had no idea how much.

Harriet patted Isabelle's hand, consolingly.

Nettie rose to visit the dessert table.

Isabelle took her first bite of the walnut cookie. Nearby, John patted Victor's shoulder, turned in their direction, and started toward them. He wasn't going to let her enjoy her cookie in peace.

Lord, trip him. Break his ankle. Anything...

"A miracle! Less than ten minutes with Victor," Frank mumbled under his breath.

"Is this seat taken?" John pointed to Nettie's chair.

"Yes." Nodding, Isabelle pressed her shoulders back in her chair.

"Nettie's at the dessert table. Sit down. You know her sweet tooth," Russell said.

Then, right in front of everyone, John sat down beside her. The shoulder of his wool suit coat touched the sleeve of her blouse.

She was going to be sick.

Albert had warned her about the big city, but she hadn't expected to find wolves in the sweet little town of Silverton.

John gently shook Russell's knee with his right hand, and then he reached across Isabelle to briefly clasp Harriett's outstretched hand.

"Have you met Isabelle?" the elderly woman asked, patting his hand.

"Yes, just a little while ago."

Isabelle felt herself stiffen.

"Can you believe her voice, Grandma?"

Isabelle lowered her cookie to her plate. Harriett was his grandmother. Out of all the elderly people at the potluck, she'd sat by his grandparents.

"A gift." Harriett nodded. With a twinkle in her eye, she held her plate over the top of Isabelle's, toward John.

"Thank you," Isabelle whispered. Why did he have to be related to such kind, sweet people? The scent of molasses and cinnamon drifted up to her before he took the cookie.

"You know these are my favorite?" He took a bite.

"They're my *Heaven-Sent* Molasses."

"They're just your plain molasses . . . Har-riet," her husband said.

John inhaled and appeared to savor it, even if it was just plain molasses.

"Have you heard, they're saying snow for Thanksgiving?" John addressed his grandfather.

"Pray it's not a repeat of last year." Frank shook his head.

Isabelle agreed. The Christmas flood of 1964 was considered a hundred-year flood. Its one-year anniversary was a common topic on the television and radio.

"What about you, Isabelle?" John glanced over his shoulder at her. "Do you have plans for Thanksgiving?"

"Yes. Mr. Hoffmeister said we'll have Wednesday and Thursday off to go home."

"And, if there's snow?" he asked.

"Albert . . ." She gripped the dessert plate tightly in her lap. "Al has chains. He'll come get me." She said a silent prayer that despite their parting words, he would make the drive.

"And, um . . . is he your boyfriend?"

He was getting right to the heart of her love life. "Yes." She nodded. "I've loved Albert since I was eight." She glanced on both sides of her to make sure everyone had heard.

"I'm sure he'll be very determined." John leaned back in his chair.

Isabelle wished Nettie would hurry back so she could offer her her chair. Instead, with her reading glasses perched on the tip of her nose, her host mother studied each plate of cookies. She was probably trying to determine if they froze well.

Hurry up, Nettie. End my misery.

"I want you to know, Russell, that your wife is one of my favorite people," John said. "Always has been."

"Mine too. One of a kind."

"Heart of gold," John said.

"Mouth of gold, too. Hasn't stopped her sweet tooth any."

Nettie approached carrying a plateful of treasures, and before Isabelle could rise, John moved to stand beside his grandfather's chair.

"Would anyone like a cup of coffee?" he asked, scanning the group.

Russell declined.

Nettie shook her head.

"It's Maxwell House." His gaze settled on Isabelle.

Her gut twisted. "No, thank you!" she said firmly enough that the nearest old-timers turned to look at her.

He retreated, grinning.

How could he even bring up that awkward moment at Roth's? He was flirting again, and at church, of all places.

***

John refilled his cup from the coffee urn.

"Isn't Isabelle the young woman from aisle three?" Seated

nearby, Virginia's gaze drifted briefly to the back of the low-ceilinged room where Isabelle, the Coopers, and his grandparents remained seated.

"You knew." He studied her twinkling blue eyes. "You had to know." Throughout the week, Virginia had spoken with all of the girls. She'd told him so on Friday.

A soft smile lit her lips.

The woman was a vault!

Someone tapped him on his shoulder. "John?"

He turned slowly, making sure his cup of coffee didn't slosh.

Darlene—choir girl number two—stepped closer, her gaze bright, steady.

"Opal, my host mother, wanted me to ask if you could drive me home."

John glanced across the room to Opal—his grandmother's first cousin. The two women were very close.

Darlene tucked her purse between her arm and side. "She'd like to leave early, something about putting her brooch in the oven?" She blinked twice and smiled softly.

He had to think about that one. His gaze roved the low ceiling.

"She probably meant *roast*."

"Oh, that makes more sense."

He scanned the room and spotted Wesley Hargett—Opal's son, and his second cousin once removed—seated amongst a group of other young people.

"Wesley's still here. You should ask him."

"He is? Oh, I didn't see him."

Surely her ditziness was an act.

John turned his back to her and focused on Virginia, who had kept the large secret all to herself since Tuesday.

Her sparkly gaze drifted to her left for a moment. Hiding

her mouth behind her coffee cup, she whispered, "That's called giving someone the cold shoulder."

"I know trouble when I see it."

"Do you think Wesley can handle her?"

"I wouldn't have sent her his direction if I didn't." John took a sip of coffee, and over his shoulder, spotted Lilly near the base of the stairs. Hopefully, she wasn't already leaving. With one foot on the first tread, she rummaged through her purse.

"Excuse me, Virginia." He made his way toward Lilly.

The young widow yanked a handkerchief out of her purse.

"What's wrong?" he asked her.

"Everything." She shrugged. "Charlie." Tears welled in her blue-green eyes.

"What'd he say?"

"He just blabbed on and on about how wonderful Tommy was. How he'd drive around town on cold days bringing shut-ins firewood. I don't need to be reminded." She sucked in a sob. "I think about how wonderful he was every day."

"Charlie meant well."

Her pain was still raw. Her first Thanksgiving and Christmas without Tommy would be tough—and with no immediate family in the area, he'd make sure to find someone she could spend the holidays with.

"I've got choir girl problems," he murmured.

Her chin lifted, and she eyed him. "What do you mean?"

"Opal Hargett had me drive Darlene, the taller brunette, to church the other day, and now the young woman thinks I'm her chauffeur. I just told her no. From now on, I'm not driving any of those girls around without a chaperone."

"That's a good idea—especially for Miss Lungs over there." Lilly nodded toward the far wall and Isabelle's group.

"She has a beau." There, he'd told her the truth. For at

least thirty seconds at Roth's grocery, Isabelle had been comfortable in his presence. She'd looked into his eyes and conversed naturally. This gave him hope.

But, it was wrong to continue his fascination. Isabelle had a beau.

"Is there a ring on her finger?"

"No." He'd confirmed that only a few minutes ago.

"The person you should be warming up to is Nettie. Remember Nettie Cooper?"

"Li-lly . . . she has a beau."

"I know. I've heard pain in your voice twice now."

She was right. He'd heard it, too.

CHAPTER 7

Tuesday morning, while the girls were at choir practice and Russell was asleep in his recliner, Nettie studied the calendar in her kitchen nook. Today was November twenty-third, Opal Hargett's birthday. She dialed her good friend's number.

"Hell-o," Opal's voice rang with its usual confidence.

"Happy birthday . . ." Nettie sang the birthday song.

"Thank you, Nettie, but you're early. My birthday's not until tomorrow."

"Oh, wait a second while I write that down." Nettie crossed out Opal's name under today's date and wrote it in the little square for November twenty-fourth instead. "While I have you on the phone, how are things going with Darlene?"

"Well . . . she is not the one for our dear Wesley."

"Oh?" Nettie pulled a padded chrome chair closer to the phone and sat down.

"When I was upstairs putting things away, Darlene hadn't even made her bed. She'd pulled the covers across, but she didn't take the time to tuck or straighten. And, her suitcase was left open, and her clothes are a jumbled mess. She'll have to iron everything to be presentable. And, if she doesn't iron them, I'll have to. I can't have my choir girl going out all wrinkled looking."

"Heavens, no." Nettie wondered if she'd been such a neatnik about the four boys she'd raised.

"What about Isabelle? All you've said about her is that she's sweet. Is she tidy?"

"I don't know. She is helpful." Last night after supper, Isabelle had wiped the counters.

"You got the best of the bunch."

"Except for our Carolyn, of course," Nettie said.

"After seeing Darlene's suitcase, I'm all the more convinced."

"Is Wesley still convinced?" Nettie bit the insides of her cheeks, curbing a giggle.

"He's sensible. Praise the Lord!"

"Is she still being bossy?"

"Yes, she's bossy. I don't know if I can iron that out of her."

She'd keep Isabelle any day over bossy and wrinkled.

"And, it's like she misinterprets everything I say." Opal sighed. "Do us a favor and run up and take a look inside Isabelle's suitcase. Either she's tidy, or she's not."

"Umph!" Nettie caught her breath at the thought. "I'll call you right back." She hung up the receiver. On her way out of the nook, she glanced at the clock. Good, it was only 10:30; she had plenty of time.

When she scampered through the living room, Russell was still asleep in his La-Z-Boy recliner; his skinny legs stretched out in front of him. Off the entry, she opened the stairwell door and, with a hand on the rail, made her way up the carpeted treads.

In the guest room, the pink chenille spreads were

straightened, and the pillows on both of the twin beds were smoothly tucked. In the small under-the-eave closet, the girls' skirts, blouses, and dresses were hung up nicely on the wooden hangers.

On the right side of the room, Isabelle's suitcase sat tucked beneath the bed.

Nettie crouched down and pulled out the old leather suitcase by its handle. Even though the girls weren't due home for lunch for a solid hour, her heart still hammered in her chest.

"I'm not stealing anything but a look," she told herself as she slid back the brass locks and lifted the lid.

Everything had its place. Even the young woman's hosiery was rolled into nice, tidy bundles. Except for the fact that Isabelle had a sort-of-boyfriend, she—Nettie Cooper—might very well be hosting the future Mrs. Hugg.

While she reached to close the lid, the corner of a small avocado-gold book caught her eye. Nettie chewed on her lower lip before pulling it out of the silk-lined pocket. *Autographs* was scored in fancy cursive across the cover. A green shoelace-like ribbon bound the left side.

She glanced at the empty doorway. Other than the faint ebb of Russell's snoring, she didn't hear a peep in their half-a-century old bungalow. Then, she flipped to the first page.

Isabelle,

I hope this little book captures a lot of memories for you of your trip.

Remember us at Wilhoit and those that love you best.

Aunt Elsie

Only one autograph in and Nettie felt like she was reading another person's soul. Fascinated, she flipped to the next page.

Isabelle,

You're going to miss me and my cooking.

Don't you fret none.
We're going to miss you, too.
Fletcher.

Hmm . . . sounds like they had their very own chef out at Wilhoit.

Nettie turned to the next page.

Izz,

Sure hope you enjoy the Christmas choir. It's going to be mighty quiet around here without you. It ain't gonna be as pretty sounding either.

—Albert

That's all? Isabelle was going to be gone for five weeks, and that's all Albert, her sort-of-fellow, had written? Even though his writing hinted at more, a sort-of-beau could easily have written gobs more.

She returned the autograph book to the same exact spot, snapped the locks into place, and slid the case beneath the bed.

What had Albert's sentiments been?

It ain't gonna be as pretty. That's all Nettie could remember, and she wanted to remember word-for-word when she told Opal. She pulled the suitcase back out, retrieved the little book, locked the case, and slid it back underneath the bed. The girls weren't due home for at least an hour, but a host grandmother couldn't be too careful.

She returned downstairs and was glad to hear Russell still asleep in his recliner; his sock clad feet pointing in opposite directions on the footrest. In her little nook area with its built-in shelves, she dialed Opal's number.

"Hello."

"Opal, it's me, Nettie," she whispered.

"What'd you find out?"

"Everything was *very* tidy."

"A very good sign. But, why are you whispering?"

Nettie cleared her throat. "She has an autograph book. And, Albert—her sort-of-boyfriend—didn't write very much."

"What'd he write?"

"Wait a second. I have it here." Wedging the phone between her cheek and shoulder, Nettie pulled it from her pocket.

The doorbell rang.

She paused for a moment and in the following silence, determined it was probably no one of importance. Then she thumbed to the third page in the recipe card-sized book. "He wrote: *Izz, Sure hope you enjoy the Christmas choir. It's going to be mighty quiet around here without you. It ain't gonna be as pretty sounding either—Albert.*"

"Hmm . . ."

"That's what I thought, too," Nettie said.

"He knows that he'll miss her voice. I wouldn't dismiss him entirely."

"Awh, but I want to."

The doorbell rang a second time.

"Wait a second, Opal." Nettie set down the phone and moved toward the doorway.

Russell had risen from his chair and taken a step toward the entry.

Nettie scurried back to the phone, her heels clicking against the linoleum.

"Russell's getting it."

"Who do you think it is?"

"Could be anyone. Could be the milkman. Could be the Fuller Brush man..."

"Could be your choir girls locked out! Hide the book!"

Nettie hadn't thought of that. Clutching it in her grip, she glanced at her open shelves of Fiestaware before tucking the autograph book between the upright telephone directories.

It didn't show one bit.

"All's well." She patted a hand to her heart.

"Nettie . . . it's time you invited John Hugg to dinner."

"I was hoping to get to the bottom of . . ." Nettie glanced toward the doorway, "her sort-of-fellow part first."

"Less than a month and it'll be Christmas. That doesn't leave us much time."

"You're right." What could she do in a pinch? Hmmm . . . Nettie strummed her lower lip.

"Nettie, the Kirby man's here." Russell's voice carried from the living room.

"Oh no!" He didn't. She stretched the phone cord to the doorway into the living room. Sure enough, a well-dressed middle-aged man was taking off his overcoat in their front room. "Opal! Russell's let the Kirby salesman in. I need to go."

"Good luck." Opal giggled.

* * *

WHEN ISABELLE and Carolyn returned home for lunch, Mrs. Cooper lay on the sofa, reading a novel, a box of tissues by her side.

"Carolyn . . ." Nettie said. And, without pulling her gaze from the page, she waved her granddaughter over. "Lilly called, out of the blue."

Isabelle halted one step past Russell's recliner.

"Lilly?" Carolyn said.

"Yes. She called just a little while ago. What do you think of inviting Lilly and John over for dinner?"

No. Isabelle stiffened. *Please, no.*

"I think that's a great idea," Carolyn said.

"Hold on a second while I finish here." Nettie turned what appeared to be the final page in the book. Her eyes traveled back and forth for half a minute before she sighed and dropped her reading arm to her side. "I haven't done a thing."

"We can help, Grandma."

Oh, no. Isabelle cringed. She'd help by hiding upstairs.

"Tomorrow's Thanksgiving Eve, so it may as well be tonight." Nettie flung the crocheted afghan aside, swiveled her legs to the carpet, and sat up.

"We should invite Ted and Ruth, too," Carolyn said.

Yes. Isabelle nodded. Invite the entire church.

"Of course." Nettie nodded. "You girls hurry up and make yourself a sandwich. Carolyn, you dust, and Isabelle can try out our new vacuum while I write out the shopping list."

"New vacuum?" Carolyn's gaze narrowed.

"Yes, Granddad let in the Kirby man this morning and let me tell you, he was quite the salesman. Your granddad and I, both of us, mind you—" Nettie glanced toward Russell "wanted the vacuum something terrible." She glanced up at Carolyn, lowering her tone. "That we used all the money we'd been saving to fix Hilda to buy a Kirby."

Isabelle's arms went limp at her sides.

There went any hope they'd had for getting to church on time.

"But, Grandma . . . your old vacuum worked fine."

"I've never wanted anything in all my life as much as I wanted that Kirby. Granddad felt the same way."

Carolyn glanced over at Isabelle with an apologetic smile.

It was their money. But this Sunday, she wouldn't let them feel bad if she walked ahead of them to service.

"What do you think about a TV dinner party, Grandma?"

Nettie nodded. "We'll have Salisbury steak and all the trimmings. We'll save the turkey dinners for Thanksgiving, in case it snows and we're stuck here."

Was she serious?

The elderly woman stretched; no change in her softly wrinkled round cheeks.

"Now, you girls do your chores, and I'll have Granddad try and get the car started, so he can drive you to the store."

A minute or two later, with a Bologna sandwich in hand, Isabelle hurried to the front entry and wheeled the shiny new upright Kirby Dual Sanitronic 50 Vacuum out of the closet.

Please, Lord, please . . . keep John and Lilly Hugg from coming tonight. You know why. She grimaced. *If they do come, I promise... it'll be the most uncomfortable evening of my life. Please, spare me.*

* * *

JOHN CHUCKLED. It was 4:30 p.m. and Nettie Cooper had just called to officially invite him and Lilly to dinner that night.

The phone rang again.

A few minutes later, Virginia knocked and poked her head inside his office. "Lilly's on line one."

"Thank you." He picked up the receiver. "This is John."

"John, my truck's still out of gas, so tell Nettie I'm not com . . . ing."

"I thought the Goffs brought you a—"

"I'm not putting any in 'cause I'm not driv . . . ing."

"Have you been drinking, Lilly?" She obviously had.

The line was quiet on the other end.

"I'll come pick you up," he said.

"If you make me, I'll tell every . . . body . . . John Hugg is in love. And he doesn't even know her."

That was a pretty solid threat.

"I'm not in love. Company and a good meal will be good for you."

Click. The line went dead.

She'd hung up on him.

He dialed the Coopers' number. It was only fair to let them know. He exhaled a heavy sigh and, while the phone rang, tapped his fingers on top of his desk.

"Hell-o," Nettie's crackly voice came on the line.

"Nettie, it's John."

"Are you calling to cancel?"

"I may have to. Lilly's been drinking."

"Oh. I just spoke with her a little while ago."

"I don't think she should be alone, Nettie." There went his hopes of seeing Isabelle. "What do you think I should do?"

"I don't think you should be alone with Lilly either, not in her condition."

She was right. He shouldn't be.

"Oh, but we've gone to all this work. You'll have to bring her."

"Okay. I'll go pick her up." But, the evening could be a disaster.

***

THE TIMER BEEPED at six o'clock sharp. While Isabelle grabbed the ketchup out of the fridge, Carolyn removed a baking pan from the hot oven and rolled Tater Tots into a Fiestaware bowl.

"Keep the oven on. We won't bake the TV dinners until John and Lilly get here," Nettie bellowed from the living room.

Isabelle set the ketchup on the table.

Seated in the recliners, Russell and Mr. Hoffmeister watched TV.

Nettie stood near the end of the couch and pulled aside the lace curtain to peer at the driveway. "Ted, what can we get you to drink?" Then with a puzzled expression, she glanced toward the kitchen. "What *can we get for him to* drink?"

"I know!" Carolyn scampered into the kitchen and soon returned to the doorway, grinning and holding a partially frozen jug of Wilhoit water up in the air like it was a trophy.

Bless her heart.

"No, not that!" Nettie frowned, waving a hand at her.

"7-Up's my favorite party drink," Russell said.

"Carolyn, get money from Granddad and hurry! They'll be here any minute," Nettie said. "The only thing I don't like about having company over is the getting ready part."

She seemed to have forgotten that Mr. Hoffmeister was company.

The doorbell rang.

"Oh, no, I forgot about my hair!" Nettie clamped her hands on top of her head and darted into the hallway.

Isabelle didn't understand the fuss. Her short, white hair was just like she'd worn it to church on Sunday.

"Buy something for the ice cream, too. I don't think Ma thought of it." Russell set a pair of one-dollar bills on the small side table between the recliners.

No one was answering the door.

With his hands folded in front of him and skinny legs elevated, Mr. Hoffmeister appeared comfy in Nettie's recliner.

Isabelle didn't want to be the one to greet the Huggs.

"Carolyn, get out the china," Nettie yelled from the other room. "And, Isabelle, answer that door!"

She strode bravely toward the entry. Silverton was an odd little town, with odd residents, and an odd pastor. Bracing herself, she swung open the door.

Mr. and Mrs. Hugg stood on the doorstep.

Lilly was five-seven, five-eight, only a few inches shorter

than John. By the dour look on her face, it was all too apparent that she hadn't expected to see Isabelle here.

"Come in." Isabelle stepped off to the side.

Cold air and a floral perfume accompanied Lilly inside. Strong, nose-burning perfume for a pastor's wife. Isabelle tried not to breathe.

"Good evening, Isabelle." John hung up his coat.

"Good evening."

John helped Lilly out of her coat before he hung it on a hanger.

Isabelle walked ahead of them into the living area.

"Evening, Russell." John made his way toward the table. "Look at this spread."

"Can you believe we forgot 7-Up? Carolyn's gone to get some," Nettie said.

A dark-haired older woman stood near the table. Isabelle did a double-take.

Nettie was wearing a shiny, dark-brown wig with a high crown and tapered sides that didn't look at all natural, but for some reason was all the rage.

Carolyn stood behind her grandmother, holding a pile of plates.

"Evening, Carolyn." John grinned.

"Carolyn?" Nettie hissed. "What are you doing here? You're supposed to be getting 7-Up."

"I was going to, Grandma, but then you wanted me to get the china." With a careful shrug, Carolyn set the pile of plates on the table.

"That's right." Nettie's gaze darted to Isabelle. "Can you run and get us seven 7-Ups?"

"Me . . . ?" Did they want her to drive the Bel Air or walk by herself in the dark?

Carolyn took her by the elbow and steered her into the kitchen until they were well past the refrigerator. Then, she handed her the two dollar bills. "It's soda pop. Comes in green glass bottles."

"I know that."

"Well, you haven't known anything else! Velveeta, Tater Tots... pot pies."

That wasn't fair. But, truth be told, the Coopers ate very differently from the way she did back home. The thought edged her closer to feeling homesick.

Silverton wasn't as old fashioned or moral as she'd imagined it would be.

"Don't worry, Isabelle . . ." Nettie said loudly from the living room. "John Hugg's going to drive you in his truck."

CHAPTER 8

*W*hy couldn't John drive and get the 7-Up by himself? Or take his wife for that matter?

She should tell him no. But, even Lilly—slumped on the sofa—fluttered her fingers goodbye.

Isabelle hurried ahead of John through the nose-crinkling cold, down the brick walkway, over crumpled oak leaves to the passenger side of his truck. She climbed in, and quickly closed the door.

A step behind her, John slid in the other side. Shoulders hunched, he turned the key in the ignition. "After Nettie's parties, I always have a story or two to tell."

"Oh. Sounds like you've been to a few of them."

"Over the years." He nodded.

"Does she always serve TV dinners?"

"Yes. And, one time she burned them." He glanced across the cab at her and exhaled a rumpled breath. "You're going to have to excuse Lilly tonight. We all are. The perfume's to cover up the alcohol on her breath."

"Wha-at?" Her mouth went dry. His wife was drunk!

Things were worse than she'd imagined. She let the truth sink in. The pastor's wife was a drunk. That's why he... She shook her head, not allowing herself to finish the thought. They were both unhappy.

While he slowly drove down the hill toward town, she stared at the dash. Lilly's drinking explained a lot about their marriage.

"By the time I picked her up, she had a Bible in her lap and was already penitent about what she'd done." He cleared his throat. "Lilly's one of the sweetest people you'll ever meet. If she says anything, well, anything odd or unkind to you tonight, try to remember that."

"Did you know?" Isabelle glanced across the cab at him and for the first time since they'd met, felt a twinge of empathy for the man.

"That she drinks?" His brows furrowed. "Lilly's not a drunk. She's going through a horribly difficult time. And..." The dash light lit his handsome profile, and she reminded herself that it was not a sin to have vision. "She needs our prayers, not our criticism."

How could he be so understanding, so complacent? "If I was you, I'd make sure there wasn't any alcohol in the house."

"That's a step Lilly has to take, not me."

"I don't agree." Lilly's drinking could harm his reputation as a pastor and his church. From the moment she'd first seen Calvary Christian, the white-steepled little clapboard chapel had grabbed her heart.

And then she'd met the pastor.

At the base of the hill, he took a left. The headlights shone on a slim street sign. McClaine.

It would be the third time she'd been to Roth's FoodLiner in a week.

He rolled into a front parking space and without turning

off the engine, leaned back in the seat. "Tell me about your sort-of beau. His name's Albert?"

Her jaw felt heavy. She didn't want to tell the man anything. And why weren't they going inside?

"His name's Albert, right?"

She'd never missed Al more than right now.

"I've known Albert Gleinbroch since I was eight." She rocked her shoulders back. "We grew up out at Wilhoit together. He's six-foot-four, an all-league point guard. One sports reporter called Al, *Mr. Fourth Quarter* and it stuck. Right when everyone else was running out of steam, Al could pour it on. He had a lot of college offers before he hurt his knee." Her memory drifted to Al being helped off the floor in the middle of the state game.

"That's too bad." John tapped the steering wheel with one hand.

"He was devastated when the doctor told him he couldn't keep playing."

"I bet he was."

"His father, Fletcher, is the cook out at Wilhoit. Even though the hotel's pretty much retired, Uncle Donald keeps him on. He makes *everything* from scratch."

"Nettie's cooking must be a shock for you then." John almost smiled.

She shrugged. "Al works at Molalla Ford as a mechanic. He thinks he's going to own the company someday."

"With that attitude, he will."

"He's studied every type of vehicle, but he's partial to Fords, and the company's philosophy of making a vehicle that the average Joe can fix."

"And . . . ?"

For some reason, he wanted to hear more.

"Well . . ." She'd dwelled more on Al in the last few

minutes than she'd allowed herself to since her arrival. "Al may have a stubborn streak wider than the Columbia, but he's kind. He's amazingly good with children. And he praises my cooking, which is generous of him."

"And, you love him?"

"Yes . . ." She peered across the cab at John. "I've loved Al since I was eight years old." She had no choice but to affirm it again in John Hugg's presence. He probably wouldn't leave her alone otherwise.

"That's what you said." He nodded. "You're very specific about that. Did something happen when you were eight?"

The old odd adrenaline coursed through her veins.

Something had. Something she wasn't about to share with him.

Yet in the debris of heartbreak, there was a memory, she couldn't let go... Albert and his fistful of purple crocuses from Aunt Elsie's flowerbed. Her world had just fallen apart. And, she'd never forget the tender look on his boyish face.

John turned off the engine and dropped the keys inside his coat pocket.

She squeezed the door handle, slid out and followed him inside the store.

Maybe it was because they were in a public place, but he appeared to be all business now.

"What is it that we need again?" He looked around.

"Seven bottles of 7-Up and Mr. Cooper wants something to put over vanilla ice cream."

"Hershey's Chocolate topping." He turned, and then she followed him down the third aisle.

"Will we be over budget?" She fanned out the two dollar bills.

"I can scrounge up a quarter or two." A few minutes later, they carried their items to the counter.

"How are you today, John?" Mr. Roth rang up their items. His green bow tie was crooked.

"Good, Orville. Temperature's dropping outside."

"Let's hope it's not anything like last year."

"I keep trying to remind folks that it was a hundred-year flood, not an annual flood." John scrounged up a dollar's worth of quarters from his pocket.

"I'll try and remember that, too." The lean, middle-aged man grinned at Isabelle. "Remember, each day is a gift—that's why it's called the present." Then he glanced at John. "Do you want your Green Stamps?"

"Yes."

On their way toward the glass doors, John stepped aside and tucked the stamps inside his wallet. "I save them for Lilly."

"Of course, you do." Isabelle braved the chilly air first.

He hurried ahead of her to the truck and set the bag of groceries on the passenger's side. With the doorframe in hand, he waited while she climbed inside the cab, quickly smoothed the back of her coat, and sat down.

"Why'd you say it like that?" Brows gathered, he remained nearby in the expanse of the door, letting in all the cold air.

"That's what married couples do." She locked eyes with him. "They save Green Stamps for each other." Chin lifted, she focused on the front of the store.

He firmly closed her door then rounded the rear of the vehicle. He climbed in his side of the cab and turned the key in the ignition and studied the front of the store.

In the time he'd just wasted, they could already be halfway to the Coopers'.

He rubbed his hands together; a smile denting his profile.

He'd found something amusing.

"Last December, Silverton was without power for a week. Some of the store's front windows were broken during the storm." John nodded toward the brightly lit building. "So, Orville and his business partner slept in the store at night to protect the merchandise. Over the course of the next week, they ate a lot of ice cream and drank chocolate milk. People weren't buying the meats and dairy products fast enough, and a lot of perishables just rotted. They had a hard go of it for a while."

"But, they made it." Isabelle nodded. She liked Orville.

"Orville's a hard worker and a great guy." John nodded, thoughtfully. "Isabelle . . ."

The soft note in his voice stirred worry. She peered over her shoulder at him.

His smile was soft. "Lilly and I aren't married."

She frowned, not sure if she'd heard him correctly. "What?"

"I've never been married or engaged."

She stared at the dash and tried to make sense of what he'd said.

"But Lilly has," he whispered. "Her husband, Tommy Crawl, was a faller for the mill, and one of my best friends."

Isabelle sucked in a breath.

"We lost him in a logging accident this past February."

Lilly was a widow. Isabelle stared at the glove compartment now.

"When you're a pastor in a small town, and your grandmother's prayer group pulls together a Christmas choir, you just assume all the young ladies know that you're a bachelor."

Isabelle shook her head. "Mr. Hoffmeister pulled the choir together."

"With a lot of help."

"But . . . your grandmother, at the potluck. . ." Isabelle tried to remember their conversation. She'd said, *Lilly? You mean . . . Mrs. Hugg?* Oh, no . . . Harriet had misunderstood her because she was Mrs. Hugg!

"It was all my mistake. I'm so sorry." She covered her mouth with one hand. "I've thought terrible things about you."

"Well . . . I'm glad it's behind us." He grabbed the gearshift knob, putting it into reverse.

Lilly, poor, poor Lilly. Her mind wove all over the place as he drove up West Main Hill.

"Is this why she was drinking?"

"One of the neighbors dropped by a bottle of wine—a widow's gift." John glanced over at her and shook his head. "She's still learning to lean on Him. And, like we all do at times, she tries to get by on her own."

He took a right on Center Street. In the Coopers' gravel driveway, he shifted into park and left the engine running. All of the lights on the main floor of the Coopers' bungalow were on.

"Are you still going home for Thanksgiving?" he asked.

"Al's coming to get me." Of course, that had been the plan before she'd thrown a rock at his truck.

She slid out her side, picked up the bag of groceries and closed the door. The 7-Up bottles clinked together as she headed toward the house.

John waited on the walkway and took the bag from her. "So, you thought I was married because of Roth's and seeing me with Lilly?" Turning, he led the way.

"Yes, and then she was at church." She followed him up the steps.

He paused, his hand on the knob. The porch light bathed his handsome features in a soft pale light.

"I have a question, Isabelle." Above the V of his wool coat, his Adam's apple bobbed in his neck. "If you love Albert so much, why do you call him your sort-of-boyfriend?"

He'd cut right to the chase. "He didn't want me to do the Christmas choir." She peered up into his keen, hazel eyes.

Lilly was a widow. John wasn't married. He'd only been doing the Lord's work. John Hugg wasn't terrible. Her thoughts tripped over themselves.

Before he could ask any more questions, she stepped past him and went inside.

CHAPTER 9

"Four 7-Ups and one Wilhoit water." Nettie entered the kitchen holding up four fingers on one hand, and her pointer finger on the other.

"Who wants the Wilhoit water?" Carolyn asked.

"John." Nettie beamed. "You girls handle the drinks, and I'll be in charge of the dinners." She nodded toward the oven.

Isabelle retreated to get the jug of Wilhoit water. On the back step, she paused, inhaled deeply and stared into the chilly darkness. In the last hour, she'd gone from thinking the worst about the man to... thinking about the man.

She shook her head. She barely knew John Hugg.

After the girls served the drinks, Isabelle sat down in one of the dining chairs that someone had moved next to where Lilly sat on the end of the couch.

Carolyn carried around the bowl of Tater Tots and ketchup and handed Isabelle a little plate.

"Hors d'oeuvres. Try and eat just one."

Curious, Isabelle dipped a tot into the sauce, took a bite, and chewed thoughtfully. She held up the next little tot, studying it. They were crisp on the outside and like a fleshy potato on the inside.

The room felt too quiet.

All eyes appeared to be on her. Had Carolyn told them to watch? Even John seated on the other side of Lilly, a soft smile on his face, seemed to wait for her opinion.

"They are good." She nodded.

"Girls! I almost forgot." Nettie rose and started for the kitchen. "I wanted you to sing happy birthday to Opal." She paused in the doorway, rolling her wrist for them to follow her. "Tomorrow's her birthday. And, I want you to sing to her now before I forget."

Isabelle followed Carolyn into the kitchen nook area.

"Have you met Opal Hargett yet?" Nettie asked Isabelle while she dialed the number.

"No."

"She's Darlene's host mother," Carolyn said.

Pressing a finger against her lips, Nettie held the receiver to her ear. "Hi, Wesley, may I please speak to your mother." She handed the girls the phone. "Soon as she gets on, start singing."

"Hello," a woman's voice came on the line.

Carolyn held the receiver between them, and the girls sang Opal the happy birthday song with Nettie bobbing her index fingers like a conductor.

While she sang, Isabelle's heart felt a hundred pounds lighter than an hour ago.

John Hugg wasn't married.

* * *

NETTIE COOPER THREW ODD PARTIES. Instead of sitting down at the nice dinner table in the living area, they sat in a semi-circle and used the skinny-legged, metal TV trays to set their food on. Lawrence Welk was on, but the volume was muted for company.

Isabelle eyed the Salisbury steak. It appeared to be a fancy name for hamburger topped with gravy. The TV dinner also came with mashed potatoes, peas and carrots, and a small serving of apple cobbler.

"The TV dinners fit so perfectly on the TV trays." Nettie steadied her mini-table with both hands.

"They designed it that way, Ma," Russell said.

"They did? Well, they're smarter than me. That's fer sure."

The phone rang in the kitchen.

"Get that for me, Carolyn. I'll dump my dinner if I try to get out of this thing," Nettie said.

Carolyn set her tray off to one side and hurried into the kitchen.

"I swear I'm shrinking," Nettie said, and taking a bite, she chewed. "Only yesterday, I could touch the molding above the coat closet and now I can't."

"Yesterday, you were wearing heels," Russell said.

"You're right!" Nettie waved a hand and laughed.

So did everyone else, except for Lilly.

"Grandma, it was Mom. I told her you'd call her back," Carolyn said on her return. "Isabelle, you didn't tell me that you brought your autograph book." She waved something in the air, smiling.

"What?" Isabelle's arm dropped against the corner of her TV tray, sloshing her 7-Up into her cobbler.

"Where did you find that?" She wanted to stand up and grab it, but... the precarious TV tray held her prisoner.

Carolyn handed Mr. Hoffmeister a pen and then the book. He set it off to his side in the recliner.

She'd never taken it out of her suitcase, not once since she'd been here. But, someone had! Who? She swallowed to moisten her dry mouth.

"It was in the middle of the phone books. Just tucked away." Carolyn smoothed the back of her dress and sat down on the couch. "This is so perfect! Everybody can sign it tonight."

"What a great idea!" Nettie clapped her hands together. "And, everyone has to write something original, none of this *sugar is sweet* stuff."

Someone had gone through her suitcase. Gone through all of her things. Her slips Her girdles. Her autograph book...

Mr. Hoffmeister paused from eating to turn to a blank page.

Autograph books should come with a key like diaries.

Had Carolyn snooped through her suitcase and found it there? If she had, her new friend wasn't nearly as wonderful as she'd thought. But her response to finding the book had seemed so sincere.

Was she an actress like Darlene?

Could Mrs. Cooper have possibly taken her book? But, why would she?

Seated nearby, Nettie spooned her last bite of cobbler. Out of the corner of her eye, the elderly woman glanced over at her.

"I can sign it anytime." Carolyn passed the autograph book from Mr. Hoffmeister to John.

"My aunt gave me the book right before I left," Isabelle informed everyone. "I didn't plan to use it. I don't even know how it got downstairs." Her gaze locked on Nettie.

The elderly woman blinked. "When I was growing up, everyone had autograph books."

"Yearbooks are more popular now, Grandma."

"You never asked me to sign your yearbook." Nettie waved a hand.

"You didn't go to my high school."

John made room on his TV tray and flipped the book

open to the first page and then the second. Was he a quick enough reader that he could read her life story? It was hard to watch.

Finally, he turned to a blank page.

Would he write something about tonight, tease her that he wasn't married. It was embarrassing. Would she ever stop being so green?

"How do I love thee," Lilly's speech sounded heavy, slurred.

"Lilly, you should try and finish your dinner," John said.

"Yeeeeah. Nettie went to *all* this work." Lilly flung a hand toward her tray then slumped back on the couch. "Sorry, I'm such a sinner."

"What'd she say?" Russell asked, looking at Nettie.

"I can't understand her mumbling either," she said.

"We're all sinners, Lilly. We all fall short," John said as he carefully moved Lilly's TV tray off to one side.

"And, Christ loves us so much, Lilly," Nettie leaned forward in the padded chrome chair, "that He left heaven to be a little baby. The miracle of Christmas."

Eyes closed tight, Lilly grimaced, shaking her head.

"That He even loves us is the miracle," Russell mumbled under his breath.

Nettie flicked her wrist, frowning at him.

With her head resting back against the curve of the sofa, Lilly no longer appeared to be listening.

"Ruth and our granddaughters had already made plans. Otherwise, she would have been here, too." Mr. Hoffmeister lifted his guitar case from the floor and flipped back the locks. While he tuned the instrument, Isabelle and Carolyn rose and gathered the dinner trays and utensils and carried them into the kitchen.

Carolyn opened the cupboard beneath the sink and pulled out the garbage can, and Isabelle stuffed the foil containers inside. "You didn't happen to take my autograph book out of my suitcase?" Isabelle asked. She didn't want to stew about it all evening.

"No. I didn't even know you had one until a little while ago." Carolyn ran hot water into the sink and set the silverware to soak.

"Then, who took it out of my case? I didn't."

"Well . . . it wasn't Grandpa. That only leaves one person. Not that I think she did it," Carolyn whispered now. "Grandma may be a gossip, but she's not a snoop."

A gossip?

"What?" Isabelle followed Carolyn back into the living room and sat down.

Nettie was a gossip? Her sweet, elderly host mother?

With a twinkle in his eye, Mr. Hoffmeister strummed the melody to "Mockin' Bird Hill" and glanced over at her.

Maybe the happy little tune was exactly what she needed to get her mind off of... She studied the carpet between Nettie and John.

Clearing his throat, Mr. Hoffmeister nodded at Isabelle.

She sat up in her chair, her hands tucked under her thighs and clearing her throat a bit tried to warn everyone that she was going to break out in song. Then she sang the opening lyrics of Mockin' Bird Hill. A loud snore emanated from the couch.

Isabelle paused.

Mr. Hoffmeister stopped strumming.

With her head tilted back over the curve of the couch, Lilly's mouth hung open. Her wheezing intake of breath sounded like a chainsaw in full throttle.

"I think Lilly ought to stay here tonight. I'll make sure she has coffee and a nice hot breakfast. Then, you can bring her home in the morning," Nettie told John.

"I think that's a good idea, too." With his arms folded in

front of him, John's gaze drifted to Isabelle, and a soft smile teased his lips.

He wasn't married.

She swallowed. And he'd just written in her autograph book, maybe something for her to brood about for the next few weeks. She dug her thumb nail deep into the palm of her other hand. She hoped not. It wouldn't be right for a man in his position to go writing just any old thing in a girl's autograph book.

People would read it.

Nettie Cooper would read it.

* * *

"I DIDN'T KNOW Lilly was a widow until tonight." Isabelle pulled the covers to her chin and waited for Carolyn to turn out the light.

"I still can't believe it. It was such a shock. Everybody loved Tommy." Standing in front of the waterfall mirror, Carolyn rolled her last swath of short, pale blond hair around a foam curler. She looked like a pink hedgehog.

"What'd John write in your little book?" Carolyn peered over her shoulder at her.

"I haven't read it." She was afraid to. She'd tucked it inside her suitcase for now until she could find a better hiding place.

"I doubt he'd write anything too personal, even if he does like you."

Her stomach fluttered. "What do you mean *likes* me?" Maybe she wasn't imagining things.

"Some fellas wear their heart on their sleeve. John's one of them."

How could he like her? He didn't even know her.

Isabelle flipped the covers back, lowering her feet to the

floor. She pulled her case out from beneath the bed and knelt down in front of it. Aunt Elsie's little book was causing problems. She should have thrown it out the window when she'd had a mind to.

She sat down on the edge of the mattress and flipped through the recipe-card sized pages to Mr. Hoffmeister's entry.

Isabelle,

You ask me for something original, and I don't know where to begin. For there is nothing original in me. But the Original Sin.

Ted Hoffmeister

P.S. God has given you a lovely soprano voice.

She appreciated his sentiments, even if they weren't original.

Turning to the next page, she spotted John's name near the bottom. Her pulse quickened.

Isabelle,

When the sun is sinking
And this path no more you trod
May your name in gold be written
In the autograph of God.
—John Hugg - 1965

It was perfect. Absolutely perfect.

"You're smiling. What'd he write?" Carolyn reached out her hand for it.

Isabelle handed it to her. Then leaning back on the bed, she giggled, relieved. If Nettie ever found her autograph book again, there'd be nothing she could read into or gab about.

Nothing.

"John Hugg!" Carolyn's shoulder sunk as she lowered the book to her lap. "Your Albert even wrote more than he did."

"When did you read Al's?"

"Before I passed it to John. Didn't take more than a second."

That meant John might easily have read it, as well.

"Well, the good news is," Carolyn sat up a little taller on her bed, "Grandma won't have much to tell the girls about."

"What girls?"

"Her prayer group. Frank Hugg—John's grandpa—who used to be the preacher, he named their group the Seven Blocks of Granite. But, nowadays, most everyone just calls them the Granite Girls."

"So, you think your grandma's the one who took my book?"

With a scrunched up look of apology, Carolyn nodded. "I found it right next to the phone. Like she'd hidden it between the directories and forgotten about it."

Things were just getting worse. "She went through my suitcase?"

"Maybe she was just putting something away." Carolyn leaned forward, handing her back the book.

Isabelle rose from the bed and paused, thinking twice about it. Then, she set the autograph book on top of the dresser in plain view.

"You're not going to just leave it there?"

"Why not? At least this way, your grandma won't need to snoop through my suitcase again searching for it."

"You have a good point."

CHAPTER 10

John awoke to a blanket of silence. He tossed back the covers and parted the gold floral curtains to peer over his fully fenced backyard. Few sights were as beautiful as freshly fallen snow.

The white fluffy stuff looked so innocent that Silverton residents often drove too fast, braked too fast, or made the mistake of stopping on hills. By nightfall, every tow truck in Marion County would be employed.

Everyone should just stay put.

Not that he could. He had to take Lilly home and chop firewood for his grandparents. Good thing he had chains and a four-wheel-drive truck.

After a bowl of instant oatmeal, he dressed and shaved. Then he trudged through the crunchy snow to the church and shoveled off the walkway and stairs leading to the main entrance and then the walkway that led to the ground level door. From there, he headed inside.

Because his grandfather would visit his office from time to time, John had gone to great care not to change a thing. Two brown, padded armchairs sat in front of the aged, oak desk. Three shelves of books lined the wall to the left of the door. Behind his desk hung a large acrylic painting of the church in spring when the yellow daffodils were in bloom. Beth Waggoner, now a mother of five, had painted it when she'd been a teen.

The phone rang.

Virginia had taken the day off to prepare for Thanksgiving, so John didn't hesitate in answering it.

"Calvary Christian Church, John Hugg speaking."

"John, this is Grandpa." His voice held good vigor. "Did something praiseworthy happen in the body last night? Was a baby born or...?"

"No... not that I'm aware of."

"Hmmm... The phone started ringing here at seven a.m., and your grandmother's been on it ever since. When I asked what all the fuss is about, she did that little wave of hers and said they're sharing recipes."

John inhaled deeply.

"If I remember correctly, it was Nettie Cooper who called here first. And, between you and me... I don't think she uses recipes."

John chuckled.

"So, you haven't heard a thing?" Grandpa asked.

"No." But, he had a pretty good idea what was being said.

Grandpa cleared his throat. "I'll do some listening and call you back."

"I planned to drive out to your place sometime this morning and cut some more firewood. In case you call, and I'm not here."

"Make sure you put chains on."

"I plan to."

"Seeing the pastor's truck in the ditch will only reinforce the notion that you're young."

* * *

When Isabelle awoke, it was like a deep-in-the-woods type of silence. Peering across the room, she blinked. Carolyn's empty unmade bed reminded her that she wasn't home at Wilhoit.

She shimmied to her knees and pulled the drapery panel aside. Through the snow-covered branches of the oak tree, the downtown area rested in a plush robe of white; at least three inches of snow decorated the Coopers' mailbox.

She might very well be stuck in Silverton for Thanksgiving and turkey TV dinners. She forced herself up and across the room to the closet under the eave, where she pulled Aunt Elsie's old, quilted, pink satin robe off of a hanger and wrestled it over her head. The garment smelled like the fir and cedar wood used to heat the hotel. She trudged through a wave of homesickness and started down the stairs.

Lilly lay on the couch with her back to the room, her coppery red hair visible above the edge of the blankets. Hushed whispers carried from the kitchen.

Isabelle braced herself, half expecting John to be sitting at the table in the nook.

Only the Coopers were seated at the Formica table.

Nettie pressed a finger to her lips, and Isabelle sat down in the vacant chair next to Carolyn.

A Corningware tea kettle sat on a hot pad beside a pile of bowls and serving-sized packets of Instant Cream of Wheat.

"I thought the air smelled like snow last night," Russell said above the rim of his cup.

"Shhh!" Nettie pressed a finger to her lips. "Lilly's asleep."

Russell mimed what he'd just said. Pointing out the window, he added a shiver, before his wife elbowed him.

The phone rang.

"It's either for Lilly, Carolyn or Isabelle," Nettie whispered. Turning, she waited for the phone to ring a third time before she picked it up and pulled the cord over her shoulder.

"Hello, Cooper residence, this is Nettie speaking," she said with normal volume. "Good morning, John." She eyed Isabelle then the ceiling. "It is beautiful. No, she's still asleep."

"I'm awake," Lilly mumbled from the front room.

"Oh, I take that back. She's awake now." Nettie covered the receiver. "John's on the phone for you."

"I'm coming."

"I don't think I've ever had a white Thanksgiving, John. Have you?" Nettie asked while Lilly wandered into the kitchen. The tails of her blouse stuck out from beneath her sweater, and her long hair was tangled.

"I agree. We're in for a treat. Here's Lilly." Nettie handed her the receiver.

Standing in front of the built-in shelves, Lilly turned her back to the table. "Hello. Uh-huh. No, I planned to make a pie tonight. Are you sure? Okay." She hung up and rubbed her eyes.

"Would you like a cup of coffee, Lilly?" Nettie whispered.

"Yes, thank you."

"The Sanka's on the second shelf to the right of the stove."

Lilly opened several cupboards before carrying a mug and the jar of Sanka to the table.

"John's taking me to Frank and Harriet's this morning." Lilly sat down in the chair at the end near Isabelle. "He said something about splitting firewood for them."

"Have some Cream of Wheat." Nettie nodded to the packets.

Lilly shook her head.

"It'd be good for you to have a hot breakfast."

"No, thank you." Yellow undertones surfaced in her pale

complexion. "I hope I didn't say anything... offensive last night."

"If you did, we couldn't understand you." Nettie lowered her voice. "You were mumbling quite a lot."

"I wasn't up for visiting. John made me," Lilly admitted for some reason.

"He didn't want you home all alone and neither did we. Honey, the next time you feel all down and out like that, call Carolyn or..." Nettie shook her head, looking around the table.

"Or me," Isabelle offered.

Lilly blinked.

"Yes, just call here, and you can talk to whoever your heart desires. Even Russell," Nettie said.

Lilly nodded and set an arm on top of the table. "Have you met Harriet yet?" she asked Isabelle.

"Yes, at the potluck."

"You should go with us."

Isabelle shook her head. "I may get a ride home today."

"Even with the snow?" Carolyn asked.

"Yes." She sure hoped so.

"Find out. Call . . . call your sort-of-Albert fellow." Nettie swished her hand over her shoulder toward the telephone.

She couldn't call Albert in front of everyone.

"Go on." Nettie swished her hand. "We need to know how many to plan for Thanksgiving."

Why? She was only making TV dinners.

"Isabelle!" Nettie's sparse white brows lifted above her glasses.

The elderly woman just wanted to eavesdrop.

Isabelle inhaled deeply and rose from the table. What was so hard about popping five TV dinners in the oven instead of four?

The tea kettle clock read 8:45. Al would have already

been at work for an hour. And, if he'd driven to work, why couldn't he drive here? She lifted the receiver and dialed, keeping her back to the table.

"Molalla Ford, how may I help you?" a male voice answered.

"Is Albert Gleinbroch in?" She rarely called Al at work. He'd know it was important.

"Yeah, Al's around here somewhere. Just a minute."

From the front office, they'd transfer the call to the repair shop in back. "Hello, this is Albert." His deep voice came on the line sooner than she'd expected.

"Hi, it's Isabelle." She gripped the curlicue phone cord with her free hand.

"Hi."

Only ten days ago, he'd bent one knee to Wilhoit Road and made his awful proposal.

"With the snow and all, the Coopers want me to try and pin down my plans for Thanksgiving." Her heart beat in her throat.

Silence followed.

"There's a good three inches here," she said, to fill the chasm.

"At least four," Russell mumbled in the background.

"I don't get off till five and if the roads are at all icy—"

"Sounds like we'll have to play it by ear."

"I'll call when I get off work and let you know. Elsie gave me the Coopers' number this morning."

"Okay. Thanks." Al sounded so matter of fact; she might very well be stuck in Silverton for Thanksgiving. She hung up the receiver.

Turkey TV dinners only came with apple cobbler. She wouldn't even have pumpkin pie if she stayed at the Coopers.

"Well . . . is he coming?" Nettie's gaze followed her as she rounded the side of the table.

"It depends on the roads. He won't get off until five." Isabelle sat down. Was she being petty about something as simple as pie? Except for Nettie's snooping and gossiping, the Coopers were wonderful, good people.

"Back in the Midwest, they think nothing of snow," Nettie said.

"Oh, is that where you're from?" Isabelle asked.

"I'm from LaCrosse, Wisconsin—where they make boots."

"I thought that's the accent I was hearing," Lilly said.

"Before LaCrosse, we lived for a few years in Missouri. Then my pappy lost his job."

"Maybe that's what I hear," Isabelle said.

"They don't get the wet stuff like we do. Black ice, freezing rain…" Russell shook his head. "Whole 'nother ballgame here."

"Where does your fella work?" Lilly eyed Isabelle.

"He's a mechanic at Molalla Ford."

"Well, if he's not picking you up until after five, you'll have plenty of time to go with us to Harriet and Frank's."

Lilly almost sounded like she wanted her to go.

Peering out the window behind her, Russell lifted his chin. "Looks like John's truck out there."

Nettie pushed back her chair and stood up. "That's him, all right."

Carolyn rose and flitted from the kitchen. Even though everyone except for Lilly was still in their house robes, Isabelle was uncomfortable that John would see her in hers.

CHAPTER 11

While John made his way up the walkway, he thought about clearing the sidewalk for the elderly couple, but no snow shovel was in sight. When he reached the porch, he began unlacing his boots.

The front door swung open, and Carolyn in her blue fluffy bathrobe and slippers stepped out onto the porch in thirty-degree weather.

"You like her, don't you?" she asked with a smile.

"Who?"

"Isabelle. I could tell last night."

"What about Albert?"

Carolyn shrugged. "She rarely talks about him."

"Well, she talks about him to me." He set his boots to right of the door and followed her inside.

"Just now was the first time she's even spoken to him since she arrived. And, not very much was said," Carolyn whispered.

Was she trying to give him hope?

In the nook area, Lilly cradled a mug of coffee with both

hands. Kitty-corner to her sat Isabelle, her face flushed and her dark hair loose about her shoulders.

He felt weak—weak in the knees, weak in the head.

"Grab a mug, John. Sanka's on the table," Nettie said.

In the kitchen, he opened the first door he came to in the row of cabinets that hung suspended from the ceiling. His guess was lucky, and he pulled out a white mug that had a Union 76 Gas Station logo on the side, a reminder to pray for Wesley Hargett. The young man needed prayer living out on a farm with Darlene whatever her last name was. John sat down near the corner of the table between Russell and Lilly in a wooden chair from the dining room.

"Do Frank and Harriet know we're coming?" Lilly loosened the lid then passed him the jar of Sanka.

He stirred in a teaspoonful. "I just spoke with Grandpa this morning." He took his first sip.

"Isabelle rang Albert, and he may pick her up after work if the roads are fine." Lilly kicked the side of his calf lightly beneath the table for some reason. "So, she'll be able to go with us, too."

His coffee almost went down the wrong pipe. He cleared his throat. "I see. Well, I told Grandpa we'd be there around 9:30."

"I should get ready, then." Isabelle rose and, carrying a bowl and mug, scooted behind them.

After Isabelle exited the kitchen, Nettie whispered, "After Thanksgiving maybe…" her gaze traveled around the table, "she won't be referring to Albert as her sort-of-boyfriend anymore—especially if he comes to get her in the middle of this snowstorm."

"It's not a storm, right now, Ma." Russell eyed the winter scape outside.

John nodded.

"Well, give the weather a little time, and prayer 'cause I'd like to keep her right here." Nettie jabbed a finger to the table.

John couldn't agree with her more.

***

THE DRY SNOW crunched beneath John's feet as he led the way to his truck. Did Isabelle want to spend the day with them or had Lilly twisted her arm somehow? He slid behind the wheel and started the engine.

"You go ahead," Lilly held open the door, waving Isabelle ahead of her. "I feel sick when I sit in the middle."

Isabelle didn't appear convinced.

"Claustrophobic, nauseated…squished when I sit there…" Lilly's voice trailed off.

"Lilly!" John sighed.

Isabelle climbed inside the cab and, keeping her gaze on the dash, scooted over until she was a hand's breadth from his side.

You'd think he was contagious.

He checked his rearview mirror. While he backed his truck onto Center Street, Isabelle sat stiffly, her profile to him.

Give me wisdom, Lord. If it's not Your will, take away this attraction.

"John, are you praying again?" Lilly was often too outspoken.

"Yes."

"I think that's wise, too." Lilly was at her finest.

"I'm glad I put on chains." He took a left on Main Street and shifted into second as he drove down the winding hill toward downtown. Blanketed in snow, the picturesque little town could carry its own line of greeting cards.

"Have you always had lungs?" Lilly asked Isabelle.

"Since the day I was born."

"What I meant is, have you always belted out beautiful music or was there a time when you went through kind of an ugly duckling quack stage?"

"I don't know. My sister's probably the best person to ask."

Isabelle had a sister, and a great-aunt and uncle, and a sort-of-boyfriend who might very well drive through the snow to fetch her.

"What are your hobbies, Lilly?" Isabelle asked.

"I work at the feed store, answering phones, payables, filing… "Hello, this is Schoenberger's Feed Store, how may I help you?' Then I go home. Eat, sleep, drink. Sometimes, I rotate the order." She exhaled a heavy breath.

"Lilly!" John moaned.

While he drove south on Water Street, he waited for her to speak truth instead of trying to shock the poor girl.

If it stayed cold through Friday morning, there'd be snow and Christmas lights at the same time. His heart wanted to take a stroll.

"I used to dust," Lilly added.

"Do you drink every day?" Isabelle asked.

"Water. Coffee. Sometimes tea. John's waiting for me to tell you the truth. I've only drunk alcohol two times in the last eight months. And, that's the truth, John. You probably don't believe me." Lilly sighed. "He's seen me both times." Then her voice rose as she added, "I tried to tell you that I shouldn't have gone last night."

"I'm glad you did."

"Well, after Barney, my neighbor, dropped by the bottle of widow's wine—"

"That isn't what he called it, is it?" he asked.

"Yes." Lilly shrugged.

Her neighbor needed prayer, too.

"After Barney left, I just sat there listening to the refrigerator hum, feeling sorry for myself, and alone. It was before Nettie called."

"You should have called John," Isabelle said.

Was she slowly warming up to him?

"Yes, Lilly. You know what I would have told you—"

"Of course. You'd have me read First Peter or some Psalm. Tommy used to call Psalms *Salve for the Soul*." Lilly inhaled deeply. "I used to knit socks when I was bored. Once, I knit the cutest little pair of cream-colored baby slippers. The needles were about the size of a toothpick—a little longer, of course. I think once when I was really bored, I tried knitting with toothpicks."

"Knitting socks involves a lot of counting, doesn't it?" Isabelle asked.

"Yes. Basic arithmetic, not calculus."

"The next time you're feeling alone, please call me," Isabelle said.

Silence followed for a minute while Lilly peered out her side of the cab. "Would you just look at this beautiful world?"

"It is beautiful," said the beautiful woman beside him.

As they left town, the setting changed from residential to frosted, towering fir trees.

"It's romantic." Lilly was getting carried away. For the drive to be romantic, Isabelle would have to be interested in him. Though she was seated beside him, she hadn't glanced his way once. Miles separated them.

Tire tracks were proof that his wasn't the only vehicle on the roads that morning.

"For Christmas, John, I'd like a big ham, a carton of ice cream, a block of Swiss cheese." Lilly was hinting that he owed her big time for Isabelle's company.

"Is she always so funny?" Isabelle glanced at him.

Finally.

He suppressed a smile. "Yes." His mind drifted to Tommy, a big lumberjack of a guy, and how he'd always been laughing.

"But, sometimes I go too far. After I'd called you *Miss Lungs* the other day, John was good about rebuking me."

"Admonishing sounds gentler, Lilly. Tell Isabelle the rest."

"I can't remember the rest. For some reason, that part stuck like cow pie to the bottom of my church shoes."

Isabelle giggled.

Thank you, Lord.

"I can usually dismiss her sarcasm," he glanced at Isabelle to find her gazing up at him, "because I know deep down she has a heart of gold." He returned his attention to the road.

"I know, but it's good to hear you say it *again*."

Isabelle giggled.

Maybe she was warming up to the fact that he and Lilly weren't married. He took a left off of 214 onto his grandparents' long gravel drive.

Does she have to go home for Thanksgiving, Lord? Would it be selfish of me to ask that she stay here?

***

HARRIET'S KITCHEN wallpaper was blue and white check, and her maple table sat beneath white, ruffled curtains.

Harriet refilled Isabelle's cup a half-inch from the top.

"Thank you," she said while John's grandmother returned the glass percolator to a burner on the white enamel stove.

"Would you care for another slice of zucchini bread?" Harriet lifted the plate toward Lilly.

"No, thank you."

"What about you, Isabelle. One more?"

"No, thank you. But, it was delicious." Harriet Hugg's hospitality was a sharp contrast to Nettie's.

"What are you smiling about?" John eyed her every thought.

"Nothing." She shook her head.

He clasped his hands on top of the table. "You were grinning about something?"

"I was thinking about Nettie's hospitality, that's all." With a sinking heart, she knew she shouldn't have said it.

"I've always enjoyed Nettie's parties, but I'm not convinced that hospitality is one of her gifts." He grimaced slightly. "Forgive me. I shouldn't have said that."

"It isn't her gift," Lilly said, peering around the kitchen. "Nettie's proof that you don't have to be good at hospitality to throw a fun party."

"I shouldn't have brought it up. The Coopers are wonderful and welcoming—"

"She's not good at hospitality, and that's the truth." Lilly cradled her cup with both hands. "It isn't a sin to speak the truth, is it? God knows Nettie's bad at entertaining, but He still loves her. Doesn't he, John?"

"Yes, of course. And, he loves me. And, he loves you, too, Lilly."

Her blue-green eyes welled with tears. "I'm not ready to talk about it yet," she whispered.

"We don't expect you to." The fingers of his left hand tapped softly on the table.

"Then, will somebody please talk," Lilly quipped.

"John, have I showed you my latest potholders?" Standing near the sink, Harriet dried her hands on a dishtowel.

"No, Grandma." He sat back in his chair. Red crept up his neck and into his cheeks. "I'd love to see them."

He was just like Al was with Aunt Elsie—attentive and sweet.

"I'll go get a few." Their elderly hostess slowly rose from

her chair and shuffled through the doorway into the living room.

Lilly's eyelids fluttered. "Sorry, everyone. I'm not ready for company . . . people yet."

"It's okay, Lilly. We're just glad you're here with us," John whispered.

He was good at saying just the right thing.

Harriet returned and set a stack of quilted potholders down on the table near his elbow.

"These are special, Grandma." John passed the top hot pad to Lilly.

An apple was appliquéd over the top of tiny quilt blocks, with an o-ring for hanging.

"Those are too pretty to use for baking," Isabelle said.

"I'm finding more time to sew, as of late," Harriet said.

John smiled softly at Isabelle over the top of his cup of coffee, and for a moment, her pulse zipped along like a sewing machine with no bobbin thread. Lilly had invited her along because of John and made her sit in the middle on the way here because of him, too. Heat filled her cheeks.

She had to be careful. Almost everyone in this little town was biased about the man. He was a little too perfect. She kept her gaze on the table.

After they enjoyed a late afternoon lunch, John went outside to cut firewood. The girls stayed behind, and Harriet shared a few recipes from her box with Lilly.

About an hour later, the phone rang.

"We have a party line." With her chin lifted, Harriet listened through the next ring. "It's mine." She rose slowly from the table and picked it up.

"Hello, this is Harriet speaking." The elderly woman toyed with the cord as she faced the kitchen. "Yes, the kids are still here. Oh, I see. I'll ask John." She covered the mouthpiece with one hand and eyed Lilly. "It's Nettie. Albert's work closed early, and he's at their place. Run and ask John if he wants to bring Isabelle home or have Albert fetch her here?"

"I'll go ask." Lilly rose from her chair.

She was going home for Thanksgiving. Isabelle curbed a smile. Albert had come to get her. Her heart clenched in an anxious knot. Maybe she'd get some questions answered.

***

JOHN HALF EXPECTED Albert to be stewing in the Coopers' driveway—but when they arrived, the cab of the shiny black Ford truck was empty. He was probably inside drinking the last bottle of 7-Up.

"Thanks again for taking me. I had a nice time." Isabelle swung open the passenger door.

John leaned forward to see past Lilly. "You're welcome. Have a great Thanksgiving."

"You, too."

The girls said their goodbyes and then Lilly scooted across the bench seat toward the door.

There was nothing to read into with Isabelle, nor had there been throughout the day. She'd barely even looked his direction—probably on account of Albert. Gripping the wheel, he watched her make her way through the snow on her walk up to the front porch.

"We should take off. You don't want to be too obvious."

Lilly was probably right.

He shifted into reverse and set his arm on the back of the seat.

"What do you think?" he asked.

"I like her. I think she has a good heart."

"Any words of encouragement?"

"I think she has a good heart. I like her."

Three miles passed in silence before he took a right into

Lilly's gravel driveway. In front of the ivy covered woodshed, he shifted into park and left the engine running.

"I can't stop thinking about her. I don't understand it." He rubbed behind one ear.

"It doesn't help that she sings like she does. You were already a little wacky over the girl at the grocery, and then... well, last Sunday didn't help you one bit. It's no wonder you're stupefied."

He peered over at her, frowning.

She shrugged. "I meant stunned to the point of . . . senseless."

The old Lilly and her odd sense of humor were resurfacing. He tried not to mind that it was at his expense.

"Do you have any advice?"

"I don't envy you. I won't say who, but word is, watching John Hugg in love is expected to be a larger draw this December than the choir."

"It sounds like something Lilly Crawl would say."

Her shoulders shook as she gave into a laugh. "Well, it's what'll happen if you're not careful."

What a difference the last few hours had made in her disposition. *Thank you, Lord.*

"Would you pray for me?" He peered over at her.

Her smile faded, and she pressed her shoulders back into the bench seat. "Right now or tonight before I go to sleep?"

"Right now." He blinked then bowed his head.

"Some people can pray out loud around others. I can't. I have no flow."

"I don't care, Lilly. The Holy Spirit intercedes on our behalf."

"I know what you're doing."

He didn't lift his head.

Lilly let out a rumpled breath. "Our dear Heavenly

Father." He heard her move around a bit on the seat, then the click of her purse. She sniffled and blew her nose.

He kept his head bowed, waiting.

"Forgive me for last night. PLEASE. Help me to not... to *never* be so dumb again. Help me. Poof, I just threw caution to the wind and gave into feeling sorry for myself. Help me to be strong like Tommy would've wanted me to be." She puffed out a breath and sighed. "Like You'd want me to be."

Thank you, Lord.

"I pray for my Christian brother, John.

"I agree. It's kind of weird how he met the girl at the grocery. I didn't have the heart to tell him, but I thought she was twelve. And then she ends up being twenty, and in the choir, and has a voice like Patti Page. Maybe even better. Why did things line up like that if she's just gonna go home to Wilhoit... and break his heart?"

John nodded and feeling the start of a tension headache, pinched the bridge of his nose. Was she done? He almost opened his eyes.

"But, when I think about it, it's probably all because of Roth's Grocery. It would have been different if he hadn't seen her there. She would have just been another girl in the choir that he was trying to avoid."

Lilly has a good point, Lord.

"But that wasn't the way things worked out." Her voice took on an airy quality.

"After her solo, you could have just put him on a plate and sunk an apple in his mouth. For all he knows, she might cook like Nettie Cooper, but John would still want to marry her. He's that far gone. And, he knows so little about her..." her voice trailed off.

He was ready for Lilly to say *Amen*.

"Help John to handle his crush on the choir girl with wisdom and... Oh, what's that word John always uses?

Discernment. And, be with me, too, Lord. In Jesus' name, Amen."

He patted the bench seat between them. "I heard the Holy Spirit's counsel at the end." He blinked, smiling at her. "Crush on the choir girl. Thank you, Lilly."

"Anytime."

CHAPTER 12

Though dusk had fallen, Isabelle could see a baseball-sized dent in the rear fender of Al's shiny black truck—his pride and joy. It was bigger than the rock had been. He'd probably left it there just to make her feel bad.

They were a few miles out of town before he loosened his necktie and unbuttoned the top collar of his shirt.

"How come you're wearing your Sunday best?" She peered across the cab at him. Maybe it was because she hadn't seen him for a while, but he looked more handsome than she remembered.

"I told you, a lot can happen in one week, much less five."

It had only been ten days.

"What are you saying?"

"I got promoted. Mr. Wentworth's trying me out in sales. Said I'm a pot of gold hidden away in repair."

"You are." Al was outgoing, confident, and people liked him. "Are you enjoying it?"

"Yeah. I just need to learn the sales side of things."

"Good. I'm happy for you, Al."

"Thanks, Izz."

He kept his gaze on the road. His jaw muscle twitched and his profile looked so serious. Like he had thoughts he was keeping all to himself. Funny, how she knew him so well.

She sighed.

"Before I forget, I want to pick your brain about Mr. Cooper's Chevy Bel Air. Half the time, it won't start. Last Sunday, Carolyn and I were so late to service that we missed half of the choir's first song."

"You're kidding!" He chuckled.

She shook her head. "It was terrible. But, at least I wasn't the only one late. Everybody was just staring at us."

"What's it sound like—the car not the choir?"

"Like a low rumble."

"Hmm . . ." His dimple deepened in his profile. "Could be the starter. Could be the battery. Could be a number of things."

"You know me; I hate being late."

They drove in silence through the town of Scotts Mills, taking the backroads home.

"Mrs. Cooper said you sounded like an angel." His soft voice thawed a bit of her reserve. Nettie's sentiments meant a lot.

"Thanks for picking me up. What have you been doing besides work?" She pressed her shoulders back into the bench seat, trying to prepare herself.

"I had my first date the other night." He shrugged.

"Oh." Her eyes felt all sting-y. "Anyone I know?"

"A gal named Sue from Melton's Mercantile."

She knew Sue. Isabelle lowered her chin, gripping her hands in her lap. Sue Chavers had a figure almost as curvy as Darlene Berry's.

She felt her temperature rise. But, it wasn't like she was just sitting in Silverton staring at the TV.

But, only ten days ago, Al had almost . . .

"No one told me that she had a voice like Minnie Mouse."

Voices had always been important to Al. She inhaled deeply and peered out her side of the vehicle at the passing snow-flocked trees.

A couple of miles passed before they were in the final curves before home.

"Slow down," she said, as they neared the east edge of the resort's property. Off in the distance, the porch lights of the two-story hotel were a beacon in the white-blanketed darkness. The clumps of snow on top of the nearby fence posts sparkled in the truck's headlights and were proof that the world had changed since she'd left.

"Nothing's been the same." Al took a right onto the poplar-lined drive.

She waited for him to elaborate, but he didn't.

"Probably been pretty quiet? Huh?"

"Your dad's been missing you more than he expected. Make sure you sing him something special. He looks over at the piano every night like he's picturing you there and gets this faraway look in his eye."

Did Al miss her, too?

"Elsie's tried to sing a couple different times, but her voice doesn't reach the high notes anymore."

Instead of heading around to the covered area in back, he parked out front and kept the headlights on for a moment so they could watch for the deer that often grazed in the campground area.

There were none tonight to welcome her home.

She climbed out her side of the cab. Wilhoit was deep in the woods, where the trees buffered them in their own little, quiet world. They walked together up the porch steps and hung up their coats in the entry. Closing her eyes, she savored the smell of the cedar firewood used to heat the hotel and…

"Do I smell sauerbraten?" She stopped in the doorway to the great room.

"Isabelle!" Near the stone fireplace, Elsie grabbed both arms of her rocking chair, rose to her feet, and ambled toward her. "We haven't heard from you. Not a word. We were afraid you'd stay for Thanksgiving with your host family."

They met halfway and hugged near the side of the old davenport.

Elsie stepped back to admire her. "You already look older."

She felt older.

"Aren't they feeding you?" Fletcher asked from his chair, adjacent to the fire.

"Not like you."

"How were the roads?" her father asked as she made the rounds, hugging everyone.

"A little bit of ice building here and there. But, not bad," Al said.

"She looks older doesn't she, Al? Like a city girl in her new coat and heels," Aunt Elsie said.

"She looks tired. They haven't been feeding her. She's been telling me stories about TV dinners, Velveeta and…"

"Swanson pot pie," Isabelle added.

"Sauerbratens are in the oven. Too bad you weren't home earlier to help with the pies," Fletcher said. Every Thanksgiving, she'd been in charge of them.

She bent to hug Uncle Donald's bony shoulders.

"Came back 'fore you even left. Homesick, were you?" His wrinkly, smooth hands gripped hers.

"I missed you." And all of his wisdom.

"At least she missed one of us," Elsie said.

"I missed you all."

"Did you read my autograph?" Uncle Donald asked.

"No." She peered down into his twinkly, gray eyes. "Did you write one? I didn't see it."

"It's on the last page of your book." He grinned.

"People used to fight over who got the last page," said Aunt Elsie.

"Oh . . ." Maybe Nettie had already read it.

Uncle Donald cleared his throat. "Remember what I told you… when a girl asks a fellow to sign her autograph book, it makes him think that she wants him to write her something special."

Even though her gaze wanted to drift toward Albert, she focused on her uncle.

"Did you write me something soppy?"

"Of course I did." He grinned.

Then, she sat down a foot away from Albert on the dark brown velvety davenport and curled her feet beneath her. Several large logs burned in the expansive fireplace. Sparks popped onto the brick hearth.

Aunt Elsie's crochet sat tucked in her bag near the couch. Uncle Donald's Bible lay open on the side table. The mending basket, as high as ever, awaited her return.

She gazed into the fire, and, for a moment her heart surprised her by remembering John's gaze that morning at his grandmother's table. Like a stitching thread drawn too tight, his attentiveness tugged at her homecoming.

Now that she was home, she understood at least that much.

"How do you like Silverton?" Aunt Elsie asked.

"My roommate's really nice. And if the roads don't improve, my host mother is making frozen turkey TV dinners for Thanksgiving tomorrow. If there were a prize for the most eccentric host parents, mine would win." She had everyone's attention. "We were late to church last Sunday for the choir's first performance. Mr. Cooper's car wouldn't start. I think I was the only one who was stressed about it."

They all laughed and encouraged her to tell more. She went on and on; and, like a broken record, she skipped over some parts.

"What new songs have you learned?" Aunt Elsie asked.

"Sing them your solo that you were telling me about." Al flicked a hand toward the piano.

She shook her head. "They know it."

He flicked his hand again. He wanted her to sing.

"Sing something, doll." Her father missed her singing, too.

She forced herself out of the old comfy couch and followed her aunt to the upright piano. "I'll be singing "O Holy Night" for a solo."

Seated on the piano bench, Aunt Elsie flipped through the pages of her songbook, and then set her fingers to the keys.

Al propped an elbow on top of the couch, grinning and acting like the old Al—like nothing had changed.

But everything had.

Albert had already dated. Even though he was smiling so sweetly at her, he was trying to forget her. Her gut twisted, and then her memory somersaulted to John Hugg and how emotive he'd been at the pulpit. The humble poignancy in his voice and words. His fervent love for their Savior.

She was already zig-zagging between Silverton and home.

She closed her eyes and tried to get her heart right for the song.

"O holy night! The stars are brightly shining.
It is the night of our dear Savior's birth!"

Halfway through, she remembered her hands. Slowly, with her palms up, she lifted them away from her sides.

"A thrill of hope, the weary world rejoices.
For yonder breaks a new and glorious morn—"

"What are you doing with your hands?" Al interrupted.

Aunt Elsie paused from her playing and set her hands in her lap.

"Mr. Hoffmeister wants me to use them more, be more expressive."

"You don't look natural." Her father shook his head.

"There's a gal, Darlene," she glanced over at Aunt Elsie. "When she onstage, she's more comfortable than Norma Zimmer. Mr. Hoffmeister wants me to mimic her, but I—"

"She's fancy with her hands because she doesn't have your voice," Uncle Donald said. "You tell this Hoffmeister-fellow—"

"Donald! Shhh!" hissed Aunt Elsie.

"Dinner's done." Fletcher slapped the arms of his chair and rising to his feet, ambled past them into the kitchen.

Elsie closed the songbook.

Everyone walked past her, except for Al. Seated on the couch, he wore a pitiful old Al look. Like all it had taken was one song to melt his mindset.

He'd been wrong not to propose because now she had questions. Questions about John Hugg. Questions she would never have allowed herself to have if Al had just gotten a ring on her finger. And not been so… AWFUL.

CHAPTER 13

John pulled into the Union 76 gas station on Water Street and rolled down his window.

"Hello, John. Fill 'er up?" asked his cousin, Wesley Hargett. He was wearing the dark blue coveralls over a shirt, tie, and the signature dark blue cap.

"Yes, and check the oil." After John rolled his window back up, he could still hear Wesley humming a catchy tune.

The young man soon returned to the window carrying the dipstick.

John rolled the window down again.

"Wouldn't hurt to add a quart." He showed him the oil line. With John's permission, he added a quart and dropped the hood. Humming again, Wesley washed the windshield and then started squeegeeing.

"How are things working out with your choir girl?" John asked.

Wesley rolled his eyes. "What we don't get is how Mr. Hoffmeister ever found her. There's not a lot of church in her choir if you know what I mean."

John knew exactly what he meant.

"Pert near every evening, she wants somebody to film her with Dad's new movie camera. Last night, Mom ended up in one of the skits by accident. Funniest thing you ever saw.

"The girl needs prayer, so I reckon that's why the Lord sent her our way."

John agreed. Darlene Berry needed prayer.

"And, you know how Mom is. She needs prayer, too."

John nodded. Opal Hargett, his mother's first cousin, was as strict of a woman as they came. After thirty-some years of teaching elementary school children, she had discipline down to a doctrine.

After the tank was filled and paid for, John started up the engine.

"I'll see you tomorrow," he said to Wesley.

"Darlene's gonna be there, too. Just to warn you."

John nodded, thankful for the warning.

From the filling station, he drove straight home. When he got there, the phone was ringing. *Dear Lord, don't let it be an emergency.*

He hurried into the small, pale yellow kitchen and grabbed the receiver of the wall mount telephone. "Hello."

"John, it's Grandpa. I need you to do me a favor," he said in a low voice.

"Sure, of course . . . anything."

"Your grandma's group needs a talking to."

"What's going on?" he asked, even though he already knew.

"Every time I turn around, Harriet's on the phone to one of the Granite Girls. She's either calling them, or one of them is calling her. I've already spoken to her about it once today. But, when there's this many involved, there's usually only one way to take care of it."

Grandpa wanted him to address it at the pulpit.

John felt the start of a tension headache. "You don't think they're just praying?"

"No-oo! Contrary to what your grandmother thinks, my stroke hasn't hurt my hearing any. Every other sentence, they're gabbing about *the Heaven Sent*. And she expects me to believe that they're talking about her Molasses Cookies. You and I both know they're talking about the dark-haired, little choir girl and her visit here today."

Grandma!

"Her name's Isabelle. And, according to Virginia, all of the choir girls are at least twenty."

"That's right. *Isabelle.* Did Grandma tell you that I cried on Sunday during her solo?"

"No." It wasn't uncommon for his grandfather to well up during hymns.

"I've never heard the old song sung quite that way before. The girl has a gift." Grandpa cleared his throat. "If your grandmother's little group has their way, they're hoping to hear her gift every Sunday, if you know, what I mean."

Grandpa was doing a little fishing of his own now.

"I want you to address the girls' blabbing. Doesn't need to be more than a line or two. Somewhere in the middle of your sermon when everyone's half asleep, slip in that *God is in control of this church, not seven little, old ladies.* The Lord knows who needs to hear it."

"You could get away with saying something like that. I can't." The majority of the congregation still thought of him as Johnny, a young pup, wet behind the ears.

"If I have to be the one to address it, they'll respect you all the less."

John's fingers did a little tap dancing on the nearby Formica. Without a doubt, Grandma and Nettie Cooper were behind a lot of this.

"Reproving, rebuking, and exhorting with longsuffering

and doctrine are all part of being a pastor." Grandpa loved quoting Second Timothy.

"You're right." He sighed.

"Pray about it."

"I will." He might even do a little fasting. The first Sunday of the Christmas season, he could very well be rebuking his own grandmother and several women who'd been his Sunday school teachers.

* * *

The savory smells of roast turkey filled John's parents' rambler. And, like he'd been warned, Darlene was at his family gathering. She carried a molded green Jell-O salad into the kitchen and set it on the counter next to where he stood slicing the turkey.

"Hello, Darlene." John turned off the electric carving knife to acknowledge her. Auburn curls framed her clear complexion; a pumpkin-orange scarf was tied around her neck.

"Hi, John."

"Darlene, we enjoyed your duet on Sunday," his mother said. Using a fork, she mixed cornstarch into the drippings for the gravy.

"Thank you, Mrs. Hugg. Are the Coopers coming today?"

"That's a good question. John, did you invite them?"

"No. Do you want me to?" He probably should have. Maybe Darlene would read something into being the only choir girl here.

"If they don't already have plans, ask Nettie to bring a card table." His mother returned to whisking gravy.

The clock on the stove read 4:15. Nettie was one of the few people he'd feel comfortable inviting on such short notice. He washed his hands and dialed the Coopers' number.

"Hello," Nettie's crackly warm voice came on the line.

"Nettie, it's John Hugg." He couldn't help but smile. "If you don't have plans this afternoon, you're more than welcome to join us at my folks'. The meal starts at five. And the roads were fine on the way here."

"John Hugg," her voice dropped to a whisper, "if you'd called twenty minutes ago, we would've taken you up on it. Our turkey dinners are already in the oven. And, you know, Isabelle's not here. Guess we can't say she has an imaginary beau anymore now, can we?"

"No, I suppose we can't." Few people were as good as Nettie at telling it like it is.

"Nope, her Albert came through a blizzard to get her."

"It wasn't a blizzard, Nettie."

"Nice young man, and tall. Russell and I were both able to speak to him for a spell. When he was leaving, Carolyn was just getting home from the beauty parlor and caught a glimpse of him. Did you have a chance to meet him?"

"No, I didn't." He wasn't sure if he wanted to hear Carolyn's opinion of the man. Behind him in the kitchen, his mother and Darlene were quiet.

"Carolyn said he's *tall, dark, and handsome.* Isabelle never said a word about how nice-looking he is. Not that it matters. Besides, you're nice-looking, too."

"Thank you, Nettie. Um, if you change your mind, feel free to drop by." He glanced behind him. "Tell Russell, there's a counter full of pies."

"Our dinner comes with a mini cobbler. You go on and enjoy the day without us. We're perfectly content."

John returned the receiver. "Uh, their dinners are already in the oven."

"Oh, that's too bad." His mother handed Darlene a calico apron. "I'll put you in charge of serving drinks. Coffee's made, and there's a ginger ale punch."

Darlene tied the apron on over the top of her camel-colored wool skirt. "Oh, John, when you have a minute, there's something I'd like to speak to you about."

"Oh. What is it?" His mother exited the room, and for the first time since their first car ride, they were alone.

Darlene's chin lifted and her mouth bunched, thoughtfully. Maybe he should get Lilly to join them.

"My uncle owns—"

A flood of relations entered the nearby dining area to find their seats.

Darlene sighed with an obvious pout. Whatever she'd been about to tell him, she didn't want to with an audience.

"Dad, will you say the prayer?" His mother's voice carried from the other room.

"Love to," Grandpa said.

About an hour later, after a delicious dinner with all the trimmings, John dished out a piece of his grandmother's banana cream dessert. He looked up to see the Coopers—Nettie, Russell, and Carolyn entering the kitchen.

"You made it." He grinned.

"Russell overheard me talking to you on the phone and said we had to come. Looks like we're here just in time." Nettie eyed the pies and then pulled a large red can out of her purse and began shaking it. "Isn't this the best stuff?" She held it out so he could read the Reddi-wip label.

"Just shake it and spray. Tastes just like homemade. And what I like best is, there's no mess."

He grinned. The party had arrived.

Nettie set the can of whipped topping on the counter near the desserts, poured herself a cup of coffee, and strolled to the front room.

"Don't tell my wife," Russell scooted a piece of pumpkin pie onto his plate, "but I've died and gone to heaven."

"I won't."

The elderly man dolloped a spoonful of old-fashioned whipped cream on top of his pie and then a crowning layer of Reddi-wip.

Carolyn paused on John's left. "I bet Isabelle's never tried Reddi-wip."

He chuckled and remembered the look on her face when she'd eyed her first Tater Tot.

"Oh, that reminds me, John." On the far side of the dining room, Darlene ran a hand over the top of the piano. "Before we leave tonight, I have an Isabelle story for you."

"Why are you acting all secretive? Just share it now," Carolyn said.

"I'll tell John first."

Was she just trying to be alone with him?

He carried his dessert toward the front room.

"It's tough being cooped up on Thanksgiving with a wife who doesn't like football," Russell said.

"That's right! The Colts against the Lions," John said.

"And today's game is in color—the first time ever."

Like Russell, John peered around the room. His parents' television wasn't turned on and, knowing his mother, was probably unplugged.

"John, would you mind giving Darlene a ride home *again?*" Opal asked. "Arnie and I would like to leave soon."

He didn't care for how she'd placed emphasis on the word *again,* especially with an audience. He scanned the room. For some reason or other, his cousin Wesley had already left—wise man that he was.

"I'll be taking Lilly home, too. So, yes, that'll work." He'd bring Darlene home first, and then discuss the evening with Lilly on the way back to her place.

* * *

"Miss Darlene Berry, in there," Lilly folded an afghan in the front room and nodded toward the kitchen, "is warming up to your mother, and she's found a way to get a ride home. You watch; she's going to find a way to sit in the middle."

"Do me a favor and don't let that happen." John tossed a pillow onto the couch.

Ten minutes later, his parents waved from the open doorway while the three walked through thin, frozen remnants of snow and patchy ice to his truck, parked behind his father's utility trailer. There was no race to the passenger door as he'd feared. John slid behind the wheel and turned the key.

"Awh." A brief gasp was followed by Lilly scooting across the bench seat toward him. She bounced on the seat a bit before setting her empty pie plate in her lap. Mouth pursed tight, Lilly appeared upset about something.

"Your pie was a hit." John rubbed his hands together and waited for the engine to warm up.

"Shoot! I forgot the Jell-O. I'll be right back." Darlene slid out and closed the door with a thud before starting for the house.

"I don't like her." Lilly inhaled deeply and scooted a few feet away from him to sit closer to the door.

"She's your sister in Christ. You shouldn't—"

"She just pinched me, *and* hip-bumped me." Lilly jabbed her thumb toward her door. "And I hip-bumped her back and I pinched her, too. Hard."

"Lilly!" He sucked in his cheeks and bit down.

"What's that verse, a hip for a hip?" She smiled, pleased with herself. "I don't think you and Miss Berry should be alone together."

"I'll drop her off first and then bring you home."

"I know I'm supposed to *love* everyone and I do. I just don't *like* her."

"Lilly."

"Maybe I'm a bad judge of character, but Tommy was good, and I liked him instantly. Actually, I loved him instantly, kind of like you and choir girl number four."

Lilly sighed. "I think your grandmother likes her a lot, too." Then she pressed her shoulders back against the bench seat. "Speaking of Harriet, Tommy used to tell me the stories he'd heard about the Seven Blocks of Granite."

"Yes." He had a pretty good sense of where this conversation was headed.

"Little things happen while I'm at work."

"Oh? What kind of *little things*?" Through the parted drapes, he could see Darlene warming up to his mother in his parents' front room.

"The wood bin's half-empty when I leave in the morning and full to the brim when I get home. There'll only be one can of tomatoes when I leave, and two cans of tomatoes, plus a can of tuna fish when I return. I may have to start keeping inventory." She glanced at him. "Little things like that. What I can't figure out is how they're breaking in."

"Who would have a key?"

"The only person I've ever given a key to is Joann Goff. But she was with me one time when it happened."

"I haven't heard a word."

Off in the distance, the front door opened and his mother stood in the porch light waving goodbye for the second time. The hem of Darlene's coat flapped as she carried the bowl of Jell-O toward them.

Lilly reached over her shoulder and locked the door.

"Lilly!"

"I was just kidding." After she unlocked it, she scooted his direction.

Darlene climbed in the passenger's side and pulled the door closed behind her.

"Sorry! Opal would be very unhappy with me if I got home without her bowl."

John waited for her to get situated before he backed out of his parents' driveway and onto the main road.

Lilly remained quiet as he drove past her large rural mailbox—the landmark for her driveway.

"Darlene, what was your news that you wanted to speak to me about?" he asked. A ribbon of moonlight rippled through the trees onto the crystallized road.

"Yeah." Darlene caught her breath and sighed. "My uncle owns Molalla Jewelers."

Her train of thought wasn't hard to follow. She'd get a sizeable discount when the right fellow came along—which definitely wasn't him.

"Uncle Leo said that Albert Gleinbroch, Isabelle's *Albert*, recently purchased an engagement ring." The brightness in Darlene's voice could easily be mistaken for glee. "Said it was as big a diamond as the *young man* could afford."

Such news so shortly after two pieces of pie didn't sit well.

"I felt it was important for you to know."

"And what's important for John to know about you, Miss... Darlene . . . ?" Lilly paused, obviously searching for a caustic word, but couldn't find the right one with her pastor present.

In the silence that followed, John's memory drifted from the warm cab to the one time he'd been alone in his truck with Isabelle and she'd told him, *I've loved Al since I was eight years old.* The airy quality in her sweet voice had been very convincing. Tomorrow, when she returned, she'd probably be engaged.

CHAPTER 14

Friday morning, they left early so Al could drop her off in Silverton before he headed to work. Only a mile from Wilhoit, he pulled his truck over to the shoulder of the road and kept his foot on the brake.

Lids heavy, he gazed over at her. "You know, I'd do anything for you."

Except apologize.

The dent in his rear fender served as a reminder that she hadn't apologized either.

"When you called me at work, and I heard your voice . . ." He inhaled deeply and sighed. "It pert near ripped my heart out of my chest."

He almost sounded apologetic.

Then, he officially shifted into park. "You know why I didn't propose?"

"No. Why?"

"Because when I got down on one knee, the first thing you did was look over my shoulder toward Silverton." His jaw muscle flexed in his profile. "All you could think about was your freedom."

"It was all or nothing. Silverton or you. You couldn't even be happy for me." There, she'd said it.

He rolled a kink out of his neck.

"Instead, you were just awful."

"Oh, and the dent," his eyes flashed for a second before he softened his tone, "shows how nice you were."

It wasn't even worth talking about. He'd already been dating. He was moving on. And, so was she. She sniffed and felt her nose drift up in the air a bit.

"When I was waiting for you at the Coopers', your host mother mentioned something about the young, unmarried pastor coming to dinner and taking you for a drive or two."

"To get 7-Up!" She stared at him.

Still . . . Nettie Cooper was a gossip and a blabber.

"She *almost* . . . made it sound li-ke . . . he's interested in you." Al's voice bounced like they were driving over potholes, but they were just sitting here. "Were you planning to tell me?"

Isabelle moistened her lower lip and swallowed. "I thought he was married and then I found out he's not. There's not anything more to tell than that."

"You used to tell me everything."

She did. She used to tell him about every boy who went cross-eyed at her. And he used to tell her about every girl.

"Well, I reckon it goes both ways . . . Guess I should tell you about Janet, then."

"I thought you went out with Sue? Who's Janet?"

"The girl at Molalla Jewelers who sold me the ring."

Her neck stiffened. The girl who'd sold him *her* ring?

He blinked, suppressing a grin. "You know how it is when you meet someone who you just kind of..." He shrugged, glancing across the cab at her.

"No . . . I don't."

"Well, I thought with you in Silverton, now would give me the time, you know, to try and figure this all out."

"Wait a second . . ." Jaw slack, she studied him. "Let me get this straight. So what you're saying is... when you were buying the ring for me, you started to like this other girl?" Her voice went a little wonky.

"I didn't know it at the time." He grinned. "When I was there, it was all about the ring and what it would look like on your finger. But, then, when I was down on one knee, and the first thing you did was look toward Silverton." He shook his head. "Well... I can't help it that something she said was the first thing that popped into my memory. Like there was a reason for the season."

If blood could boil.

"What'd she say?" She'd probably flirted, batted her long eyelashes while Al slid the ring on her finger for size.

"She said the diamond might not be big enough."

Al had bought her a diamond. Her heart stretched a little at his expense, and she felt her eyes do the water dance. "That's a terrible thing to say." She gripped her purse in her lap.

He shifted into first, glanced in his rearview mirror, and drove onto the main road.

She had her answer now. The reason he hadn't proposed was because of Janet. The girl who'd sold him her engagement ring.

Al was no longer her sort-of boyfriend.

She peered out her side of the truck at the blur of Douglas fir.

"Wait a sec . . ." He didn't make sense. Only a few minutes ago, he'd confessed to... "I thought hearing my voice on the phone ripped your heart out?"

"Yeah." He toyed with an upper eyelash. "I talked to

Milton, an older salesman at work, about that. And, he said that I'll pretty much always feel that way hearing your voice 'cause you're the first gal I ever loved. He said it gets easier. And, it already has."

Al had loved her.

Arms crossed and jaw tight, she tried to make sense of it all. Al had never come right out and said he loved her before.

It hurt being told in past tense.

* * *

Friday afternoon, while the girls were at choir practice, Nettie pulled the last boxes of Christmas ornaments out of the cubby hole in the girls' room upstairs. On her way to the door, she spotted something out of the ordinary on top of the waterfall dresser.

It almost looked like Isabelle's autograph book.

Turning, she set the stack of boxes on top of Carolyn's bed.

It most certainly was the autograph book.

Next to the milk glass lamp, the little book sat perfectly at an angle, almost like a decoration. Nettie paused for a moment, studying its exact placement before picking it up. Then, she sat down on the edge of Isabelle's bed and, curious about what John had written, thumbed through the opening pages.

Ted's autograph was the first new one. Even though what he'd written sounded original, she'd read it somewhere before.

She turned to the next page of cursive.

Isabelle,
When the sun is sinking
And this path no more you trod

May your name in gold be written
In the autograph of God.
—John Hugg - 1965

"Oh, pooh!" Nettie lowered the book to her lap. While John's sentiments were lovely, they probably weren't his own original work. And, what was he thinking? Here was his chance to say something special, something about his feelings for Isabelle. Even if the dear girl wanted to, there was nothing for her to read into.

The situation needed prayer and . . . Opal Hargett's opinion.

* * *

NETTIE KNEW that she'd never remember it all, so she'd slid the little autograph book inside her apron pocket, and carried the ornament boxes downstairs.

Russell had finished putting up their aluminum Pom Pom Sparkler tree in front of the picture window in the living room and then returned to his recliner for a mid-afternoon nap. Already, he was softly snoring.

Nettie set the ornament boxes on the dining table next to the tree. She'd decorate later. Now was the time to call Opal.

In the nook area, she dialed her good friend's number.

"Hello." It was Wesley.

"Is your mother home?"

"Yes, Mrs. Cooper, I'll get her for you."

He was such a nice, young man. Hopefully, he wouldn't fall for Darlene.

"Hello, Nettie," her good friend's voice came on the line.

"Opal, I spoke with Virginia, this morning, and we have a praise—Ralph Ferguson got a new job."

"Praise God!"

"But, he'll only get one paycheck before Christmas."

"That's wonderful news! We'll keep them on the list to ensure the children have a little something. Are there any more items to add for Lilly?"

"Yes, Virginia called about an hour ago. New dishcloths and V05 hairspray." Nettie cleared her throat and looked around. "Opal, is anyone else in the near vicinity?"

"*Near vicinity* is redundant, Nettie. It would be better to say *vicinity*?"

"Is anyone else in the *vicinity*?"

"No, I'm alone in the kitchen," Opal said.

"I thought I better call you now before it gets any closer to suppertime."

"Why?"

"Isabelle's autograph book was just sitting out on the dresser. And, as you know, Ted and John signed it when they were at our place last Tuesday."

Opal laughed softly. "What did John write or dare I ask?"

"I have it here, and I'm going to read the whole thing to you, in its entirety." Nettie pulled the little book out of her apron pocket and flipped through the pages.

"Good."

"Here, it is. This is John's." Nettie cleared her throat and read it clear through to John's signature and 1965. "That's it. Nothing else."

"The thoughts are lovely, but I don't believe they're his own. Hmm… Dear, dear, dear John." Opal sighed. "Harriet thinks he's smitten. And Virginia, who avoids gossip of any kind, agrees."

"He should have written something for her to read into. Don't you think?"

"Yes." Even Opal agreed. "Or . . . at the very least for us," she added, drily. "But, he is a pastor and he needs to be wise. And, fortunately for John, there're still four Sundays before Christmas."

Opal was good about putting things into perspective.

"How are things going with your . . . Darlene?"

"We are in a season of prayer." Opal lowered her voice for some reason. "The other night, I saw Wesley staring a little too long if you know what I mean. Arnie sent him out to chop wood. The girl is a performer on and off the stage. You should see her wash windows."

Nettie giggled and then cleared her throat. "Don't you think that one of us needs to speak to John about his autograph?"

"Why?"

"Well, he likes her and, she'll never be able to tell from what he wrote. He's new at courting. And, it's obvious from the times he's been here that he plum doesn't know what he's doing."

Opal sighed. "Harriet will want to be the one to speak to him. And, I should be the one to call her. She's told me before that Frank is on high alert when you ring."

Nettie did a triple blink. Frank had once told her if the *Spokesman Review*—the local paper—had a gossip column, it would be called *Nettie Gossip*. She'd tried to be better for a while, but she must be slipping.

"Nettie, please keep our Wesley in your prayers. He truly loves the Lord. I can't tell you how troubling it's been to have Darlene here. Never have I seen him delve into the Word like this. He's quoting scripture all the time. But, I am a bit worried by all his mumblings."

"Oh. What is he . . . mumbling?"

"First John. The lust of the flesh, and the lust of the eyes, and the pride of life, is not of the Father, but is of the world."

"Oh, the three temptations." Wesley's trials tugged at her heart. "I'll keep your dear boy in prayer."

"Nettie . . . you don't have a young man at home anymore. What about trading choir girls with me?"

"No, I can't do that, Opal." Nettie glanced to the doorway. "We already love Isabelle. She and Carolyn are already the best of friends." And, if Nettie were completely honest, she found hosting the possible future Mrs. Hugg to be very entertaining.

CHAPTER 15

After she decorated the tree, Nettie pulled back the lever for the footrest and relaxed deep into the corduroy comfort of her recliner. Seated nearby, Russell read one of his Louis L'Amour cowboy novels.

The phone rang.

She opened one eye. It might be the milkman. She'd forgotten to leave the collection envelope in the bottle rack that morning. Or it could be one of the Granite Girls… or one of her choir girls. It could be anyone.

"That's probably one of your girlfriends." Russell turned the page.

"You're probably right." She pushed the lever forward, lowered her slippers to the carpet, and hurried to the nook.

"Hello," she breathed into the receiver.

"Nettie, it's Rose." Rose Carlton rarely called her first.

"Hello, Rose." Nettie laughed softly. The news must have already made the rounds.

"Opal called and told me about John's autograph."

"Yes." Nettie patted at the pocket of her apron and was

surprised to find the little book still there. She'd purposefully gone upstairs to return it, but she must have got distracted by something.

"I spoke with Harriet, and she feels the same way I do," Rose said. "A lot of people may read John's autograph, and if he'd written something too personal, well, it would only provide fodder for gossip. John was only being sensible, writing what he did."

"Yes, I understand both sides." Nettie tried to enunciate clearly as Rose's hearing was poor.

"What do you mean?" Rose asked.

"I understand John's side and Isabelle's. Girls often want a fellow to write something a little more personal. And, when they don't... well, she could very easily write him off. Girls can do that, you know, when they don't have encouragement."

"Well, I'm sure John Hugg can figure out a way to give her encouragement outside of an autograph book."

The other night, when John had been here, had he said anything for Isabelle to read into? Nettie didn't remember him acting or saying anything special or out of the ordinary. She narrowed her gaze at the tulip-checked wallpaper.

"Nettie, do you remember back to when we had autograph books, how sometimes, someone might hide one further toward the back. You know, folded in half, secretive-like."

"You don't think?" Nettie fumbled in her pocket and pulled out the little book.

"Ever since Opal called, I can't get the thought out of my head."

"I'll look through it right now, Rose, while I have you on the line."

"I'm not going anywhere."

Nettie held the receiver between her shoulder and ear, and beginning near the front, flipped through the pages.

"I thought Lilly looked better on Sunday than she has for a while," Rose said.

"I did, too." Nettie realized that might have sounded wrong. "I mean, I thought Lilly looked better, too. How are things going for you with your choir girl? What's her name, again... Evelyn?"

"Yes. Evelyn is very sweet and timid as a mouse," Rose said, lowering her voice. "Half the time we don't know when she's in the house.

"I suppose Opal's told you how she has her hands full with her choir girl—and, how she leaves her bras and girdles in the bathroom to drip dry. Do you know their poor Wesley has already chopped three cord loads of firewood since their choir girl's arrival? He's growing stronger physically and spiritually."

"Yes, and I told Opal we'd keep him in prayer." Nettie sighed. A slight gap in the book grabbed her eye.

One page was folded in half toward the spine with cursive across the face.

PRIVATE

What causes tears?

Nettie's heart leaped to her throat. "Rose, I found something."

"I just knew it! What'd John write?"

"He folded the page in half, just like you said, and *PRIVATE* is written in capital letters, and underneath it, he wrote *What causes tears?*"

"Oh, wait til I tell Harriet! What's inside?"

Nettie opened it.

Onions was written on the upper side of the fold.

"Onions." Her shoulders slumped. *"He wrote onions."*

"Wha-at . . . in the world is he thinking?"

It was official—John Hugg needed help with courting.

"Wait a second. There's more . . ." On the lower side of the fold were several lines of cursive. She held it toward the sunlight streaming through the nearby window.

"*Izz,*

If you do go ahead with the Christmas choir..."

That was odd; it didn't sound like something John would write.

"I'll be living for the day you come home."

A large lump formed in Nettie's throat.

"I love you, Al."

Oh, what a kettle of fish they were in.

"Who? What . . . did you say?"

"It's from Albert." She lowered the book to her side. "Isabelle's sort-of-boyfriend is head-over-heels in love with her."

"Oh, dear!" Rose sighed. "Read it again, and louder, this time."

Nettie yanked on the telephone cord, and taking a few steps toward the doorway, glanced toward Russell's recliner. Good, he hadn't moved. Then, she returned to the nook and the little book.

"Izz," Nettie read slowly through Al's autograph, trying to clearly enunciate each word. *"I love you, Al."*

"Oh, dear." Rose sighed.

"Rose! Maybe Isabelle isn't the one we've been praying for." Nettie sniffled and pulled a handkerchief out of her apron pocket. "She's been so quiet about Albert that well... we almost thought he was an imaginary beau. And, she didn't even have a picture to show us. But, then he came and picked her up for Thanksgiving. He's a nice, tall, good-looking young man, a Christian, and has a good job with Molalla Ford. He didn't even hug Isabelle when she came in the house. But, he watched her, you know. Russell noticed, too. He said that Albert couldn't take his eyes off of her."

"Oh, dear . . . dear, dear." Rose sighed. "According to Harriet, John can't take his eyes off of her either."

"I don't think Isabelle's seen this yet." Nettie slid the book inside her apron pocket. "Maybe I should just tear it out and throw it in the fire. Save us all a lot of heartache." Her eyes flashed wide. "What do you think?"

"You'll do no such thing." Rose's voice was so commanding it was like it was straight from God. "We'll continue to pray for God's will to be done. Not Rose Carlton's will. Not Nettie Cooper's will…"

Nettie nodded, wiping aside a tear.

"Pray with me," Rose said.

Nettie sniffled and bowed her head.

"Our dear heavenly Father, You are in control, not us. Not Rose, not Nettie, not Opal…" She named all seven of the Granite Girls. And, then she concluded with what over the years, the group had coined the *Grandmother's Prayer*. "We're not giving up, Lord. We pray for a young woman who loves Jesus, who loves others, and who loves Harriet Hugg's grandson—John Hugg."

* * *

THAT AFTERNOON when Russell was reading a western in his recliner, Nettie rose from her comfy chair and moseyed back to the kitchen nook.

Even though Rose had been a Sunday School teacher for thirty years, Nettie wasn't sure if she agreed with her about not ripping Albert's autograph out of the book. She picked up the phone and, without giving the situation another thought, dialed her good friend's number.

"Opal, it's Nettie. Is now a good time to talk?"

"Yes. I've been looking for my peanut brittle recipe all morning. I hope I didn't lose it."

"I hope you didn't either." They looked forward to Opal's peanut brittle every Christmas. "When was the last time you made it?"

"I only make it in December."

"Did you file it under Candy?"

"No, I don't have a Candy file."

"Hmm... did you check under *Cookies*? Maybe you stuck it there."

"Yes. I checked there."

"What else do you make *only* at Christmastime?"

"My fruitcake. I'll check under *quick breads* while we're talking. And, once I find my recipe, I'm going to make a *Christmas* category. What's new?"

"Well . . ." Nettie tried to collect her thoughts. "About an hour ago, Rose and I discovered an autograph that was hidden in Isabelle's book." She kept an eye on the doorway, in case Russell should wander in. "We were looking for one from John and stumbled across one from Albert instead. Oh, Opal, it's just plum terrible."

"What do you mean . . . *terrible?*"

Nettie explained everything, how the page was folded in half toward the spine. What the cover read and then how, inside, Albert had poured out his heart.

"He wrote, "I'll be living for the day you come home. I love you, Al."

"Oh, no!" Opal's voice deflated. "You're kidding?"

"No, I wish I were."

"Hallelujah! Here, it is. It was stuck to the backside of my fruitcake recipe by something sticky—probably Karo Syrup." Opal laughed. "I'm going to make a *Christmas* divider right now."

"That's a great idea. And, speaking of great ideas, I was

thinking I could just rip Albert's autograph out and throw it in the fire. It—"

"Nettie . . . don't be ridiculous!"

"But . . ." Opal's response surprised her. "It would save us all a lot of grief."

"Nettie . . . it's not yours to tamper with."

"Now, just hear me out. The way the binding's set up, she'd never even know it was there."

"God knows! And . . . you know. *And,* her fellow Albert knows. Nettie, you remind me of a third grader. Keep your hands in your own desk and be respectful."

Even though Opal's voice was firm, Nettie's mind had wandered. Who would know if she were to rip it out? It wasn't like Harriet or Opal would ever read Isabelle's autograph book. And, even if they were ever to sign it, she doubted very much if they'd take the time to search through *every* single page.

"You're awfully quiet, Nettie. Have you already burned it?"

"No. I wanted your opinion first."

"How could you live with yourself?"

She thought she could; probably, because it was easy to imagine John and Isabelle together and happy—married, living in Silverton, pushing a stroller down Water Street.

"Nettie, if you don't tell Isabelle, I WILL. I'll tell Isabelle that you tore a hidden autograph from Albert out of her book."

There was the voice of reason, she'd been waiting for.

"And besides," Opal's voice softened, "I think we all need to prepare ourselves. There's the strong possibility that Isabelle is not the one we've been praying for. And, you know what this means?" Her voice climbed gradually like an escalator. "There's still a chance for Darlene."

"Opal!" She just didn't want Wesley to end up with her.

Heaven forbid Darlene Berry ever being a pastor's wife!

Nettie would be doing her church family a huge favor if she ripped Albert's autograph out of the book and threw it into the fire. She stared at the nook's wallpaper. But... could she live with herself?

CHAPTER 16

Saturday afternoon, Isabelle used the telephone in the Coopers' kitchen nook and called Al. While Aunt Elsie went to find him, Isabelle couldn't help but wonder who he was in love with now? Was it still Janet?

"Hey," Al said, sounding like his usual self.

"Hi. Remember how I told you about Mr. Cooper's Bel Air? Half the time it starts, and half the time it doesn't."

"You need to find out what year it is."

"Hold on." Stretching the phone cord, she paused in the doorway to the living room. She could see the top of Russell's thinning gray hair over the curve of the recliner. "Mr. Cooper, what year is your car?" she said loudly.

There was no movement.

She raised her voice. "Mr. Cooper, I have Albert on the phone. We're trying to figure out what's wrong with your Bel Air."

Nettie leaned around the side of her recliner to peer at her.

"Do you know what year it is?" Isabelle asked.

"1965," Nettie said.

"No. I meant what year is your Bel Air?"

"Russell," Nettie poked him. "What year's our car? Isabelle has Albert on the phone. He's a mechanic."

"I don't remember," he mumbled, and his arms rose above the chair as he stretched. "It was the first year that they made the Bel Air with the full-width grill."

While Isabelle repeated the information to Al, she returned to the nook area.

Mr. Cooper mumbled something else.

"Wait a second, Al."

Carolyn carried a glass through the doorway on her way to the kitchen. "Granddad said to tell him that it has a V-8 engine."

"Al, it has a V-8 engine."

"I wonder what came first, V-8 Vegetable Juice or the V-8 engine?" Nettie asked, loudly from her recliner.

"Not now, Grandma."

"Is the gas cap hidden behind the driver's side tail light?" Al asked.

"Why would they do that?" She laughed and then relayed his question to Carolyn who'd stood in the doorway to the living room.

"Yes, it's underneath the tail light." Carolyn didn't need to ask her grandfather that one.

"It sure is, Al."

"Sounds like it's a '56."

Covering the phone, Isabelle said, "He thinks it's a '56."

"Grandpa, Albert thinks it's a '56."

"That's right! It's a '56 2403, 4-door Chevy Bel Air."

Isabelle repeated the information to Al.

"Does the battery crank over?" he asked.

"Yes."

"What's it sound like?"

"Kind of a high-pitched grinding noise."

"Hmm . . . sure sounds like the starter."

"What do I do?"

"You don't start with the starter. It's expensive and a lot of work. You always start with the battery. Get a pen and paper and write down everything I tell you."

Albert knew her well.

"You know, I hate this kind of stuff." Would he take the hint and pop over with his toolbox?

"I'll be out tonight."

"Oh." She didn't want to know who with.

"And, this is something even you can handle."

She was good at handing him tools. She'd never had to use one.

The Coopers' detached garage trapped all of the icicle air and was colder than the world outside. Wearing Nettie's gardening clothes, an old wool coat of Russell's, and a Russian-looking fur hat, Isabelle opened the door to the old Bel Air.

Carolyn, who'd volunteered to help, wore a long wool coat and heels and stood nearby holding a clipboard and pen. "Start with the battery," she said.

After turning the key in the ignition, Isabelle twisted on the headlights and could tell by the light on the wood plank wall that they were working. She walked to the front of the car, squinting in their glare. The lights were plenty bright.

"Make sure the lights are nice and bright," Carolyn said.

"They are, which means the battery's fine."

"Good!" Carolyn checked off the box.

"No, not really. The battery would have been an easy fix." She lifted the release latch for the hood.

"If the battery's fine," Carolyn continued, "you need to disconnect it, or you'll electrocute yourself later. Wha-at? Is he kidding?"

"No."

"I think we should call a man." Carolyn pleaded with her. "I know, we'll call John Hugg."

"We don't need a man for this," Isabelle said. "Even I can do this," she mumbled under her breath. "Shine the light on the battery for me."

While Carolyn held the old metal flashlight steady, Isabelle slid on a pair of Russell's yellow-lens shop goggles. Using a socket wrench, she loosened the nut on the negative terminal first.

"Are you sure you wanna do this all by yourself?" Carolyn's breath puffed like smoke signals.

"I'm not. You're helping me. Now, I have to take off a tire to inspect the starter wiring."

"You're kidding!"

"Nope." Isabelle returned to the driver's side of the car and set the parking brake. Then, she put a piece of firewood behind the back tires, and centered the jack under the front, near the radiator support bracket.

"We should call a man," Carolyn said. "I know, we'll call John Hugg."

"We don't need to. I've been helping Al on and off for years." She only wished she'd paid more attention. "We'll be fine."

"Don't you want to see John?"

"No, not right now." She didn't want him to see her. Not in her present garb. After removing the hubcap, Isabelle crouched down near the front tire and, using a socket wrench, loosened the first bolt.

Carolyn rounded the front of the Bel Air, joining her on the passenger's side. "The first thing you're supposed to do is remove the hubcap."

"Check."

"Loosen the lug nuts—a half turn—while the tire is still on the ground."

"Check."

"Boy, your fella knows his cars."

Carolyn had dropped the sort-of fella part, probably because she was fishing for information.

Isabelle cranked the jack until the wheel was a good half inch off the ground.

"You never did tell me how it went at Thanksgiving."

Carolyn was fishing.

She didn't want to think about Al right now. "What's next?"

"Make sure the stand is secure and put the wheel under the chass-is to protect yourself. What's a chass-is?"

"It's pronounced Chas-ee. The chassis is the frame."

Bending her knees, Isabelle lifted the tire off and slid it under the front of the car.

"What does he mean *protect yourself?*"

"A lot of people have been crushed when working on their cars. So don't go leaning against it while I'm under it."

"I'd feel better if we had a man here."

"No. I'm fine." Isabelle lowered herself to the cold, hard earth and wished she'd put a towel down first.

"At least let me call John. He can pray."

"So can you." Isabelle shimmed her way beneath the car.

"Not like John."

She'd always been in Carolyn's shoes before, talking to Al while he worked. Being underneath the car was more claustrophobic than she'd expected.

"Keep talking to me, Carolyn." She shone the flashlight at the starter—a bullet looking thing attached to the side of the motor. Like Al had warned, the posts were all white and powdery—not a good sign.

"I don't know why Ted put your duet first. Granddad's late every Sunday like clockwork." Carolyn tap danced around a bit, trying to stay warm.

Please, not tomorrow. Isabelle pulled the yellow goggles out of her pocket and slid them on. Then, she used an old wire paint brush to clean the powdery corrosion off the posts.

"Too bad they went and spent all their money on their new Kirby Vacuum," Carolyn said.

Isabelle couldn't agree more. "What's next?" The power posts were as clean as she could get them.

"Let me see. Make sure no wires are hanging loose. There's a lead 3/8-inch bolt that holds the red wire from the battery and hooks in right there. Sometimes the cable corrodes. Take 'em off. Clean them with a wire brush, and put it back on. Sure sounds easy enough to me," Carolyn said. "That's it. Do you mind if I go in? Get a cup of coffee. I'm freezing."

"No. Go right ahead."

The cold, hard earth had numbed Isabelle's backside clear to the bone. She loosened the bolt and tried not to feel sorry for herself. It was Saturday night, and while Al was probably out on a date with Janet, she was half-frozen under a car, looking like a goofball.

"How you doing under there?" Carolyn had returned to the garage, probably to see if she was still alive.

"I'm almost finished." Isabelle slipped the cable back on the starter post. Then, rocking her hips from side to side, she shimmied her way out from under the car. She was glad to see daylight and Carolyn, who was holding a cup of coffee like it was her lifeline.

"Now, for the moment of truth." Isabelle rose to her feet, opened the car door and slid behind the wheel. She pumped the gas pedal a couple of times then turned the key.

Absolutely nothing. She tried one more time then slumped back in the seat, and stared at the hood visible through the windshield.

"Duh!" She hadn't reconnected the battery!

Her lovely assistant hadn't remembered either.

From her prior sessions with Al, she remembered to reconnect the positive terminal first and then the negative. Lastly, she dropped the lid.

She slid behind the wheel, said a prayer, pumped the gas pedal a couple of times and turned the key.

The same old high-pitched grinding noise followed.

"Come on, Hilda." She pumped the gas pedal again, turning the key.

Three more failed attempts followed before she leaned back in the seat, defeated. She'd have to call Al again.

"What's wrong?" Carolyn asked.

"It's not the wiring."

"But . . . what do you mean? Don't tell me we just did all that work for nothing!"

"No-oo. Now, we know it's not the battery or the wiring." Isabelle tried to look at the bright side.

"But . . ." Carolyn said as she followed her back to the house. "But . . . we just did all that work."

"Car repair is a matter of elimination.

The kitchen was night-and-day warmer than outside. Nettie was on the phone in the nook area, so while she waited for her turn, Isabelle poured a cup of coffee and cradled the warm mug between both hands.

"Yes, Opal, that's what I said. Isabelle's been outside fixing our car. Her sort-of-boyfriend, Al, is a mechanic. We might just be to church on time tomorrow." Nettie pressed the receiver against her shoulder. "How'd it go, girls?"

"It's not the battery," Isabelle said, taking off Russell's old coat.

"Even I could have told you that." Nettie flicked a hand before uncovering the receiver. "Oh, and, Opal, when you're praying for Lilly, say a prayer for Hilda, too. It wasn't the battery."

After Nettie exited the nook, Isabelle lifted the receiver and dialed Wilhoit's number.

Aunt Elsie answered.

"Is Al there?"

"No, honey. I'm sorry."

"Did he already leave?" Isabelle turned her back to the room as Nettie and Carolyn were still standing close by.

"He said if you called to tell you that he's going to town to get engaged."

Probably to Janet.

Aunt Elsie lowered her voice. "We've all told him he's a fool, but in the meantime, he thinks he can just fill this hole that you left in his heart."

"I see. Well, thanks, Aunt Elsie. I love you." She hung up the receiver and turned to face her audience. "Al's not home."

Carolyn shook her head and turned. "Granddad!" She called out as she started for the doorway to the living room. "Tomorrow morning, you have to start Hilda early. Isabelle has a duet first thing that we don't want to be late for."

"Okie dokie, smokey, wokey." Russell yawned.

He probably didn't even know the meaning of the word *early*.

* * *

RIGHT AFTER BREAKFAST, Isabelle slid her saddle shoes on, determined to walk.

"You stay right here and go with us. You're a Cooper now, and we're family," Nettie said. "We're all in this together. Russell, go get Hilda started. We need to get our girls to church on time."

Russell put on his Sunday hat and went out the back door. Then, for several minutes, Nettie looked for two heels of the same color and came out of her room wearing one black and one blue again.

The Cooper women finally exited the house together.

The rhododendron-lined path funneled an all too familiar grinding noise. They followed it to the detached garage.

"For the last ten minutes, she's been like milking a dead cow," Russell said. "Come on Hilda." He turned the key for the umpteenth time.

Isabelle tried not to worry, but her stomach flopped around like a fish on dry land.

Carolyn glanced at her. "Did you plug the battery back in?"

"Yes." She nodded and glanced at her wristwatch. Their duet started in two minutes. Darlene was probably on stage waiting for her.

Please, Lord. Please.

"It's okay," Carolyn whispered. "It'll be fine. Ted will probably just have Darlene sing it as a solo. They won't even wait for you."

She didn't find that very comforting. They'd worked hard on the piece. And even though her arms were often wonky, Mr. Hoffmeister was very excited about their duet. She gripped the door handle. Running in high heels would be better than just sitting here.

"Say a prayer, girls." Mr. Cooper patted the dash with one hand and turned the key with the other. "Come on, Hil-da. Come on, baby doll."

"Boy, she's having a bad day today," Nettie said.

Instead of a grinding noise, the engine actually revved.

Nettie threw her hands into the air. "Those were the magic words! I've been sitting here racking my brain. *Boy, she's having a bad day today* worked once before. Remember?"

"I've been praying, Grandma. It's my prayers that worked."

"You tried, honey," Nettie said from up front. "It's not your fault that Albert told you to work on the battery instead of the starter."

"I worked on both, Nettie."

"Well, no one can say that you didn't try."

Isabelle inhaled deeply.

"Your hair looks real nice like that." Carolyn eyed her bouffant bun. "You don't need to worry about Mr. Hoffmeister. He'll know it's not your fault."

"Thank you."

Russell set his blinker and turned left onto Jersey Street.

"Granddad . . ." Carolyn patted his shoulder. "Poor Isabelle's going to be late for her duet. Drop her off out front, will you?"

Out front? That meant she'd have to walk up the center aisle and like a bride late for her own wedding, everyone would turn and gawk at her.

CHAPTER 17

The tires of Mr. Cooper's Chevy Bel Air rubbed against the curb out front of Calvary Christian Church. Isabelle popped out her side of the car. Unbuttoning her coat, she dashed up the church steps.

"Good morning, Isabelle." Dressed in a dark suit and striped tie, John held open the door.

"Are they waiting for me?" She whisked past him.

"We took the offering early, so—"And because he was the nearest coat tree, she turned and flung her coat at him. "You don't need to worry." He grinned.

Heels clicking on the hardwood floor, she made her way through the sanctuary's double doors. Just like she'd feared, people on both sides of the aisle turned in the pews to stare at the choir girl late for her duet.

"I'm sorry," she said to the folks on her left and to the folks on her right, repeating her sentiments as she made her way to the front.

On the podium, Mr. Hoffmeister and Darlene stood, waiting.

Isabelle rounded the side of the front right pew, then met

Ted's solemn gaze as she climbed the steps. "Sorry," she said again, and then turned to stand shoulder-to-shoulder with Darlene. Flush cheeked and slightly winded, she faced the packed, little church.

A purse snapped closed.

A baby whimpered.

Isabelle's gaze settled on Frank Hugg. The elderly man sat several inches higher than anyone else on the left side of the room. Beside him sat his wife.

Harriet's gentle smile and nod helped to calm her a little.

On the guitar, Mr. Hoffmeister strummed through the first stanza of "Blessed Assurance."

Still wearing their coats, the Coopers—Russell, Nettie, and Carolyn—walked up the center aisle and sat in their usual pew—the third from the front.

Only three more Sundays and she'd never have to drive to church with the Coopers ever again. This odd little town and its... young unmarried pastor—her gaze followed John as he walked up the center aisle—would all be twenty miles behind her.

She flinched as Darlene pinched her in the side.

Why couldn't Mr. Hoffmeister have paired her with Evelyn? She was sweet as pie and never pinched.

Mr. Hoffmeister cleared his throat for some reason.

Crud! As if things weren't bad enough, Isabelle had missed her cue.

"The hymn the girls are about to sing . . ." He paused and took a folded handkerchief from the chest pocket of his suit coat and patted beneath his black framed glasses. "...was written by Fanny Crosby."

Isabelle closed her eyes. Then reopened them to... John looking right at her. Their eyes locked.

She blinked twice. Why was he staring like that?

Darlene pinched her hard.

Out of pure instinct, Isabelle elbowed her.

A few snickers followed.

Darlene pinched her again.

She'd had it!

Isabelle snaked her right hand beneath the elbow of her left arm and pinched Darlene good right below the hem of her Cross Your Heart bra.

"Fanny was blind from birth, yet she wrote thousands of hymns. The hymn we're about to sing was inspired by Hebrews 10:22. And for the life of me, do you think I can remember how the verse goes?" Mr. Hoffmeister patted at his brow.

Several people flipped through their Bibles.

A middle-aged fellow near the front raised his hand. "I got it." He peered down at the text. "Let us draw near with a true heart in full assurance of faith."

Oh, Lord! . . . The verse was exactly what she'd needed to hear. Isabelle closed her eyes. *Help me to sing for You, for my heart to be right.*

While Mr. Hoffmeister strummed the chords again, the girls entwined their nearest arms as rehearsed, and when he reached her cue, this time Isabelle was ready.

"Blessed Assurance, Jesus is mine!" Then, Darlene's contralto voice joined in. *"Oh, what a foretaste of glory divine!"* And, the worries of the morning slipped away.

Both girls raised their free hands palm up and shoulder high. And even though Isabelle felt like an organ grinder's monkey, she kept it there.

"This is my story, this is my song. Praising my Savior all the day long." Maybe it was the adrenaline of performance, but they harmonized together better than they ever had in practice.

Darlene, the more expressive of the two, helped to pull the limelight off of Isabelle, for which she was glad. The unmistakable reverence in the cathedral-ceilinged room made her feel like her soul had been here much longer.

"This is my story, this is my song. Praising my Sav-ior," she caressed the note, *"all the day long."*

When they were finished, the congregation clapped.

On their way to their seats, Darlene leaned toward her. "Why were you so late?" she whispered.

"The Coopers' car wouldn't start."

"Then, you should have walked."

For once Darlene was right.

"Next time, I will."

* * *

Arnie Hargett was mid yawn. Russell Cooper was asleep. Beth Waggoneer employed her fan. All were signs that John was in the third quarter of his sermon. It was time to ever so subtly slip in that God was in control, not seven little, old ladies.

His gaze drifted to his grandparents in the middle of the fourth pew. Grandpa tilted his head ever so slightly toward Grandma. Like John could possibly forget.

Oddly enough, John's long pause had opened a few eyeballs.

The Hargetts' youngest boy, Clark, bobbed his head to one side, wiggling a finger in his ear, either to get out the cotton or the ear wax.

Maybe he should take long pauses more often.

Someone must have elbowed Russell, for he'd stopped snoring.

"Is it over?" The elderly man righted himself.

John ignored the chuckles, locking eyes with his grandmother.

Her brows furrowed. The slight lift of her chin knotted his internal organs.

From his grandmother, his gaze traveled across the aisle to Opal Hargett. Beneath her wide-brimmed Christmas hat, the one with red roses, the broad-shouldered woman stared back. She'd been his third and fourth-grade teacher. The woman knew him a little too well.

He zigzagged across the aisle to the Coopers' row. Ted had only had to stall for nine and a half minutes this morning, waiting for the girls to arrive. In the middle of the third row, he eyed Nettie Cooper.

With a quick shift of her shoulders, she hid behind Bill Roluff, seated in the pew in front of her. Her reaction proved that she was the guiltiest of the group.

And, for the conclusion of his silent lecture, John locked eyes with Rose Carlton.

His former Sunday School teacher's countenance was angelic. She even smiled.

According to his grandfather—a trusted source—the other three women who made up the Granite Girls didn't require a silent lecture. Virginia, Velma Knapland, and Joann Goff were better about the telephone and gossip.

Then he glanced at his notes and gripped the edge of the lectern. "Before He was even born, the world was already telling baby Jesus, 'There is no room for you here.'

"There is no room for you here." John shook his head. "We struggle with this spiritual battle every day. Will we give him the cathedral of our heart?" He held a flat hand to his chest. "Jesus said, 'I stand at the door and knock.' How often are we like the innkeepers? 'There is no room for you here. Not right now. Try again tomorrow.'"

He looked down at the lectern and his notes.

"Christmas is a season to celebrate the birth of Jesus, the Son of God—the greatest gift ever given." He glanced briefly at Lilly, seated in the second row, trying to prepare her, but at the same time knowing he couldn't. "And it's a season for us to give of ourselves. For at least six years, our dear brother, Tommy Crawl, made it a point at Christmas, to deliver firewood to the needy in this area. He'd cut and stack extra cords of wood during the summer so he could give it away in December." He gripped the wooden edge of the lectern, as tears filled his own gaze. And here, he'd been so worried about Lilly.

"Tommy was always trying to love like Jesus." His voice broke for a second. "The Christmas season inspires us more than ever to give to those in need. To reach out to our neighbors. In Matthew five, Jesus calls us as Christians *to be the light of the world.*

"Pray that we are not like the innkeepers. Instead, may we follow Him like the shepherds. And, may we give like kings."

Lilly wiped her cheek with one hand.

"The Christmas choir will host two afternoon performances next Sunday. One at five o'clock and one at seven. Not tonight, folks. Next Sunday." He smiled. "Invite your friends and neighbors." He closed in prayer. Then, he strode toward the front and shook hands as people exited the sanctuary.

"You're getting better, so much better." Bill Roluff chuckled, patting him on the shoulder.

The Waggoner family was next—all six of them—and then his grandfather.

"You should have just said what I told you to." Grandpa shook his head. "Women need words." He nodded toward the middle of the church where Grandma remained seated. "Tell Harriet that I'll be in the car."

"I will." He sighed.

After the sanctuary emptied, John took a seat beside his grandmother in the fourth pew from the front.

"Just because you look at me, doesn't mean I can read your mind." Holding her purse in her lap, one forefinger tapped—up and down.

"Do you have plans after church?" he asked.

"Yes. Velma and Cecil have invited us to their home for lunch."

"Well, how 'bout I take you out for a piece of pie tomorrow then?"

Her features softened. "Tomorrow's fine. And, there's something that I need to talk to you about, too. Something to do with Nettie."

"Good." If it had anything to do with Nettie and her choir girl, he didn't want to put it off any longer than he had to.

CHAPTER 18

The opening chords to "She's Got You" played from a nearby radio, and then Patsy Cline's rich voice filled the air. Beneath the table, Isabelle's ankle bobbed.

Brown vinyl booths lined the periphery of Leona's Café. Bottles of Heinz Ketchup were on every table. Large, tea-colored spots stained the white acoustical tiled ceiling.

Across from Isabelle, Carolyn peered over Darlene's shoulder to eye the menu. "I want a chocolate milkshake."

Darlene shook her head. "When Mr. Hoffmeister gave me the money, he said that we're all to have a piece of pie on him."

"He won't mind if we have a milkshake. He only wants us to be together," Carolyn said.

"He said *pie*. We all have to have pie." Swaying her shoulders to the song, Darlene watched the door.

"What can I get for the four of you?" The middle-aged waitress's thick, short hair was the color of Kellogg's Frosted Corn Flakes. She wore a powdered blush and light blue eye shadow.

Darlene eyed her nametag. "We're all having pie, Leona."

Carolyn pouted and met Isabelle's gaze across the table.

"You don't have to," Isabelle whispered.

"We're down to apple, cherry, peach, and there's one piece of chocolate cream."

"Apple, please," Darlene and Evelyn said at the same time.

"I'll have the chocolate cream." Carolyn gave in, adding a shrug.

Then, everyone was waiting on Isabelle. She hardly ever went out for pie. Living out at Wilhoit, she rarely went anywhere, except to town once in a while for groceries.

"I guess I'll just have apple, too, heated, with ice cream, please."

"Apple ala mode," the waitress murmured as she wrote on her notepad. "Coffee, girls?"

"No, it's bad for the vocal chords," Darlene said. "And, I'll have my pie heated with ice cream."

"Coffee's not bad for you!" Carolyn frowned at her. "Bing Crosby drinks it all the time."

"I'll have coffee." Evelyn held up one finger.

"Do you girls sing?" their waitress asked.

Darlene was giving Evelyn the evil eye, so Isabelle piped in, "We're a Christmas choir."

"Also known as Ted's Girls—Ted Hoffmeister. Do you know Ted?" Carolyn asked.

"Yes. Do you need cream?"

"Yes, thank you," Evelyn's gaze rolled right over the top of Darlene's.

Their waitress paused to wipe a table on her way to the kitchen.

"Ted's Christmas Choir Girls isn't going to sell any records." Darlene shook her head. "We need a new name."

Isabelle waited for her to spout, *Darlene and the Christmas Choir.*

With her elbow on the table, Darlene appeared thoughtful

for a moment; then she tapped a finger to her chin. "I can't think."

"When was your first solo?" Carolyn asked, looking at Evelyn.

"You go first." Evelyn waved a hand.

"Well . . . I was seven. And, my grandma, Nettie," she smiled at Isabelle, "told Rose Carlton, the Sunday School teacher, that she wanted her to listen to me sing a little something for a part in the Christmas play. So, Mrs. Carlton had me sing her a line from "The First Noel," and I got the part. It was short and sweet, but I remember standing on stage in my new patent leather shoes."

"Were you afraid?" asked Evelyn.

"Not at all." Carolyn flicked a hand. "Your turn."

Their waitress returned with a tray of ice waters and one cup of coffee and a bell-shaped creamer.

"My two younger sisters and I have been singing as a trio at our church for years—and, only as a trio. The only solo I've ever had was the first day here when Mr. Hoffmeister made us sing up front. I never want to do that again." Evelyn's voice trailed off. She nudged Isabelle. "Your turn."

Their waitress finally left the table.

"I was twelve." Isabelle clasped her hands in her lap. "Every summer, the Aurora band members hold a reunion out at Wilhoit. They bring in a large brass band and have a big potluck. I knew that I was supposed to sing during their intermission. As my solo grew closer, I felt so sick to my stomach that I hid down by the creek under this little bridge." Her gaze lifted to the ceiling. "I think I just planned on staying there 'til their intermission was over, but Albert saw a patch of my white dress sticking out. He's always been tall—bigger than me, and he carried me over one arm through the crowd. Of course, I was upset." She laughed softly at the memory. "Then he set me down near the backstage of the pavilion.

"His dad was already on stage, playing the guitar. Fletcher's the cook out at Wilhoit, and he'd just been strumming the same chords over and over, waiting for me."

"Kind of like Sunday when Ted and I were waiting for you." Darlene shifted her shoulders a bit in the booth.

The girls laughed.

"Were there a lot of people?" Evelyn asked.

"A couple hundred. It was terrible and wonderful at the same time." Isabelle thought about her father out in the crowd in his wheelchair, but she wouldn't tell the girls about that. Too many questions would follow.

"No wonder you were nervous," Evelyn whispered.

"Did Al say anything to you or just plop you down?" Carolyn asked.

Isabelle paused at the cusp of one of her fondest memories. "When he set me down backstage, he was real serious for Al. He said, 'Now, get up there and show 'em what God gave you.'"

"Oh, I just melted," Darlene breathed.

Evelyn patted above her heart.

Carolyn was quiet.

"And, I bet you just did wonderful," Evelyn said.

"After I finished the first song, several people in the crowd hollered for me to sing another. Al was blocking the backstage, so I couldn't escape."

"He was like your first stage manager," Carolyn said.

Everyone laughed.

"Your turn." Isabelle looked across the table at Darlene.

"How old is this Albert? Maybe, if you end up with John Hugg, I can have him."

"Darlene, you're rude!" Evelyn exclaimed.

"She can't very well have two." Darlene shrugged.

"I don't have either." Isabelle's cheeks warmed. She glanced at Carolyn. Now that she knew, would she be just like her grandmother and tell everybody?

Darlene waved a hand. "Let's see, I sang in the school choir and musicals, and in an underground ballot taken in our senior class," Darlene set a hand above the V in her Cross Your heart bra, "I was voted the most likely to land a wealthy husband."

"That's terrible!" Evelyn said.

"Let me see," Darlene said, "I can't remember the first time I sang on stage, but my mother does. I was little, and she said I ate it up. My grandfather was on the lighting crew for Fox Film Corporation, so Hollywood runs in my blood like… Jell-O."

The girls laughed.

"After this trip is over, I'm going to Hollywood to live with my Uncle Fred and his family. I plan to get discovered. I . . ." Mouth agape, Darlene looked toward the front and patted at her heart. "Pitter patter. Pitter patter."

Carolyn leaned toward her. "Darlene, whatever is the matter?" She repeated Mr. Hoffmeister's usual sentiments.

"It's John Hugg and another woman. Girls, we have competition," Darlene said.

Isabelle leaned out the side of her booth and glanced behind her toward the entry.

It was John, and the other woman was his grandmother—Harriet Hugg.

He briefly waved their direction and headed for a booth in the far corner of the cafe.

He looked all business.

* * *

"The choir girls are here, John. Did you see them?" his grandmother asked.

"Yes." He took off his coat and set it off to the side of him in the booth.

"Is that why you seated us in no man's land?" She sat down across the table from him and shrugged her shoulders out of her dark wool coat.

"Yes." Usually, he preferred the window area, not the back wall of the well-lit café.

"Do you need to look at the menu?" Leona, their waitress and the owner, set two glasses of iced water on the table.

"No, we're just here for pie and coffee," Grandma said.

Leona looked over her shoulder toward the lit display of pies on the back counter. "We're down to cherry, apple, and peach."

"I'll have apple ala mode, heated, please," Grandma said.

Leona nodded. "And, what about you, John?"

"Peach."

"Do you want it heated?"

"Yes, thank you."

"With ice cream?"

"Yes, please."

"Is it always like pulling teeth with him?" Leona asked.

"Sometimes." Grandma regarded him thoughtfully.

"Someday, John, if you're not careful, you'll get a cold piece of pie all by its lonesome," Leona said. "Two coffees and I know to bring cream."

John said *thank you* before she stepped away. Then he folded his arms on top of the table and regarded his grandmother—her short, white curly hair, her powdered complexion, her gray-blue eyes steady behind her wire-framed glasses.

"So, you didn't like the look I gave you on Sunday?"

"No. I didn't care for it at all." She wrinkled her nose.

"Opal said you looked directly at her, too. Nettie's afraid you did. Like I told you on Sunday, *women need words*, John—young and old."

"That's good for me to remember." He glanced across the three rows of tables and chairs toward the front of the café. The girls appeared to be enjoying themselves. Seated near the aisle, wearing a jumper and long-sleeved white blouse, Isabelle was every bit a vision as the first time he'd set eyes on her.

There was a click as Grandma opened her purse and pulled out a little memo book. "What you wrote in Isabelle's autograph book, I've read somewhere before. The sentiments are very nice, but…" she scooted her napkin of silverware off to her right and lifted her gaze, "they aren't going to win her heart."

"I knew that whatever I wrote would be broadcast by Nettie. And I was right."

"Did you read what her Albert wrote?"

"Yes, in passing," he admitted. Once he'd seen Al's signature at the bottom of the page, he'd scanned the rest. "He didn't write much."

"Neither did you."

Leona set a stainless steel creamer on the table, turned over the mugs, and poured dark coffee.

Grandma waited until Leona was several tables away before she said, "In my day, autograph books were very popular, amongst the young folk, especially." She slowly poured cream into her cup and stirred it with a spoon. "And, there were tricks to the trade." She took her first sip and lowered her mug to the table. "People used to fight over the back page and put cute little sayings like…" With a quirk to her mouth, she eyed the corner of the booth, *"By hook or by crook, I'll be the last one to write in this book.* Most often, it was simply nonsense."

Grandma took a sip of her coffee and then studied him.

He added cream to his coffee and stirred and ignored the knot in his gut. Her abrupt silence usually meant something.

"Sometimes," Grandma pressed a finger to her lips, "if someone had a secret to share, or just wanted to make it feel secretive, they'd fold a page back toward the spine, somewhere in the middle, tucked away."

Was she hinting at something?

From the left sleeve of her cardigan, she pulled out a folded piece of paper and held it toward him like a stick of gum.

"This is what Albert wrote in the middle of Isabelle's book."

His insides felt like a pinball machine.

"You tore it out?"

"No-oo." She shook her head. "Nettie told me what it said over the phone, and I wrote it down—word for word."

He lowered the cup to the table. When Grandma Hugg was on your side, she firmly believed that God was on your side, too. He couldn't begin to guess how many sermons she'd inspired his grandfather to preach over his three decades at the pulpit.

"It isn't right . . . Grandma." He tried to break it to her.

She set an open hand on top of the table and then laid her other hand on top. "I discussed this with your grandfather."

"What'd he say?"

Her head wobbled slightly. "He didn't want to read it, at first... either. But, after he did, he agreed that you should know."

John pressed his shoulders back into the booth, and then he leaned slightly to his left to view the narrow hallway to the payphone. For a dime, he could get his grandfather's side of the story. When Grandpa dropped Grandma off at the church, they hadn't had a chance to chat. But, he was probably home by now.

"It's my handwriting, not Albert's." Grandma leaned across the table and propped a white recipe card, folded in half, to the side of his coffee cup like it was a nameplate at a dinner party. There was writing across the front of it.

Isabelle wouldn't want him to read it. He knew that much about her.

"Three Sundays, John. The girls are heading home in three Sundays. December nineteenth—after their final performance. You may never see her again."

He knew that, too.

Whenever the girls were in the building, his pulse picked up. He found himself walking out front of the church to get the mail—something Virginia had always done. Instead of being locked away in his office, he was often walking—to pick up his messages from his secretary's office, grab a fresh cup of coffee, any chance he could to hear Isabelle's voice... to catch a glimpse of her.

His gaze drifted to his left to where Isabelle sat, conversing and smiling amongst the other choir girls. Then, returning his attention to the table, he read his grandmother's tight pointy cursive.

PRIVATE

What causes tears?

His chest felt like it was in the stranglehold of an anaconda.

He flicked the card, and it landed a few inches away on its side—at an angle that he couldn't see its contents.

But, mid-air, he'd seen one word.

Onions.

Grandma had played him.

"That was cruel." He met her gaze.

"If you only saw *Onions*, there's more."

He could walk away now, and not be guilty. And, for all he knew, the other half of the card could be a pun as well.

But, Albert had bought a ring.

John reached out and swiveled the card. On the other side of the fold were several handwritten lines.

"Izz, If you do go ahead with the Christmas choir,
I'll be living for the day you come home.
I love you, Al."

He felt himself age twenty years.

He lifted his gaze to his grandmother's. "I don't know if I needed to read that. Maybe I have no business even thinking about her."

"Maybe you don't." She nodded. "The girls, we've all been praying. But, now you know what you're up against."

He set his forearms on the table and leaned heavily against them.

"Nettie doesn't think Isabelle's read it yet." Grandma cradled her mug with both hands. "I don't think so either. If she did, do you think she'd just leave her autograph book lying around like a decoration?"

He shook his head.

He'd wanted to address the Granite Girls' gossip, and now... he was a part of the problem, too. He inhaled deeply and heard his fingers tapping on the table.

Their waitress strode toward them and set down Grandma's apple pie ala mode in front of her. And, while Leona set his slice of peach pie and ice cream down in front of John, he picked up the little slip of paper, folded it again in half, and dunked it deep into his coffee.

Grandma's eyes flashed wide.

"How are we doing on coffee?" Leona clasped her hands in front of her, eyeing their mugs.

"Fine. Thank you, Leona." John set his hand over the top of his cup.

She nodded and stepped away.

Grandma eyed her ice cream, and then pushing the dessert plate slightly to her left, folded her arms on the table. "The reason that I wanted to talk to you, John, is, Nettie may have torn Al's autograph out of the book. We're not sure."

His hand dropped to the table. "What?"

Grandma closed her eyes for a moment and nodded. "Nettie brought up the idea with both Rose and Opal."

Nettie!

"She's very biased about her choir girl. And—"

"She has no business." Jaw slack, he shook his head.

"This all happened on Friday. The phone hadn't rung like that since the Hundred Year Flood—which was only last year," Grandma said, thoughtfully. "But, there I was stuck in the middle of it all and Frank getting mad at me for *Nettie gossip*."

"Nettie's the one who needs a lecture."

Grandma moved her pie plate back in front of her. "Remember how Frank wasn't afraid to speak the truth?"

"Yes."

"Nettie needs a dose of truth."

Sometimes, when his grandfather got behind the pulpit, his congregants were afraid of what he'd say. Yet, they loved him for it.

"I'll speak to her in person, first."

"Of course. And, you can't be afraid of offense, not in your position. Speak the truth with love. Deep down, Nettie truly is a tender soul.

"Now, what about our pie?" She smiled, reaching for his hand. "I'll say the blessing."

They gripped hands above the table and bowed their heads.

"Our dear Heavenly Father, we have so much to be thankful for, especially Your Son and the Christmas season at hand. Be with Isabelle and Albert, Ted's choir girls, Lilly, Frank with his hand…" Grandma's prayer went on and on as they often did, including nearly every member of the congregation. "And, be with my grandson. You know how proud we are of him, even though we're not supposed to be proud. But, You know what I mean." She sighed. "If one of these choir girls is the one You've planned for him, then bless John with Your encouragement and the words, Lord, that she would understand the sincerity of his heart. In Your Son's name, Amen."

"I heard the Encourager's counsel at the end, Grandma. Thank you." He smiled past the knot in his gut. Already, he was feeling a heavy dose of remorse and was kicking himself. He shouldn't have read Al's autograph.

CHAPTER 19

*T*uesday afternoon, John sat at his desk and toyed with an ink pen. He shouldn't pursue Isabelle. She'd already told him that she loved Albert. And Albert had written *I love you* in her autograph book and bought her a ring. She might be wearing it now, for all he knew.

Someone tapped on his door and then Emmett Baker stuck his head inside. "You have time to talk?"

"Come in, Emmett." He rose halfway out of his chair, waving a hand. Every couple of weeks, the middle-aged mechanic stopped by to tell John about the vehicles he was working on and then they'd pray that he'd be able to fix them.

"The fourth vehicle is a '38 Ford four-door." Emmett had a voice that could carry across a shipyard.

A rap on the door was followed by Virginia poking her head inside.

"The engine's rusted like they were storing it at the coast with the hood up for the last twenty years." Emmett kept on talking.

John held up a finger, and then met his secretary's gaze.

"Nettie's on the phone for you. She said it's not urgent or life threatening, just important."

That sounded like Nettie.

John pushed down on the blinking red button and lifted the receiver to his ear. "Hello, this is John." He scanned the bookshelves lining the wall on his left.

"John, I just had a great idea! Why don't you come to dinner tonight, and we'll surprise the girls."

"Nettie . . ." He chuckled and glanced at Emmett. "Why *surprise?*"

"Isabelle's only with us for a few more Sundays. That doesn't give us a lot of..." she lowered her voice, "Courting time."

"Nettie!" He kept his gaze on the desk.

"I spoke with Russell, and we've decided that she'd make a fine pastor's wife. She's bright, sweet, and, boy, can she sing."

He drummed the fingers of his left hand on top of the desk. Nettie had conveniently left out Albert's second autograph.

"Does she have a ring on her finger?" He couldn't wait any longer to find out.

"No." Nettied giggled. "As soon as she got home, I made sure of that."

"What time should I arrive and what can I bring?"

"Six o'clock and bring 7-Up. Oh, and there's still plenty of Wilhoit water here for you." The line went dead. It wasn't hard to imagine Nettie in her little nook area, smiling.

"The fifth vehicle," Emmett continued, "is a one-of-a-kind Chevrolet roadster. The fellow at Molalla Ford referred it to me."

"Oh!" John nodded.

"Looks like you're a roadster man, yourself."

John nodded. "Do you remember the fellow's name?"

"Albert Gleinbroch—smart, young man—had a cup of

coffee with him once at the Molalla Ford garage. Sure knows his Fords."

"I see. Well, before I forget to ask, what do you think is wrong with the Coopers' Bel Air?"

"Don't rightly know. Russell said 'it's still getting him where he needs to go.'"

"Yes, just not on time." John chuckled.

Emmett settled his beefy forearms on top of the desk and toyed with one ear like he usually did before he shared something profound. "There are two types of people: Those who work on rigs," he held up a dark, grease-stained finger, "and those who don't. Russell's one of them who don't."

John nodded, his mind elsewhere. All it had taken was one phone call from Nettie, and he was up and swinging. He needed prayer.

* * *

"My friend Burt Cohen thinks your duet . . ." Arms raised in the conducting position, Mr. Hoffmeister eyed Darlene and then Isabelle, "has a chance of making it on the Lawrence Welk Show."

Be still her heart.

"What, what do you mean?" Darlene rested a hand on Isabelle's shoulder.

"An old music pal of mine with connections was here on Sunday and, heard you girls sing. I didn't want to tell you. Didn't want to make you feel nervous, but with your girls' permission, he'd like to send a copy of the duet to Lawrence Welk."

Carolyn gripped Isabelle's arm.

Was Mr. Hoffmeister teasing?

"What do you mean a copy?" Darlene asked.

"We had a tape recorder set up onstage. I turned it on

right before, well about ten minutes before," he glanced at Isabelle, "your duet started. The quality is surprising good."

Jaw slack, Isabelle stared at him. He wasn't kidding.

"Well, are you *both* interested?" His gaze drifted back and forth between the two girls. "If you are... the pinching needs to stop. You'll embarrass the entire town if you get on TV."

Isabelle couldn't believe it . . . Lawrence Welk!

"Of course we're interested," Darlene said.

"What about you?" Lowering his arms, he studied Isabelle.

"I'd kick myself forever if I said *no*."

"That's what I wanted to hear." He grinned.

If it took every ounce of willpower in her, she'd never pinch Darlene again.

* * *

"Now, Carolyn give me a G," Mr. Hoffmeister said.

Carolyn could hum any note he asked her to. She was a human pitch pipe.

Lilly Crawl entered the sanctuary and took a seat in the second row from the back.

Carolyn nudged Isabelle.

Isabelle blinked and shook her head. She didn't know why Lilly was here. But, she didn't look mad. She almost appeared happy for Lilly.

Carolyn nudged her again. This time so she'd focus.

"*Si - lent night ho - ly night all is calm all is bright Round yon vi – rgin moth –er and child.*"

"Girls!" Ted lowered and shook his head. "Be sure you all clip the D in child off at the same time. Let's try again. And after this Sunday, I want to have this be the duet you girls work on." He eyed Darlene and Isabelle.

After they sung it through once more, Mr. Hoffmeister lowered his arms. "Time for a break. My wife made cookies, and there's apple cider for you girls downstairs. And, absolutely no talking. Your voices need a rest."

"Awh!" Darlene and Carolyn moaned.

"No moaning, either."

Isabelle trailed behind the girls on their way to the foyer.

Lilly locked eyes with her, fluttering a hand. "I was hoping to speak to you for a minute." She scooted over in the pew, setting her purse on the other side of her. "I wanted to ask you over for supper. I know its last minute, and all. If you don't have anything planned, that is."

Isabelle sat down in the space beside her. "I'm not supposed to talk," she whispered, glancing at Mr. Hoffmeister. Then she mouthed, "My voice," and pointed to her throat.

"Oh," Lilly whispered. "I could bring you home to the Coopers' afterward. If you want to, that is."

"Yes." Isabelle mouthed, smiling.

"Really?" Lilly smiled. "That's wonderful."

"But . . ." Isabelle mouthed and then pointing at Mr. Hoffmeister fluttered her fingers in front of her open mouth.

"You still have to sing a few more songs? I'll just stay here and listen if that's okay?"

Isabelle nodded. She knew it was. Virginia, the church secretary, sat in here all the time and listened.

***

They'd stopped at Roth's before leaving town and Isabelle had purchased whole cream butter to make biscuits at Lilly's.

"How do you make a beef gravy when the beef is already cooked?" Lilly asked stirring the start of their stew. Joann Goff had given her some left over roast beef and they'd chopped an onion and carrots.

"I dunno." Isabelle stood beside her at the stove. "You have any Worcestershire?"

"No, I wish."

"What do you have?"

"There's some red wine. I found it the other day in a corner cupboard. Tommy used to marinate his elk meat with it."

Lilly also found a can of Campbell's Cream of Mushroom soup. The stew was an interesting mix of carrots, onions, cubed roast, cream of mushroom soup, and a splash of wine.

Lilly poured in another splash of wine while Isabelle added the final seasonings.

"I saw that. How much did you add?"

"About a mouthful." Lilly smiled.

The biscuits came out puffy, lightly golden... beautiful. Thankfully, Isabelle knew Fletcher's recipe by heart.

Lilly pulled tin plates out of the cupboard. "I love these old plates. Feels like you're sitting around a campfire when you eat off of them. It's nice to have company."

A steady fire crackled in the hearth. Three miles out of town, Lilly's cabin had electricity, running water, and what looked like many years of firewood split and piled in the nearby woodshed.

After Lilly said a prayer, Isabelle took a bite of stew. It wasn't half bad.

"You're lucky you were able to go home for Thanksgiving." Lilly buttered a biscuit. "Did you hear that the Coopers were at John's folks for dessert?"

"Yes, Carolyn told me."

"Did she tell you that Nettie declined the main meal because she already had the TV dinners in the oven when John called?"

"No!" Isabelle giggled.

A dimple briefly surfaced in her cheek before Lilly's

expression dimmed. "One minute, I'm laughing and the next I'm not. I've always heard that the Lord doesn't give us more than we can handle. But, this past year, I've wondered if He has a Lilly Crawl clause."

Setting down her soup spoon, Isabelle lowered her hands to her lap.

"You know, the little asterisk they put in ads to inform you that there's an exception?"

"Yes."

"Except God is perfect. He never forgets a thing." Tears welled before Lilly swallowed. "So, if there was supposed to be an asterisk by my name, He would have put one there."

"And He knows us completely. He knows every hair on our heads. Every tear."

Lilly dangled her spoon over her soup, studying her. "I saw something in you at the potluck that first Sunday that made me think all's not right. Pretty girl like you, voice like yours, a fella like John Hugg being obvious about the way he feels about you."

John hadn't told her.

"I thought he was being unfaithful."

"To who?" Lilly blinked.

"You're young, pretty, wearing a wedding ring, and always with him."

"What are you saying?" Lilly's jaw hung slack.

"I thought John and you were married . . . for several days, I thought it." She shook her head now at the memory. "No one told me. All I knew is that you were always together."

"You thought I was the pastor's wife?" Lilly sat back in her chair and laughed softly.

"Yes."

Lilly set a hand on the table. "How . . . when did you find out?"

"John told me the night we went to Roth's for 7-Up. I thought he'd tell you."

"Oh... that awful night." Lilly gazed sullenly at the table.

"Was it a turning point?"

"Every day is a turning point for me right now." Lilly chewed on her lower lip. "I didn't know how much I needed to be around people until the next day at Harriet's."

Over the next hour, Isabelle told her more about Roth's, and from there, the conversation traveled to the autograph book. "Nettie must have gotten into my suitcase to find it. I never took it out."

"Nettie Cooper!" Now that Lilly had a little color in her cheeks, and sparkle in her blue-green eyes, she was pretty—really pretty. "You have to be careful around Nettie. With her, your life's pretty much an open book."

Isabelle laughed. "Except for the autograph book, there's not much snooping she can do."

"Well, consider yourself lucky." Lilly smiled briefly before adding: "I've needed somebody to talk to... besides John." The corner of her mouth twitched. "The morning Tommy left for work, the day of the accident, he rubbed my shoulders in bed, and I was so tired, I mumbled in my sleep that I hoped he didn't want me to get up.

"I always tried to get up early with him—five o'clock. And make him coffee and something to eat, and I did that morning. Over breakfast, he laughed about what I'd said when I'd been half asleep. But, it doesn't seem very funny now."

"You were half asleep. And, he laughed about it."

"Tommy laughed about everything. Everything but God." She propped an elbow on the table.

"I believe in love at first sight because of Tommy. The first time I ever saw him was at his brother's wedding." Lilly's gaze shifted toward the fireplace. "I knew the bride. Tommy was the best man... He truly was." Tears ebbed then she swallowed. "He had a full beard—trimmed, all nice and tidy. I thought he was fine looking from a distance.

"At the buffet, he was on the other side of the table from me, and at the same time, we both reached for the Parkerhouse rolls." Her eyes shimmered with memories. "You know what he said to me?"

"No."

"He said, 'You really ought to put some of those little chicken wings on your plate. My Aunt Elna makes the best chicken wings you've ever tasted.' Big, brown eyes. Without saying a word, I set two chicken wings on my plate and looked at him. Tommy laughed. He was always laughing.

"And, it was the same way for John." Lilly folded her arms on top of the table, studying her.

"You can't speak for John." Isabelle's rib cage knit together tightly.

"He was so shook up when he couldn't find you again at Roth's. I told him to calm down. I told him what Tommy used to say to me: 'If it's supposed to happen, it will, 'cause God has His hand in all that happens.'" Lilly folded over the cuff of her flannel sleeve. "Funny, having to remind your pastor about God."

Isabelle eyed her remaining stew. "We should have sautéed the onions before we added them."

"We'll know better next time. You know what you need to do?" Lilly glanced up from buttering her second biscuit. "Kiss John Hugg before Christmas."

Isabelle shook her head confused. "I misunderstood you. That first Sunday in church, I thought you were upset that I was there."

A blank look replaced the mirth in Lilly's eyes. "It was Tommy's birthday and, I remember sitting there, envious of you girls. How your happiness is right in front of you, and the best of my life is behind me."

"No, Lilly—"

"You never knew my husband." Her gaze shifted to the entry area behind Isabelle. "He wasn't any taller than John, but Tommy's shoulders filled that doorway."

Isabelle glanced to the wood-framed doorway behind her.

"A big guy, with a big sense of humor. Last year, when I had my miscarriage . . ."

Isabelle sucked in a breath. "I didn't know."

"He cried like a baby, and I *loved* him for it."

"My life hasn't been all roses, either . . . Lilly. You've just seen some of the highlights." Isabelle's shoulders felt all jumpy at what she was about to share. "I lost my mother when I was eight."

Reaching across the table, Lilly took her hand.

"She died in a car accident." Her admittance was accompanied by the all too familiar adrenaline. "And, my father, who'd been driving, lost the use of his legs from the waist down. That evening while our aunt held my sister and me, she told us, 'Your Momma's now an angel, and she's watching over you from the balconies of heaven.'"

Tears slid down Lilly's cheeks.

"I was a little girl trying to come to grips with loss, but I accepted the Lord as my Savior that night." Tears warmed the corners of her eyes. "I felt a peace that I otherwise would never have known." She swallowed tears. "When we trust in Him, Lilly, the best is before us."

"I know." Lilly sniffled and nodded.

CHAPTER 20

*J*ohn showed up at the Coopers' at six o'clock with five bottles of 7-Up. He carried the grocery bag to the kitchen and set it on the counter. By divine intervention, he had Nettie alone. This was his chance.

"Nettie, I want to be sure and reiterate to you that my visits here are to remain private. I would appreciate it if you didn't speak to the other Granite Girls about them."

"Is that why you singled me out on Sunday?"

He nodded.

"As a pastor, I need to guard my reputation. And, I need your help in this matter."

"Of course, John. Absolutely." Nettie transferred the bottles of 7-Up to the fridge. "And, I'm sorry I invited you tonight."

"Wha . . . what do you mean?"

"Didn't Carolyn tell you?" She looked up at him.

"No, Russell answered the door."

"Well . . . Isabelle isn't even here. Supposedly, Lilly

stopped by the girls' practice and invited her over to her place for supper."

"Oh . . . I see?" He tried to collect himself. "That's wonderful for Lilly."

"And, Carolyn didn't know I'd invited you over for supper. Otherwise, she would have told you." Nettie motioned to the plates on the counter. "Here, carry these in for us."

He delivered golden brown chicken pot pies to the living room, first to Russell and then to Carolyn who was now seated on the right side of the couch, her legs tunneled beneath a TV tray.

"Carolyn, Isabelle didn't happen to say what time she'd be home?" he asked.

"No. But, I don't think she'll be out late."

He sat down on the other end of the couch, and lifted his TV tray a bit. Wilhoit water sloshed in his glass onto the tray, just missing his pot pie.

"John, would you like to say the prayer?" Nettie asked.

"Yes. I'd be happy to."

Carolyn rose and dimmed the volume on the television set. Then, they bowed their heads, and he said the blessing. Near the end, he prayed for Ralph Ferguson to find employment and for Lilly that the Lord would continue to strengthen her.

Carolyn spun the dial to the normal volume and returned to sit down.

"I took Lilly grocery shopping awhile back. She was down to one can of tomatoes." John took his first bite of the pot pie.

"We have some canned tomatoes we can give her. Don't we, Ma?" Russell asked.

"I meant her cupboards were bare except for the *one* can of tomatoes."

Brows gathered, Russell peered over at him.

"No need to worry, the Granite Girls have her covered," Nettie said.

"Everybody!" Carolyn sat up and clapped her hands together. "I just remembered something exciting."

"Shhh! It's on!" Nettie pointed to the TV and the start of the Lawrence Welk Show.

"It's exciting news, Grandma."

"It can wait." Nettie pressed a finger to her mouth.

From across the room, the colorful lights on their aluminum tree reflected off the window, adding a strobe light of color to the black-and-white picture. Champagne bubbles floated across the screen. Lawrence Welk held a conductor's baton, "Ah-one, ah-two!"

John glanced across the sofa at Carolyn and smiled, apologetically.

"Remind me during commercials," she whispered.

He'd try.

He'd never been much of a big band guy. Though he'd never spoken about it in a sermon, he'd learned endurance and perseverance during his teenage years when his grandparents used to watch the show. Unlike Russell, he could at least make it through the one-hour program without falling asleep.

Onscreen, the Champagne Lady, Norma Zimmer, wore a loose blue dress with a big, red bow. She painted a picture while she sang "Whistle While You Work." In between brush strokes, she strolled about a cozy set complete with a fireplace and couch.

John relaxed deeper into the sofa, and pictured Isabelle walking about his living room, singing the same song.

"Uh . . . John. Earth to John."

He blinked, looking at Nettie. "Yes."

"Russell's talking to you." She bobbed a finger toward her husband.

A Polident Denture commercial played.

"Yes, Russell, I'm sorry."

The elderly man lowered his chin. "Nettie was saying that Lawrence Welk is still looking for a new Champagne Lady. Don't you think Isabelle would look pretty on TV?"

Nettie peered over at him, too.

"She doesn't need to be on TV to look pretty."

Carolyn giggled.

"Can I tell you my big news now?" she asked her grandmother.

"And that's to stay in this room, Nettie," John said, already feeling sorry for his admittance.

"Oh, John, of course." Nettie flicked a hand. "What is it, Carolyn?"

The phone rang in the other room.

Carolyn's shoulders slumped, and she heaved a heavy sigh. "I'll get it." Then she rose and hurried to the kitchen.

"Norma, the Champagne Lady, gave her notice years ago because she wanted to stay home with her boys," Nettie said. "Every week, Lawrence interviews a new girl and still hasn't found the right one."

"Sounds like he doesn't want to replace her," John said.

Arms folded in front of him, Russell bobbed his head in agreement.

"Grandma, Opal's on the phone." Carolyn picked up a magazine off the side table before returning to the couch.

"Oh?" Nettie lowered her footrest and glanced over at John. "Kind of an odd time for her to be calling." Then with her back slightly bent, she started for the kitchen.

"I know what Opal's calling about." Carolyn eyed the two men. "Mr. Hoffmeister had one of his old pals visit our church on Sunday."

"Burt Cohen." John nodded. He'd spoken with him briefly after service.

"Yes. Supposedly, Mr. Cohen has connections. He liked Isabelle and Darlene's duet enough that he's going to send Lawrence Welk a tape of it."

"You're kidding?" The news was huge.

Carolyn shook her head. "I almost thought the same thing at first, but, well, you know how Mr. Hoffmeister is. He never jokes about a thing."

"The girls' duet on Sunday was nice," Russell said.

It had been amazing. A knot formed in John's chest. The Lawrence Welk show was recorded in Los Angeles, almost a thousand miles away.

"I know, it just flowed," Carolyn said. "Isabelle's so reserved compared to Darlene. Mr. Hoffmeister's always trying to get her to use her hands, be more expressive. I remember thinking she almost looked relaxed like Darlene—"

"Nettie thought the girls were pinching each other when they were onstage," Russell interrupted.

"Darlene likes to pinch." Carolyn thumbed through her magazine.

"Wait until Nettie hears this." Russell eyed the television. "Lawrence Welk."

"Most likely, Opal's telling her right now." John picked up his water glass and rose to his feet. Halfway to the kitchen, he paused and eyed the smiling soloist onscreen. Did Isabelle have the gumption to make it on the show? Darlene certainly did, but did she have the voice?

"That was wunderful. Just wunderful." Lawrence Welk tapped his baton into his open hand, preparing the audience for another commercial break.

John continued toward the kitchen.

"John's at my house for dinner tonight," Nettie's whisper

carried from the nook area. "I didn't know that Lilly had invited Isabelle over for dinner. Yes, it's unfortunate."

John paused before the doorway.

"I agree. Yes, I like Isabelle, too. I told John earlier that I wouldn't discuss their relationship. But, I agree, he's not going to like the news—Los Angeles!"

Nettie! He'd just spoken to her. Rerouting himself, John returned to the sofa to sit down.

Russell's head turned; with furrowed salt-and-pepper brows, the elderly man peered over at him.

Tipping his empty water glass, John pretended to take a sip.

Nettie returned soon enough and sat down in the recliner next to her husband's.

"Who was on the phone, Ma?" Russell asked.

"Just Opal." Nettie wiggled her shoulders deep into the corduroy and got comfortable.

"Did she tell you the news?" Carolyn asked.

"What news?"

"About sending a tape of Isabelle and Darlene's duet to Lawrence Welk?"

Nettie glanced at John for some reason. "Yes, she did. It all sounds very exciting and a long ways away to me. I've decided we ought to do everything in our power to keep the girls here. Well, to at least keep Isabelle here. Don't you agree, John?"

"I don't know, Nettie. Seems like it might be a once in a lifetime opportunity for them." He tried to be diplomatic.

He should head home. He'd work on his sermon, pray and read his Bible—maybe Psalms, or as Tommy had called them, *salve for the soul.*

The phone rang in the other room.

"Not again." Nettie sighed.

"I'll get it, Grandma." Carolyn tossed her magazine aside and hurried toward the kitchen.

"You'd think it was Christmas," Russell eyed him, adding a chuckle.

"It's for you, Grandma," Carolyn said from the doorway.

"Probably something to do with the Granite Girls," Russell said. "You know how they are—always planning and praying about something."

John's fingers tapped the side of his empty water glass.

What had his grandfather's wording been . . . *God is in control, not seven little old ladies.* The short, little sermon was starting to sound better all the time.

***

That evening, John waited until nine thirty to ring Lilly at home. Then, he waited through three rings on the other end before she picked up.

"Lilly, it's John."

"I thought so."

"Nettie invited me over for dinner tonight, and, lo and behold, Isabelle was at your place."

"Sorry about that. I tried to put a good word in for you, though."

"How'd it go?" He waited through a stretch of silence. And then added, "What do you think?"

"You can't be in such a rush."

"I'm not rushing anything. I'm just trying to get to know her. Besides, the girls are only here for a couple more Sundays."

"Listen to yourself. You, of all people, should know that you don't rush a good thing. I could see it happening, and I had to step in."

"What do you mean?"

"I had to give her some breathing room, a chance to think. You're hoping to get this romance of yours all wrapped up by Christmas. When really, it's going to take her the rest of her life to forget him."

His chest tightened. "Do you mean Albert?"

"Yes, Albert. You never forget your first love."

CHAPTER 21

Sunday evening, while the choir girls sang "Silent Night," John didn't see anyone unusual in the crowd—no one he didn't know—except for a tall, broad-shouldered, young man seated in the back. His gut told him it was Albert Gleinbroch. He looked like he could play tight end for the Oregon State University football team, and his eyes were full of love for the same young woman John had spent the last few weeks thinking about.

After the song ended, Ted stood up and read aloud Luke 1:30-35. "But the angel said to her, 'Do not be afraid, Mary; you have found favor with God. You will conceive and give birth to a son, and you are to call him Jesus. He will be great and will be called the Son of the Most High.'"

Darlene's and Isabelle's duet, "Angels We Have Heard on High," followed and received a loud applause.

The girls sounded beautiful. They might very easily make it on the Lawrence Welk Show.

Near the close of the evening, John stood up to address the audience. "After the next solo, which is our final song of the evening, you're welcome to stay for refreshments downstairs.

He drew in a slow, deep breath as his gaze lingered on the sea of faces. "Two thousand years ago, the Light of the World left heaven and the glory of His Father's side to be born. It's this miracle of love that we celebrate at Christmas.

"If you feel inspired to know Jesus as your Lord and Savior or desire prayer of any kind, my grandfather, Pastor Frank Hugg, and I will be up front to pray with you."

While John stepped off to his right, his grandfather rose in the audience and ambled over to stand beside him.

The back row of lights dimmed and a halo of light encompassed Ted, seated on a stool, and Isabelle standing beside him. Her hair was pulled up in a high bun. Like the other choir girls, she wore a red cashmere sweater over a black skirt. She looked stunning, yet, he couldn't help think, a little fragile.

"*O Holy Night!*" Isabelle's poignant voice held unusual clarity and depth.

Ted's guitar joined in as an accompaniment.

"*Fall on your knees!*
Oh, hear the angel voices!
Oh night divine,
Oh night when Christ was born."

Grandpa rocked back his head and sniffled. Then, he pulled a folded handkerchief out of his back pocket and dabbed at his cheeks.

John couldn't look at him. He felt the same way.

* * *

Praise be to God, an older man and Rose Carlton's granddaughter came forward during Isabelle's solo. His grandfather's tears only added to the heavy emotion in the room.

Following the performance, John turned from speaking with Rose to see Isabelle with Albert seated nearby in the back pew. His stomach dropped.

Ben Armstrong, a middle-aged logger who hadn't been to church in a while, strode toward John.

"Question, Pastor." Ben vigorously shook his hand. "If I hang a carved wooden fish on my wall, is that an idol?"

"As long as you don't bow down to it." Out of the corner of his eye, he saw Isabelle and Albert exiting. "We're... to love the Lord with all our heart, soul, and mind." He focused on Ben. "Now, don't go looking at that fish more than you do your Bible."

Ben slapped him on the shoulder, grinning.

A few minutes later, John passed Albert and Isabelle in the foyer. They were deep in conversation near the picture window.

John started down the stairwell. Not only had Al driven through the snow to drive her home for Thanksgiving, he was also here for the choir's first performance.

A bitter dose of reality walloped him.

In the basement, he poured himself a cup of coffee and nabbed one of his grandmother's molasses cookies. He conversed with Charlie Waggoner for a few minutes, and then excused himself to grab the vacant seat next to his grandmother on the far wall.

Sitting down beside her, he rested his coffee cup on his knee.

"My Heaven Sent Molasses always been your favorite," she nodded toward the cookie, "ever since you were young."

"Plain ole molasses," Grandpa murmured, seated on the other side of her.

"Grandpa saw Isabelle earlier with a tall, young man," Grandma whispered under her breath.

"Yes... Albert."

"Oh-hh!" Grandma rested her hand on his arm, consolingly.

John held the cookie beneath his nose, inhaled, and closed his eyes. The molasses-gingery smell brought back a treasure trove of childhood memories—and his grandmother's kitchen at Christmas. Still, the cold hard truth remained; before the evening was through, Isabelle might very well be engaged.

"Delight yourself in the Lord," Grandpa said.

"And He will give you the desires of your heart," added Grandma.

"In the meantime, try not to wear your heart on your sleeve so much."

Grandpa was one to talk. John's gaze drifted to the stairwell.

"John's always worn his heart on his sleeve. That's who he is," Grandma said.

"But, he's a pastor now."

"Our church family loves that he's just like you."

John peered into his grandmother's pale blue eyes and did his best to change the subject. "Any chance you've been to Lilly Crawl's home recently?"

Years of working anonymously for the Lord helped her to not even break a smile. But, he saw a twinkle in her eye, all the same. "Why do you ask?"

Her gaze drifted across the room to where Lilly stood near the food service window, speaking to Joann Goff.

"Little things change when she's at work. She asked me if she should be concerned."

"What kind of *little* things?"

"The wood bin's empty when she leaves and full when she returns. A can of tuna in the back of the cupboard that she could have sworn wasn't there the day before. A light bulb that was burnt-out in the morning is lit when she gets home."

"Born again," Grandpa said.

"Little things . . . mainly." John nodded.

"It doesn't sound like anything to call the authorities about." Grandma's gaze remained on Lilly.

"You're probably right. Sounds more like do-gooders." John's gaze drifted to the stairwell. The ring that Albert had purchased was probably searing a hole in his pocket and heart. Right now, he was probably down on one knee, giving it to her.

* * *

"Thanks for coming tonight." In the foyer, Isabelle gazed up into Albert's blue eyes.

"Sure looks like you're fitting in." Al's grin didn't quite reach his gaze. "You should've heard the folks around me. For some reason, they're afraid that you're going to make it on the Lawrence Welk Show. When..." For a second, there might've been a glassy sheen in his eyes, but then he blinked, "they all want to keep you right here... in Silverton."

Chest knotted, she lowered her gaze to the V of his collar.

"Izz, there's something I need to tell you."

"What?" There was the strange aloofness that she'd sensed last week.

"Maybe it was meant to be that you never saw the ring."

He'd already found a girl to give it to. She should have thrown two rocks.

"Is it Janet?"

He shook his head and smirked. "That was me being dumb again."

"What do you mean?"

"What's going on with you and the pastor?"

"Not much."

"Has he signed your autograph book yet?"

"Yes, but, I didn't ask him to. Mrs. Cooper got into my suitcase and had it sitting out by the phone."

Al stepped back a few inches.

"Carolyn found it during the TV dinner party that I already told you about."

He looked all serious. She wasn't used to seeing him that way.

"Was it any better than . . . the mushy one I wrote you?" His voice cracked a bit.

"It was more pastoral." She shrugged and rolled her eyes. Al's autograph had been anything but mushy.

He glanced around the foyer. His Adam's apple bobbed.

Was he telling her goodbye? It sure felt like it for some reason.

While she waited for him to spit it out, her heart unearthed a memory that it didn't want to let go. "Remember…" she swallowed past a clump of tears, "your fistful of purple-crocuses from Aunt Elsie's flower bed?" After her parents' accident—when her family had first moved out to Wilhoit—Al, just a boy at the time, had seemed to worry about her the most.

The corner of his mouth twitched. "If it's any help, Elsie told me to pick them for you. I didn't think it up on my own."

All these years, she'd believed otherwise. Still, she couldn't forget how carefully Al had set them on the porch railing beside her any more than she could forget the tender look in his eyes.

He rolled a kink out of his neck and began buttoning his coat.

"Hey." She looped her arm in his. "I need to pick your brain." She wasn't ready for him to leave. "It wasn't the battery." She steadied herself against his side. "Headlights were bright. I checked the wiring underneath, cleaned everything, and the car still wouldn't start."

"That's too bad." He grimaced. "The next thing you gotta do is get a hammer."

"A hammer?"

"Yep, a hammer."

"Are you lying?" She'd never seen him use a hammer on a vehicle.

"Nope. You tap the solenoid with the hammer. If the engine starts right up, that's the problem."

"The solenoid's that can-looking thing on the starter?"

He nodded and his Adam's apple bobbed above the V in his dark wool coat. Then, he lingered like he was waiting for her to say something.

"So you didn't like what I wrote?" He stared down at her.

Still holding onto his arm, she shook her head. "Do you blame me? I always wondered how you really felt about me."

"Now, you know." His brows gathered as he swallowed. "Goodbye, Izz." He kissed her forehead, turned and started for the double doors.

"Al!" He was almost acting like it was goodbye.

"Al . . ." She started after him, but he just kept walking.

In the door's upper glass, she watched through a sheen of tears as he crossed the street. Gold Christmas lights twinkled in the distance, outlining the two-story buildings downtown. He climbed inside his cab. Did he see her?

"Al!" She lifted a hand.

He drove out of the parking lot, taking a right onto Jersey Street before his tail lights disappeared from view.

He'd just said goodbye. And, he'd almost acted like it really was.

CHAPTER 22

When the girls returned home from choir practice Tuesday evening, they hung their coats in the front entry.

Wearing her shiny brown wig, Nettie stood near the living room window, peeking out of the curtains. They must be having company.

"Who's coming over?" Isabelle asked. She followed Carolyn through the front room on their way to the kitchen.

Nettie shook her head. "Carolyn, get the china out, and, Isabelle, set the silverware for five."

"Okay, Grandma, but there's only four of us."

"Set the table for five."

"Five means company, Grandma."

"Set the table for five."

Whoever they were having, Nettie wanted to keep it a secret.

"Maybe Santa's coming." Carolyn winked at Isabelle.

Totino's Pizza boxes and empty cans of Green Giant creamed corn littered the Formica counter.

"Is the oven ready?" Nettie asked, entering the kitchen.

"No, it's preheating, Grandma."

The doorbell rang.

Had she invited John, again?

"Russell, get the door," Nettie bellowed, pulling her best white apron over her head. Her wig hung cockeyed, covering her eyes. She shifted it to where she could at least see.

When Isabelle carried silverware to the dining table, Russell was still seated in his recliner, his back to the kitchen. This time, she didn't want to be the one to answer the door. Instead, she took her time folding paper napkins and tucking them under the right edge of each plate.

The doorbell rang a second time.

"Russell, get the door!" Nettie bellowed.

His spindly arms flew skyward like he'd just awoken from a deep sleep.

"Huh?" Yawning, he peered over at Isabelle. "Do you need me to start the car?"

"No. Stay where you are." Isabelle started toward the entry. She paused for a moment to make sure her blouse was tucked into her skirt. Then, she pulled open the door.

John Hugg stood on the front porch, holding a grocery sack. "Good evening, Isabelle." He stepped past her into the entry, the necks of green 7-Up bottles visible in the open bag.

"Hi, John. Did Nettie invite you?" Of course she must have. Isabelle glanced toward the truck.

It was empty.

He was here all by himself this time.

She closed the door.

"Yes. Don't be mad at her. Be mad at me. I didn't require much prodding." The corner of his mouth twitched.

"Why?" She moved ahead of him to pull open the closet door. Then she took the grocery bag from him so he could hang up his coat.

"Isabelle . . ." He chuckled and hung up his coat above the

new Kirby vacuum. "That question might take me a lifetime to explain…" Turning, he met her gaze. "Or understand."

His answer bordered between vague and terribly romantic.

He retrieved the bag from her, and held it off to one side. "Would you like me to be more specific?"

Was it a trick question? She already knew he was a lot smarter than her.

"O . . . kay." Then, she inhaled like she was about to sing the National Anthem.

A hint of Lifebuoy soap drifted in the air between them.

"All right." He leaned his head slightly to peer past her toward the living room.

She knew only Russell was seated, his focus inevitably on the TV.

With the edge of the closet door slightly between them, she lifted her gaze to John's.

"It all began at Roth's. I think you know that." He inhaled. "And, each time I've seen you on stage, I understand a little better why."

He wasn't making sense.

"There's a look in your eyes, Isabelle—a fragility about you—that I've pretty much fall—"

"Stop!" He was about to say the unthinkable.

"Isabelle . . ." His dark brows furrowed. He was every bit as stubborn as Al, she could just sense it.

Turning, she felt heat climb her neck as she made her way through the front room. It wasn't right. Only two nights ago, Albert had said his odd goodbye. And now John was trying to twist her heart into thinking about him.

* * *

Isabelle beelined to the kitchen and, following Nettie's

orders, she took glasses down from the cupboard. One tumbled onto the counter and from there to the floor. Luckily they were plastic and didn't break. Then she dropped another one.

"Isabelle, get a grip!" Nettie said.

It was easy for her to say.

"John, I hope you like homemade pizza," Nettie bellowed, tucking a Totino's Pizza box in the garbage beneath the sink.

"Grandma, you know it's not homemade," Carolyn whispered.

"It most certainly is. I'm making it in my *own* oven."

"I love pizza," John said loudly from the front room.

"And Isabelle." Nettie giggled and gripped the jelly roll pan of pizzas and lowered the oven door.

Had she really said that? Isabelle's head swiveled.

"Grandma, it's still preheating."

"What was that?" Nettie slid the pan of pizzas inside, turning her good ear up.

"I said *it's still preheating.*"

Isabelle knew she hadn't been imagining things. John had been about to say—

"Grandma!"

While Nettie peered up at her granddaughter, the upper element sent a wave of heat over Nettie's dark hair. The front and sides of her wig melted to her head like a swim cap and her glasses fogged up in the center until her eyes looked like Orphan Annie's.

"Grandma!" Carolyn shrieked.

Hands fluttering, the elderly woman flung the wig to the far side of the kitchen. The waxen blob hit a lower cabinet and slid to the floor.

Isabelle stared; half expecting it to scurry behind the fridge.

"Are you okay?" Carolyn closed the oven door and stepped closer to her grandmother.

"I don't know. Am I?" Nettie gulped and ran a hand over her short white hair.

"Nothing's red or bubbly." Carolyn studied her forehead.

"Everything okay in there, Ma?" Russell bellowed from the front room.

"Yes." Nettie patted a hand above her heart. "Except my hair."

She'd just witnessed a miracle in Mrs. Cooper's kitchen!

"God was watching over you, Grandma. You weren't burned. Not even a dot." Carolyn turned back to the stove and spun the egg timer a quarter turn.

"It's a miracle!" Isabelle said.

"It was the webbing. The webbing saved me. It was the only thing that wasn't plastic." Nettie wrestled a pair of tongs out of a drawer and ambled across the kitchen. She picked up what remained of her wig with the long-handled utensil.

The girls followed her to the living room doorway and watched as Nettie halted in front of the television.

"Look." She held up the waxen blob. "I got too close to the element, and look what it did to my wig."

"What!" Russell laughed. "I thought it was a rat!"

From the couch, John also chuckled.

"I know what I want for Christmas." Hand on hip, Nettie pointed the tongs at her husband. "A new wig. And it's not something you can pick out for me. You'll need me there."

"Things are going to get downright boring after the girls go home," Russell told John.

"I agree." The color wheel on the aluminum tree reflected little dots of light on John's face. "But, you'll still have Nettie." Then, his gaze drifted to the doorway where, right in front of everybody, it settled on Isabelle.

She felt like she'd swallowed a candy cane sideways.

"One Wilhoit water, coming up," she said. And then, like the awkward choir girl that she was, she strode to the back door and pulled it closed behind her. She lingered on the back step. "What's going on with Al?" she whispered into the brisk December air. "And, what's going on with me?" She lowered her voice. "I *know* what's going on with John. Lord, help me to get a grip!"

She picked up the glass jug of Wilhoit water off the top step and returned inside.

At the counter, she poured beverages and inhaled deeply, trying to summon the nerve to deliver them.

Carolyn stepped beside her and carried out the task for her.

Whiffs of Aqua Net Hairspray accompanied Nettie's return to the kitchen. Her short hair was pulled up on the sides with bobby pins. "Carolyn, carry the pizza to the table in the living room," she barked. "Isabelle, you take the bowl of creamed corn. Turn off the television, Russell, and we'll all sit down."

They were sitting down at the nice table?

"The television's not on, Ma."

"Well, that's a change."

Isabelle sat down in the chair on John's left, kitty-corner to Russell, seated at the head of the table.

"What's the sermon about this Sunday?" Russell asked.

"You asked that the last time he was here." Nettie held her hands out for prayer.

"I must be a creature of habit."

"Do me a favor, Russell"—John gripped both Isabelle's hand beside him and Carolyn's hand across the table—"and remind me what the sermon was about last Sunday?"

All too aware of John's warm, strong hand, Isabelle kept her gaze riveted to Mr. Cooper on her left.

"Oh, that's easy . . ." Russell's gaze roved the ceiling. "Nettie, help me."

His wife appeared frozen, but her mouth moved, "Carolyn."

"It wasn't about me." She giggled. "It was something about..." Carolyn's gaze traveled to the Pom Pom Sparkler aluminum tree in front of the picture window.

Russell jabbed a finger into the air. "Was born to give them second birth."

Was he remembering "Hark the Herald Angels Sing" or was it also a line from the Bible?

"Yes." John nodded. "Through miraculous conception, Jesus was born on earth. He laid aside His glory to become a baby."

Heat climbed into Isabelle's cheeks. He was always saying just the right thing. Well, almost always... her thoughts returned to the entry.

John Hugg was in a hurry. He was trying to get her all wrapped up before Christmas.

CHAPTER 23

"*S*ing through the last refrain one more time and hold the last "O night divine." Mr. Hoffmeister cleared his froggy throat. "Chin up and shoulders relaxed."

Seated in the fourth pew from the front, Virginia was Isabelle's solo audience. It was Thursday and Isabelle had stayed late again to practice her solo which meant John would be driving both of them home.

She readied her stance and with a slight lift of her chin, sang:

"*Fall on your knees!*
O hear the angels' voices!"

John entered the sanctuary, his coat folded over one arm. He walked down the center aisle toward the front and sat in the pew beside Virginia.

"*The night when Christ was born.*" Isabelle's gaze settled ever so briefly on the two, before she focused on the entryway.

"*O night, O holy night, O night divine!*" She caressed the last note.

"Wunder-ful. That was just wonderful." Mr. Hoffmeister did his Lawrence Welk impression.

"Thank you."

"That song's very taxing. That's why it's the last one of our performance," Mr. Hoffmeister said. "Rest your voice for at least the next hour." Then he turned and informed the others, "Isabelle needs to rest her voice for the next hour, which means absolutely no talking."

She wouldn't have to worry about conversation tonight. She chuckled at his timing. In the foyer, she put on her coat and gloves.

"Goodnight, everyone." Carrying his guitar case, Mr. Hoffmeister went out the front double doors.

She waved briefly.

John entered the foyer and locked the upper doors. Virginia tidied pamphlets on the entry table. Then they all started down the steps to the ground level door.

The phone rang in John's office.

"I'll get it." He started back up the stairs. "Go ahead, ladies, I'll catch up."

"It could be anyone," Virginia said as they ventured into the damp evening air. "I could name ten people it could be, but you just never really know." She made small talk while they crossed the street to John's truck. The elderly woman climbed in the passenger side first, and scooted to the middle.

"Hopefully it wasn't an emergency," Virginia added. They were in the cab for a minute or two before John joined them and started the engine.

"Who was on the phone?" Virginia asked.

"Bill Roluff."

"Oh."

"I hope you ladies don't mind if I take a slight detour on the way home."

Isabelle shook her head, even though he probably couldn't see her.

"That's fine," Virginia said.

"Bill saw Lilly driving through town with a load of firewood."

"Oh... you don't think?"

"He seems to think that Lilly may have taken my sermon a couple of Sundays ago to heart." Out of the gravel parking lot, John took a right on Jersey Street.

"You'll have to remind me."

"About giving to the less fortunate this season... and I mentioned Tommy."

"Lilly is the less fortunate."

"Yes. But, she has firewood."

Virginia sighed and peered over her shoulder at Isabelle. "Every Christmas, Lilly and her husband, Tommy, used to deliver firewood to the shut-ins and needy families. But... she has no business giving it away. Not now."

Isabelle shook her head.

John made a right on Water Street. Twinkly gold lights outlined the store fronts. A banner with a huge, cursive *Merry Christmas* in silver tinsel stretched high above the street. They stopped behind another car at the four-way intersection and a man dressed up like Santa rang a bell and paused outside John's window, holding a red metal bucket.

John scrounged for change in his ashtray. Virginia and Isabelle found some loose coins in their purses, and handed them to him. He rolled down the window, and dropped the coins into the bucket. Bing Crosby's "Silver Bells" drifted over from Weisner's TV and Appliance on the corner.

"God bless you, Pastor Hugg." Santa leaned over and waved to them in the truck.

"God bless you, too." John rolled up the window.

"Do you know who that was?" Virginia asked.

"That was Santa." John chuckled. "Bill thought Lilly might be headed toward the Fergusons' Place."

"She might not have heard that Ralph started his new job last week—praise God."

"Things will be still be tight for them this Christmas."

Over her shoulder, Virginia said, "Ralph and Betty Sue have four little girls. These past couple of years, they've had their share of hard times."

"But, if . . ." Isabelle leaned forward in the seat.

"Shh!" John shushed her. "And, you're right. Lilly has a lot of firewood. But, she'll need it this year and the next. But... there are others in the church who can help others with firewood this year. Rest your voice, remember?" He grinned at Virginia. "How often can I get away with saying that to a woman?"

"Just once," Virginia said.

Isabelle sat back in the seat and exhaled. It was Christmas. And, out of the goodness of her heart, Lilly wanted to help others. Isabelle wanted to argue with him and she wasn't supposed to even talk.

"Isabelle . . ." Leaning toward the steering wheel, John glanced over at her. "What do you think of dinner at Leona's Café and a piece of pie?"

Her heart caught in her throat. He'd asked her right in front of the church secretary. Hopefully, she wasn't like Nettie.

Holding her purse in her lap, Virginia's posture had noticeably stiffened.

"She can't talk right now. Remember? Ted wants her to rest her voice," the elderly woman said on her behalf.

"That's right."

Isabelle stared at the dash.

"And, you weren't very specific. Are you asking her to dinner for tonight or next week?"

"Well . . . I was thinking I'd drop you off first, and then drive Isabelle back down the hill to Leona's Café." He leaned forward to eye her again. "What do you think?

She couldn't think.

"Shake your head or nod," he said.

She shook her head.

"I see." He sat back in the seat.

If she did go, by the time they reached Leona's, it would have been an hour. She could argue with him, remind him that it was Christmas and Lilly should be able to give firewood to whomever she wanted to.

But, then . . . someday, she'd have to tell Al about going to dinner with the young pastor. He probably wouldn't mind anymore, now that he had Janet. The two were probably sitting in front of a cozy fire right now, staring into each other's eyes.

She nudged Virginia and when the elderly woman looked over at her, Isabelle nodded.

"Why are you nodding?" Virginia whispered, narrowing her gaze. "Did you change your mind?"

Isabelle nodded.

"You want to go with him now?"

Isabelle nodded.

"Uh, John . . . Isabelle's changed her mind. Women are allowed to do that, you know."

"I don't mind, especially, when it's in my favor." He chuckled.

Her pulse quickened.

She already wanted to change her mind again.

* * *

IN A DIMLY LIT neighborhood at the north end of town, John parked behind an old gray truck. Near the open bed, Lilly stood cradling an armload of wood, squinting in the glare of the headlights.

He left the engine running and closed the door behind him.

Isabelle thought about getting out, too. But, what good could she do, when she couldn't even talk?

Was Lilly drunk? Wearing a red and black mackinaw, her movements appeared normal enough as she grabbed another piece of wood.

Leaning toward Virginia she whispered, "Do you think she's been drinking?"

"No-oo. Now, shhh!"

Shaking her head, and moving away from John, Lilly stepped toward the curb.

He set his hand on her nearest arm.

She shirked away from him.

"Lilly! You can't give it away." They could hear him from inside the cab. "Not this Christmas."

"Oh, dear." Virginia cupped a hand to her mouth.

John was wrong. She could!

Piece by piece, he took the firewood from her, returning it to the messy pile in the bed of her truck.

Arms free, Lilly waved one toward the firewood, then the other toward the house half hidden in the shadows of the tall trees.

Isabelle and Virginia couldn't hear or make out what was said.

Lilly lowered her head, arms folded in front of her, and shoulders shaking.

Hold her, John. Didn't he see it? She needs to be held.

Tears burned Isabelle's throat.

It was so difficult to just sit and watch. *Please, Lord...*

Finally, John pulled Lilly into his arms; and she buried her head into his shoulder, sobbing.

Virginia made muffled sounds and dabbed a handkerchief to her eyes.

Tears dripped down Isabelle's cheeks. She sniffled and searched her purse for the packet of Kleenex.

"Oh, look!" Virginia sat up taller in the seat. "John's helping now."

With his back to them, he stacked firewood, piece by piece, into Lilly's cradled arms. Then, he gathered a load for himself before disappearing into the shadows.

"Dear, dear John," Virginia whispered. "He's no different from any of us. He makes mistakes, too. I've known him all his life. And, he's a very special young man." Virginia looked over at her now and, in the dimly lit cab, her eyes were keen. "We're all a bit protective of him, you know, because of that."

What was Virginia telling her?

"I saw you in the hallway last Sunday with a young man. I believe his name is Albert." The elderly woman gripped the handles of her purse and cleared her throat. "And... I think you have tender feelings for him."

It was a reprimand that she wasn't ready for. Isabelle squeezed her eyes closed and tried to trap the tears.

"I'd gone to my office for my sweater and when I returned down the hallway, I saw you... gripping his arm and gazing up at him like a young woman very much in love."

She shouldn't have told John *yes*. She shouldn't have nodded. Virginia was right. It had always been that way. She'd always loved Albert.

CHAPTER 24

John pulled into a short, gravel driveway in front of a well-lit bungalow, shifted into park, and climbed out.

"Would you call Nettie for me?" he asked Virginia while she scooted across the bench seat toward his open door. "Let her know that Isabelle won't be there for dinner, and that I'll get her home by nine o'clock, ten at the latest."

The elderly woman nodded. "Thank you for the ride home." Then she glanced toward Isabelle. "Goodnight."

Isabelle waved from inside the cab.

John slid behind the wheel and pulled closed the door. The porch light was on and he waited until Virginia disappeared inside before backing out of her gravel driveway.

They weren't more than fifty yards down the road when Isabelle cleared her throat.

"John..."

She was already having second thoughts.

He glanced at his wristwatch. "In ten minutes, it'll be an hour." He glanced across the cab at her and smiled. "I guess I got lucky. About the time we're seated, you'll be able to talk."

Then, without looking over at her again, he drove down west Main hill. He passed the Coopers' street. "I do not feel bad," he mumbled under his breath.

"You should," she whispered.

"Shhh!" He reminded her.

She'd already told him yes—she'd nodded. He wasn't going to let her change her mind three times.

This was his chance.

* * *

"What'll you have?" Flora, their middle-aged waitress, paused in front of their booth and held the order pad a few inches below her chin. Isabelle was still studying the menu, so John went first.

"I'll have a hamburger and fries, and a cup of coffee."

"Cream?"

He nodded.

"I'll have a hamburger and fries, too," Isabelle said.

"Coffee?"

"No, thank you."

Flora gathered up the menus and strolled toward the kitchen.

"Boy, she's friendly," Isabelle actually smiled across the table at him.

He couldn't help but feel forgiven.

"That *was* friendly for Flora." He grinned.

"I'm glad that Lilly ended up giving them the firewood," Isabelle said. "She wanted to. And, it is Christmas. It's probably good medicine for her to be able to help others."

John nodded. "I wasn't thinking of it that way."

"Why was she crying?"

He shook his head. "It was something I said." He picked up a spoon and stirred cream into his coffee. "She's bent on giving to every needy family in town that Tommy used to give to. I wanted her to see the flip side... that this time around, Tommy's hard work needs to be a blessing for her."

Tears welled in Isabelle's gaze before she looked away.

"I'll make some calls tomorrow. There are others who can help."

While they waited for their order, Isabelle used the powder room and John sunk a dime into the payphone in the hallway. He wanted to check on Lilly, make sure she'd made it home all right.

"Hello."

"Good, you made it home."

"Yes. Thanks again for worrying about me."

"Anytime." He cleared his throat and kept an eye on their empty booth. "Isabelle almost backed out on me, but we're here now at Leona's. I told Nettie that I'd keep her out until ten. Any suggestions?"

"Don't just stay there. After dinner, take her to meet someone you love."

"What was that?"

"I said *take her to meet someone you love.* On our third date, Tommy took me to meet his Aunt Elna. I learned about the impish little boy he was and... well, trust me, John."

"Thanks, I'll do that."

John sunk another dime into the payphone then dialed his grandparents' number. Of course, Isabelle had already met them, but this visit would be different. This time, he was courting her.

***

"John, I don't want them to think . . ." Isabelle felt all knotted up inside as they drove up his grandparents' long gravel driveway. "I mean, I'm just not ready..."

"Would you stop worrying?" He chuckled. "They know about Albert. You told them yourself that day at the potluck."

"Then why I am here?"

"Because I was just lucky enough to catch you during a quiet time in your life." He grinned.

The soft way he said it made her insides flutter. John had a very sweet way about him, but she wasn't over Albert.

Even though, he might be over her.

John parked behind the boxy ranch-style home. His truck's headlights shone on an empty clothesline.

Off in the distance, the back porch was lit by a soft light bulb. While they walked, she kept her hands in the silk-lined pockets of her coat.

John went inside first and held the door open for her. In the backroom, they took off their shoes. Then, in her stocking feet, she followed him through the dimly lit kitchen. Molasses and ginger fragranced the air. A yellow oven light revealed a pan of cookies baking inside.

On the cusp of the living room, John took her hand.

An uneasy knot formed in her gut. This visit was far more serious than her first had been. She wasn't ready.

She retracted her hand from his grip.

A floor lamp illuminated the Zane Grey novel that Frank was reading and cast shadows on the papered walls. Silver tinsel decorated a noble fir that was only a few inches shy of touching the ceiling.

Harriett sat in her rocker. With an embroidery hoop in her lap and a needle in hand, she peered over the top of her spectacles at them. The grandfather clock chimed the half hour. Time slowed in this room, reminding Isabelle of the pleasantly slow evenings at Wilhoit.

They sat down on the upholstered couch.

"What are you embroidering?" she asked Harriet.

"A Christmas dishtowel. A little holly and the year." She pulled the needle through the muslin.

"Harriet likes to keep her hands busy." Frank set his open novel to his knee. "What's your sermon about Sunday?" he asked John.

"Christmas."

"That always makes for a good sermon." His grandfather smiled before his gaze shifted to her. "What church did you grow up in, Isabelle?"

Her pulse quickened. "My great-Uncle Donald owns Wilhoit Mineral Springs. He holds a small service in the hotel. Aunt Elsie plays the piano, and we sing hymns for worship. The first Sunday of the month, we usually attend Molalla Baptist Church."

"Pastor Cordill." Frank nodded.

"Yes. Three summers ago, he baptized me in the Molalla River."

Frank nodded as he rocked. "So your folks know Christ?"

The retired pastor had already pried to the heart of her testimony.

"Yes." He'd already reached the point of no return. She clasped her hands tightly in her lap. "My mother died when I was eight… in an automobile accident."

"Awh!" Harriet pressed a hand above her heart.

Isabelle rolled her foot at the ankle, waiting for the wave of emotion to pass.

"And your father?" Frank asked.

"The same accident left my father paralyzed from the waist down."

"Isabelle, I'm so sorry," Harriett breathed.

"They were on their way home, and it was raining hard when their car hydroplaned into a telephone pole, about a mile before Molalla."

Somehow or other John had taken her hand again in his, gripping it firmly this time.

"I remember hearing about it, Isabelle," Frank's voice deepened. "And, praying for your family as a church body the Sunday after it happened."

Tears burned her throat and welled thick in her eyes.

"I do, too," Harriet whispered.

Isabelle swallowed past the tears.

A look was shared between John's grandparents.

"I remember reading about it in the paper." Frank moistened his lips. "For years, Isabelle, your family has been in our prayers. Harriet, go get the box."

Isabelle peered over her shoulder at John.

He shook his head and smiled softly.

His grandmother rose and disappeared into the kitchen. She soon returned, carrying a metal recipe box. Once seated in the padded rocker, she set it in her lap and flipped back the lid.

"I know it's under Sunday." Harriet thumbed through recipe cards looking for something. "Here it is." She pulled a card out of the box, rose again from her chair and carried over to Frank what appeared to be a newspaper clipping glued to both sides of the card.

He held it in his good hand, read it and wiped at his eyes.

"Isabelle, we've been praying for your family. We've been praying for you girls—you and your sister Mabel—every Sunday afternoon since you were eight years old." He sniffled and, turning away from them, patted a folded handkerchief to his eyes.

"It's been years since we've read the entire story," Harriet said, standing in the middle of the room, arms folded in front of her. "But—we've prayed for your father—for Lawrence and his two girls every Sunday since it happened." Her voice trailed off.

Frank cleared his throat. "No wonder you've tugged at my heart since the moment I first laid eyes on you."

* * *

When everyone had dried their eyes, Frank said, "Now, Harriett, take Isabelle into the guest room and show her that pretty quilt you made with all those scraps of clothes."

Leaving the warmth of John's side, Isabelle rose and followed his grandmother down the dimly lit hallway. They passed a sewing room with tidy piles of folded fabrics. Harriett opened a door on the right and flipped on the overhead light.

A beautiful quilt covered the queen bed. Various-sized pieces of fabric were stitched together with dark threads in a crazy quilt design.

"I made this from our five children's clothes and a few of the grandchildren's things." Though it was cold in the room, Harriett closed the door behind them.

"Kind of like a scrapbook." Isabelle set her hand on top of the wrought-iron frame and studied the intricate hand stitching.

"Yes." Harriet nodded. "The dark blue wool was from John's first blazer. He wore it to church when he was six or seven. He always wanted to be a pastor like his Grandpa Frank." Off of the top of the highboy dresser, Harriet picked up a picture frame before sitting down on the edge of the bed, her back to the door. "From a young age, John would turn over apple crates in the barn and stand on top of them and belt out John 3:16 and other verses that he knew by heart." Harriett inhaled deeply like the memory brought her great joy.

Smoothing the back of her skirt, Isabelle sat down beside her.

"You know, you have a special grandson when he wants to be just like his grandfather." With the hem of her apron, Harriet dusted the glass and the wooden frame. "And, he is so like Frank." She handed Isabelle the picture.

Frank, twenty years younger, and John, as a boy, were seated together on a tractor. With his cheek pressed against his grandfather's shoulder, he shone with a look of adoration on his already handsome boyish face.

"This fabric," Harriett pointed off to her left to a deep red-and-blue checked flannel diamond, "was from one of John's favorite shirts. He was about seven. He wore the shirt *everywhere*. I remember seeing him playing in it on Friday and Saturday and then wearing it to church on Sunday. Finally, he outgrew it."

Isabelle gazed at the precious photo.

"It was when he was about this age," Harriet's gray-blue eyes lifted from the photo and locked on hers, "that I began praying the Grandmother's Prayer."

Unfamiliar with it, Isabelle shook her head.

"For his bride to be a young woman who loves Jesus, who loves others, and who loves my grandson."

Isabelle's throat burned. She couldn't say she was the one. Even though he might already be another gal's, she wasn't ready yet to let go of Albert.

Harriet blinked softly and fastened her gray-blue eyes on hers. "Am I wrong in believing my prayers have been answered?"

"Mrs. Hugg... I don't know..."

"Don't worry, honey. I'll let you tell John how much you adore him in your own sweet time." Harriet softly patted her hand. "Frank and I just hope we get to see him married... in our lifetime.

CHAPTER 25

From the driveway, the lights from the Coopers' aluminum Christmas tree twinkled in the picture window. There was also the flicker of the black-and-white picture on the television. The Coopers were up past their usual bedtime.

"Thank you for dinner and . . ." Isabelle chewed on her lower lip. Their visit to his grandparents had been difficult for her.

John shifted into park. "I had a nice time, Isabelle."

"So, did I. It's just that . . ."

"I know." He smiled over at her. "You thought about Albert a lot tonight. But… I can't help thinking that he has a twelve-year head start on me. And, I can't help but hope that in twelve years, there's the possibility you might say, I've loved John ever since I was twenty years old."

She laughed softly, meeting his gaze. For the first that evening she felt herself relax.

"Hallelujah!" he whispered. "There's the girl I've been waiting to see."

He was prolonging the difficulty of the evening.

"You don't need to walk me up."

"That's not the way I was raised." He chuckled under his breath.

He was going to be trouble all the way to the door. She could sense it.

"No hand holding," she said, firmly.

"Why not?"

"Because I don't want to."

"Hmmph. That's no fun."

"If you want fun, Darlene Berry has a very large crush on you. Every time she sees you enter a room, she says, 'Pitter patter' several times in a row under her breath. If you winked at her, I think she'd faint." Isabelle giggled for a moment at the thought.

"While I could feel flattered," his voice got all soft-like again, "I don't have a crush on Darlene."

She knew what he was saying—loud and clear.

And, she knew what he was doing. He was trying to corral all of her thoughts of Albert into one tiny corner. And, he was trying to fluster her to the point that all she could think about was… John Hugg.

It wouldn't be too hard to let him convince her.

He had a nice genuine way about him. And, she sure liked Silverton. She studied the front of the cozy bungalow. She liked the Coopers, too. And, she liked Lilly a lot. Then, with no warning, she remembered Al on one knee in the middle of Wilhoit Road looking up at her. There'd been a sheen of love in his eyes.

Hadn't there?

One minute, he was almost proposing and the next, he was talking about Janet.

But, was Isabelle any different?

One minute, she was crying over Albert and, the next, she was letting John Hugg confuse her. She squeezed the door handle and without a word, exited into the brisk December air.

"Isabelle, what are you thinking about now?" John closed his door behind him and followed her up the walk.

"Nothing." She kept her hands in her coat pockets.

He caught up with her on the porch steps.

"Goodnight, John." She paused, before the door. "Thanks for dinner and…"

"And, thank you . . ."

She glanced up at him.

". . . for not insisting that I bring you home."

He was right. If she'd really wanted to, she could have demanded that he take her home.

Then, John leaned toward her, and eyes bright, he wrapped an arm around her shoulder, pulled her close and kissed her on the mouth. Without asking.

Out of curiosity and a slight case of confusion, she let him.

John's kiss wasn't fleeting like Albert's first kiss had been when they'd been fifteen. But, it was just as stolen and equally surprising. John stepped back, a halo above his head from the porch light. "Goodnight, Isabelle."

"Goodnight." Then feeling very mechanical, she turned the knob and closed the door behind her. In the unlit entry, she proceeded to the closet and hung up her coat. The television blared. The Coopers were watching *The Smothers Brothers Show*.

With the closet door as her curtain, she stared blindly at the Kirby vacuum.

Oh, why couldn't he have asked? She would've simply said no? But, no!

He was a pastor. He was supposed to behave. Be more sensible than the rest of the human race. Not kiss her on the Coopers' front porch! She pressed the palms of her hands against her eyes. She'd just been flustered enough that she'd let him.

Oh, she just wanted to hide in the closet!

"Did you have a good time?" Nettie's voice carried from the front room.

Inhaling, Isabelle stood up taller. "Yes. We um . . ." She closed the closet door and took a few steps into the living room, "went to Leona's Café for hamburgers and then afterward, we went to Harriet and Frank's home."

"Oh, how nice." With a hint of a smile, Nettie's gaze returned to the television.

"I think I'll turn in early," Isabelle said.

"Okay, honey," Nettie said.

"I'll be up as soon as . . ." Carolyn's gaze drifted back to the television, "this show's over."

Feeling confused, Isabelle made her way up the stairs. Back home when she'd needed advice or someone to just listen, she'd sought Uncle Donald. If only she could talk to him now. Then, she remembered the autograph book and that he'd written something in the very back.

Steps lighter now, she reached the landing.

After she changed into her flannel nightgown, she sat down on the edge of her bed and opened to the back of the book and her uncle's loopy cursive. Clutching the ruffled neckline of her gown, she read:

Isabelle,

It has been my privilege to pray for you and your kin since the day you were snuggled in your mother's bosom. And it has been a privilege to help raise you as our own. His voice was so clear; it was like he was sitting right beside her. She wiped her tears on her sleeve.

She thought about calling home. But, the only telephone was in the nook, and she didn't want anyone to overhear her when she spoke with Albert. Knowing the Coopers, one of them would try. Before she spent any more time with John, she had to get to the bottom of what was going on with Al and Janet—the gal from Molalla Jewelers.

She continued reading. *Always remember that Prayer changes things. Truer words were never uttered if you believe it and ask according to the Lord's will.*

We love you,

Uncle Donald

She fingered his sentiments—*Prayer changes things.*

Kneeling down beside her bed, she gripped her hands in prayer and leaned her forehead against the side of the mattress... *Lord, if John is the one you've meant for me to be with then why I am thinking about Albert every other breath?* Her admittance brought a flood of tears, and she wept quietly into the side of the chenille bedspread.

Please, help me not to make too big of a mess while I'm here.

* * *

AFTER ISABELLE JACKED up the chassis and took the passenger tire off, she scooted under the vehicle, shone the flashlight on the starter and got to the fun part.

Tap. Tap. Tap. Tap. Tap. She tapped the solenoid with a hammer.

Albert wasn't home when she'd called. He was working his sixth day in a row at Molalla Ford. But, he'd left notes for Aunt Elsie to read to her. Far as Isabelle knew, Albert might very well be kidding her. She'd never seen him use a hammer on a vehicle.

"What's next?" she asked Carolyn.

"Let's see, after you tap it five times, you're supposed to get out and see if it starts."

Isabelle set the hammer aside and slowly shimmied her

way out from beneath the car. Happy to see the overhead lights.

"I think you only tapped it four times." Carolyn peered down at her over the side of her clipboard.

"I tapped at least five." Rising to her feet, Isabelle dusted off her hands.

"Well . . . what do you think?"

"If it starts right up, it's the solenoid." Isabelle slid behind the wheel and left the door open.

"And, if it doesn't?"

"Then, we've got bigger problems. Say a prayer." Isabelle pumped the gas pedal a few times and patted the dash. "Come on, Hilda. Come on, sweet sugar pie pumpkin with whipped cream on top," she said sweetly, and then turned the key.

The old girl started right up.

Leaning back in the seat, she grinned.

Carolyn squealed and threw her arms up in the air, kicking her legs behind her like a cheerleader. "We did it!"

Imagine that! Maybe she was going to be able to fix Hilda after all.

"Granddad's never going to believe how easy it was. Who ever would have thought it would just take a hammer?"

Isabelle leaned toward the door a ways to stare at her. "It's not fixed. Now, we know it's the solenoid."

"Oh . . ." Carolyn's expression dimmed.

Hopefully, tomorrow morning, Hilda would start right up, now that she'd had a good tapping.

* * *

READY FOR CHURCH, Isabelle waited by the back door. "Mr. Cooper, would it be all right if I go ahead and start Hilda?" she asked for the second time that morning.

"Soon as I'm done here, I'll head out there." Russell hummed. In the reflection of the door's upper glass, he crossed one end of his necktie over the other.

The tea kettle clock in the nook already read 9:50. She was reliving the last three Sundays and, there was nothing she could do about it but pray.

Lord, as You know, we're already late—later than Mr. Hoffmeister wanted us to be. You can do anything. Will You do this little something for me: Will You freeze time? Right now. So we're not late. You know me. I'm shy. I dislike being late. I dislike it a lot... She swallowed.

"Look at what Carolyn found for me!" Nettie entered the kitchen, pointing down at her matching black pumps. "It was tucked behind my suitcase. Heaven only knows how it got there."

"Grandpa!" Carolyn exclaimed at the sight of him. "What are you still doing in here? You're supposed to have the car warm and ready! The choir has the opening song."

Isabelle glanced at the clock. While she'd been praying, three more minutes had passed. Being a Cooper was hard, especially on Sundays.

"I can't believe the trouble I've had with my tie." Russell patted at the off-center knot, and giving up on it, pulled open the door. "After you, ladies." He swished his hand.

In the cold garage, Hilda was her old cantankerous self. Isabelle wasn't about to take the tire off in her church clothes and crawl under to tap it again. After ten minutes of incessant prayer, the old Bel Air finally started.

Carolyn needed to be upfront this morning, too. So instead of dropping them off out front of the church, Russell drove the narrow crunchy gravel driveway to the back. Again. Hopefully, the congregation was singing something loud and wouldn't be able to hear them roll by.

Mr. Cooper brought the vehicle to a jerky stop.

"Here's your peppermints, girls." Mrs. Cooper doled out the candies. "Carolyn, if you can, try and hold off on singing until we're seated."

"Grandma! We're already late."

"Oh, never mind." Nettie waved a hand.

Just like their first Sunday here, they hung up their coats in the back hallway. Ever so quietly, Isabelle pulled the door to the sanctuary closed behind them. She followed Carolyn across the stage to their places in the front row. Darlene and Evelyn stood waiting on the step behind them.

Isabelle tried to prepare herself for Darlene's pinch. It stung, all the same.

Seated in the front row, Mr. Hoffmeister glumly shook his head. He pointed up to remind them *to sing for the Lord*. Then he gave them a couple of seconds to catch their breath.

This is the part Isabelle didn't like, facing an audience that was unhappy with you. She scanned the back pews. Albert wasn't here.

He was probably at church with Janet.

Her gaze drifted to the very front where John was seated. The soft dreamy smile that he wore made her feel anxious. She shifted her gaze to the other side of the aisle.

Chins lowered. Dimples appeared. And, there was a hint of giddiness in the room as elderly women smiled. Maybe it was just her imagination getting the better of her, but... it was like all the old ladies had already heard about the kiss on the Coopers' front porch.

Had someone seen? Had Nettie made six phone calls?

Harriet Hugg smiled softly at her and nodded.

Sing for the Lord, Isabelle reminded herself. She inhaled deeply and waited for Mr. Hoffmeister.

Nettie and Russell finally entered the sanctuary.

Mr. Hoffmeister nodded—their cue to begin.

While the girls sang "When We All Get to Heaven," Mr.

and Mrs. Cooper made their way up the center aisle toward the third pew.

Isabelle was glad they weren't seated in time. It was nice to share the limelight a little.

* * *

As the girls were walking to their seats, Darlene leaned toward her and whispered, "You need to talk to John. I heard Opal talking on the phone—something about an autograph."

Darlene was a week behind the times.

She suppressed a giggle and sat down next to Carolyn in the third row.

Halfway through John's sermon, she remembered her peppermint and pulled it out of her pocket. The crinkly cellophane was loud as she unwrapped it. Then she gave one end a good tug and popped the candy into her mouth.

"I've heard a lot of mumbling lately," John said and then paused for an uncomfortable amount of time. He almost appeared to be looking right at her. She swished the mint off to one side and kept it there. But, upon closer inspection, he was looking right at Nettie.

Head bowed, the elderly woman toyed with a loose string on the front of her dress.

"Especially amongst the older women in our congregation," John said.

He was singling Nettie out.

His gaze shifted to the other side of the aisle. "Over and over, I've heard *Heaven Sent*. Sometimes it's in reference to cookies..."

His own grandmother had referred to her Molasses Cookies as *Heaven Sent*.

"Sometimes choir girls."

Isabelle almost swallowed her peppermint.

Thank heaven he hadn't looked at her!

"As of late, it seems the only thing our church family talks about is the Christmas choir." His sweeping gaze more natural now. "Yes, our little congregation has been blessed to host such talent. But, our Christmas choir was not supposed to get our focus off of Christ."

Ooh. Isabelle bit her lower lip.

"I want to remind every one of you that the one true Heaven Sent has already been sent. His name is Jesus."

Thank you, Lord.

CHAPTER 26

Tuesday afternoon, someone knocked on John's office door.

"Come in."

Isabelle poked her head inside. "Is now a good time for you?"

"Yes, come in and have a seat." The brief time she'd held the door open, he could hear the choir girls singing.

She turned and quietly clicked the door closed behind her.

He'd spent time in earnest prayer, asking the Lord to give him discernment. It almost seemed like she'd avoided him on Sunday. He'd seen her briefly after service then she'd skirted out of the sanctuary. But, now she was here in his office.

Isabelle smoothed the back of her woolen skirt and sat down in the chair closest to the door. Her dark hair was up in one of those round, smooth buns near the top of her head.

"Darlene said that I need to speak to you . . ." Her voice trailed off.

"About?" He swallowed. Was she going to apologize for the kiss?

"She's going on and on and said there's something I don't know about. Something about Nettie and my autograph book. She won't tell me. She just said I need to speak with you. Knowing Darlene, she's trying to cause trouble." Hands clutched in her lap, Isabelle sighed.

John nodded.

Nettie hadn't told her yet.

He took a sip of cold coffee.

Most likely, Darlene had overheard her host mother—Opal Hargett—talking on the phone to Nettie. She'd probably overheard their entire conversation regarding Albert's hidden autograph and his love for Isabelle. Darlene might very well be able to tell Isabelle more than he could.

And then again, maybe not.

Him seeing Al's autograph was not in his favor.

"It'll take a little while." Off to his left, his fingers made a tapping sound on the top of his desk. He stopped them. "Can Ted spare you very long?"

Isabelle nodded. "Evelyn's working on her duet with Carolyn at the moment." Then, she leaned to her right, and peered past him at the painting behind him, and then to the bookshelves on her right.

"My grandfather had this office for thirty-three years. I've tried not to change anything about it."

Her ebony gaze met his. "Why?"

"He's made remarkable improvement in the last year since his stroke. We all continue to hope that he's going to fully recover, that he'll someday be back behind this desk. This really is his office." But even more than that it was God's.

With a look half sympathy, half surprise, she shook her head.

"You've never seen my grandfather preach. He has a way

about him when he's up there. He's not afraid to say it like it is."

Isabelle held her shoulders stiffly now, her hands in her lap.

"Sorry, the chair's not more comfortable." He tried to gather his wits about him.

"It's okay." She shifted a tad.

"There's a group of senior women in the church. They crochet. They bake. They pray. They pull together funds for those in need—"

"The Granite Girls?" She nodded.

"Yes."

"Carolyn told me a little. I know that Nettie's one of them and that she's often on the phone to Opal—Darlene's host mother."

He nodded. "There are seven of them. They have a wonderful ministry. Yet, from time to time, they busy themselves with conversation that borders on gossip. On several occasions, my grandfather has had to speak to one of the women, in particular—"

"You mean Nettie?" Isabelle curbed a smile.

"Yes. Grandpa warned her once that if there were ever a gossip column in *The Spokesman Review*, it would be titled *Nettie Gossip*." Mouth dry, he swished it around. "The other day, Nettie stumbled across Albert's second autograph."

Her gaze locked on his. "What do you mean. . . second?"

"This one was hidden, somewhere near the middle of the book." He half expected her to exit and slam the door behind her. "It was folded in half toward the spine."

"They called you, too?" Her voice was gut-deep.

"I found out about it from my grandmother—the day we were at Leona's Café when the choir girls were there."

Mouth pursed, she stared at the front of his desk. And,

then while she mulled over the truth, red crept up her neck into the hollows of her cheeks.

"Why didn't you tell me?"

He shook his head. "I was hoping you knew about it."

The truth was glaring. He'd known about Albert's autograph before he'd kissed her.

"One minute, my grandmother was talking about hidden messages in autograph books then the next she's passing a copy of what Albert had written across the table to me." A guilty chuckle escaped him.

"Wh-hy?"

"It wasn't Al's original. You see, she'd folded a small piece of paper and written what Nettie had told her over the phone."

He cleared his throat. "*PRIVATE* was written in capital letters on the cover. And beneath that, Albert had written: *What causes tears?*"

"*Onions.*" Her voice sounded far away. And, if he wasn't mistaken a mist of tears followed, but only for a second. Then jaw stern, a deep somberness filled her gaze "That's just like Al. He's written that in a note to me before. He thinks it's funny. Well, it isn't." Her voice wavered. "Not when you're expecting… tender thoughts."

Were *tender thoughts* what she *still* wanted from Albert? Maybe it was because they'd grown up together or… maybe her longing for Albert's words was now a part of who she was. Twelve years was a long crush.

"Sadly, Isabelle, I was curious enough about Albert's feelings that I read the note. I should have told you, gotten to the bottom of it and made sure you knew about it, too." She'd looked away from him, and he wasn't sure how much of it she'd heard. Her mind was probably spinning.

"I almost brought it up on Friday night. But, I didn't want to ruin our date." He shook his head.

"What'd he write?" She lifted her chin a bit before her ebony gaze locked on his.

"Tender thoughts." He could barely get out the words.

"Al . . . ?" Her dark brows gathered.

"It's in your book—about halfway through." At least, he prayed it was.

"I can't believe Nettie went through my book again." She set an elbow on the arm of the chair. "I've always wanted to live in a small town—where I could walk to everything, and attend a little church like this one. But, boy… everybody is into everybody else's business. Even you."

"I'm sorry, Isabelle. Don't base Silverton on Nettie Cooper." He added a grin, but Isabelle didn't appear to notice. "Though, she does have a heart of gold. And, she is one of my favorite people."

"Nettie's been wonderful. Except for getting into my suitcase and going through my things, she's made me feel like family." She patted the top of his desk like she was ready to leave.

"Can I say a prayer before you go?"

She nodded and bowed her head.

His prayer flowed. One word came to mind—discernment—that the Lord would give Isabelle discernment. "Amen."

She remained seated, filling her lungs with air. But, she wasn't going to sing. Something else was on her mind.

"I think you're wrong about not changing things in this office." Her gaze roamed the wood-paneled walls. "For one thing, when you're sitting in this chair, you can't see that wonderful painting that's behind you. Not fully. If it was on this wall," she pointed to the bare wall on their left, "you'd be able to see it right now, and so would I."

He nodded. "Beth Waggoner painted it for my grandfather when she was in high school. She has five kids now, and her family attends this church."

Isabelle rose, and clasping her hands in front of her, paused in front of his desk. "I'm sorry about Friday. I—"

"Hold on a second." He chuckled. He wasn't ready for this admittance from her so early—before she'd even read Al's autograph. "I'm not ready to come down to earth yet." He managed to smile past the knot in his chest. "I've been enjoying Cloud Nine."

Chewing on her lower lip, she looked pitifully apologetic. "And, those big shoes you're so worried about filling, I think you already have."

"Isabelle . . ." He caught himself. He had to wait until she at least read Albert's autograph to pour out his heart. "Thank you."

* * *

WHILE THE COOPERS were watching *The Lawrence Welk Show* after supper, Isabelle excused herself and went upstairs. She didn't want to read what Albert had written in front of Carolyn, or anyone for that matter.

Her autograph book lay atop the dresser next to the milk glass lamp—the same spot she'd set it weeks ago. But, oh, how it had traveled in the meantime.

With a heavy sigh, she sat down on the edge of her bed and gripped the little book in her lap.

Beginning in the front, she flipped through the pages. On the page that followed John's autograph, Carolyn had written one, also.

Isabelle,
U-R2 sweet
+2 B
4 got-10

Your friend,
Carolyn Cooper

She'd miss Carolyn when the choir was over. She'd miss a lot of people in this odd little town; although, she wasn't so certain about Nettie Cooper at the moment. She carefully turned the slightly glossy pages, careful not to miss a one.

Near the middle of the book, she breathed past an uneasy knot in the center of her chest.

Curious about the binding, she pried the pages apart to inspect it. Laced through three paper-punched holes, the dark green ribbon bound the book together. If Nettie had wanted to, she could have torn it out without leaving a trace.

She turned the page and, just when she'd been thinking the worst about her host mother, Isabelle noted a gap. Laying the book flat, the half page sat like a sailing ship in an open sea. She swiveled the book ninety degrees and read:

PRIVATE

What causes tears?

"This little book." She inhaled deeply, trying to prepare herself. The page appeared worn like it had been fingered a hundred times.

She unfolded the hidden message part way.

Onions was written in the center of the half page.

Several lines of writing lay below the fold.

In small, tight cursive for Al, he'd written:

"Izz, If you do go ahead with the Christmas choir,
I'll be living for the day you come home.

She brushed aside her tears.

I love you, Al."

Tears blurred her vision and the pain in her chest went bone deep. She stared—unblinking—at Carolyn's side of the room. This is what he'd tried to tell her the night of their first performance. She'd misunderstood him.

And, he'd misunderstood her.

Oh, Al. What if she'd never found it?

How could he say write something like this and already be sweet on Janet?

For the first time since she'd left home, she let herself dwell on the look in Al's eyes when he'd bent his knee on Wilhoit Road.

Tears had rimmed his gaze. "Stay." He may have even sucked in a breath if she'd looked at him long enough to tell.

She'd been so set on Silverton that nothing was going to hold her back. Not even Albert, the boy she'd loved since she was eight. And, now she'd turned him away, and he'd taken up with some young floozy from the jewelry shop.

* * *

Isabelle studied her reflection in the mirror. Her eyes were only a little puffy. She made her way downstairs.

"Is everything okay, Isabelle?" Carolyn asked as soon as she entered the living room.

"Yes. Does anyone need anything in the kitchen?"

Nettie shook her head, watching her.

Russell did the same.

"I'm going to make a quick phone call." She tried to sound matter of fact.

"To who?" Nettie asked.

"Wilhoit." Then, she made her way through the doorway to the nook.

Russell, who never got up for anything but meals, flicked on the lights in the kitchen and ambled over to the fridge. For the first time since her stay in their home, he pulled it open.

Crud! He'd hear her.

The line rang once and then a second time.

"Hello."

"Hello, Aunt Elsie. How is everyone?"

"Oh, we're all fine. Donald's asleep by the fire. Your father's looking through his tackle box. He's going fishing in the morning with Trevor. And, Albert's working late, honey. A sales meeting."

"Can you tell him I called?"

"I sure will, honey. Oh, Fletcher's mad that I left him out. He's looking through his tackle box, too."

"Aunt Elsie . . . Has Albert ever talked to you about a girl named Janet?"

"No. None of us know what's going on with you kids right now..." She lowered her voice, "Though, Albert did say that your church pastor is young and unmarried. You failed to mention that at Thanksgiving."

"Oh." The subject was even trickier than it had been at Thanksgiving. She glanced over at Mr. Cooper. His face illuminated by the light inside the refrigerator. "Give everyone my love."

"I'll do that, honey. Your uncle's awake now. And, he knows I'm on the phone with you. He's asking if you've read his autograph yet?"

"Ye-es. Tell him that it made me cry."

"She did, Donald." Aunt Elsie didn't cover up the receiver. "And, it made her cry."

Now was her chance to say that she'd read Albert's, too. But, she wanted to tell him in person.

"Tell everybody that this Sunday, Darlene and I are being filmed. Mr. Hoffmeister is sending it to Lawrence Welk. If he likes it, there's a chance..." Her voice trailed off.

"That's right! Lawrence Welk! Albert told us all about it." Elsie sighed. "Donald said to remind you to 'Sing for the Lord, Isabelle, not Lawrence Welk.' We love you and we can't wait until you're home. That includes Albert."

Isabelle nodded and sucked in a fishbowl of tears.

Returning to the living room, she sat down across the couch from Carolyn and stared at the television. The Lennon Sisters were singing "May You Always." The quartet had pretty much grown up on The Lawrence Welk Show and America with them.

"How is everyone at Wilhoit?" Russell plunked down in his recliner with a bottle of 7-Up.

Isabelle shrugged. "Everyone's well and good." She glanced ever so briefly at Nettie. She'd called Wilhoit. Would she be inspired enough to make six phone calls?

"If you don't mind, I think I'll go lay down. I'm not feeling very well."

"Sure, honey," Nettie said as Isabelle rose to her feet. "Let me know if you need anything—cough drops, Vicks... tissue."

Tissue? She glanced back at Nettie.

The elderly woman kept her profile to her.

Isabelle continued toward the entry.

"Hopefully, there's not a bug going around," Nettie said.

"Only the love bug," Russell mumbled under his breath.

Isabelle halted. He'd really said that! She thought about saying something smart. Then she bit down on her lower lip and started up the stairs.

"Of all the host families, Lord . . ." she closed the door behind her, and threw herself down on her bed, "why did you have to place me here?" Hugging her pillow, she gave into her heartache with abandon.

She'd kissed John Hugg!

Albert loved her! Or he had.

"Five weeks, Lord. I've made such a mess in five weeks!

She'd finally stopped sobbing. As she sniffled, her stomach did the wiggly Jell-o thing.

Someone set a box of Kleenex within reach.

Out of the corner of her eye, she glimpsed the gray pleats of Carolyn's skirt.

"What's going on?" She sat down on the side of the bed.

She couldn't tell her. The Coopers were all in this together.

"Grandma thinks you may have found Albert's autograph. Is that why you're crying?"

Isabelle sniffled. "How long have you known about it?"

"All of one minute."

"I'm fine. I just need—"

"You are not."

"Yes, I am." She snagged a tissue.

"What's going on?"

"I just need time alone."

"O-kay." Carolyn rose to her feet. "If you need *anyone* to talk to, Grandma and I are right downstairs."

She'd rather open the window and yell on a megaphone than ever tell a Cooper her feelings.

"Grandpa feels bad about what he said. He has an odd sense of humor. I know it probably isn't very good timing…" Carolyn sighed. "But, he wanted me to tell you that he caught the love bug once, too. And, that's why he calls her Nettie Bug."

Isabelle buried her face deep in the pillow and tried not to laugh.

CHAPTER 27

"Hello, Nettie. It's John." Holding the phone against his ear, he pressed his finger on a nearby dime, and traced it around the surface of his desk.

"Hello, John. Only three days and our choir girls will be heading home. Really four days, but, Monday morning doesn't count." She sighed. "Why are you calling?"

"You've been pretty quiet." He'd been hoping she'd invite him for supper.

"I've been a good girl."

"Uh . . . in what way?" He chuckled.

"I've been on the phone less and praying more."

"That's wonderful to hear."

"Yep. After you walked Isabelle to the door the other night, and Carolyn saw what she did, I didn't go calling all the girls about it. Even though I wanted to. I prayed."

"What do you mean, what Carolyn saw?"

"Well, we were wondering what was taking you kids so long to come in. Carolyn parted the curtains for a little glance, and she was so shocked that she clamped her hand to her mouth. Wasn't hard to guess what her giggle was about."

"I see." He swallowed. He should never have kissed Isabelle on the Coopers' doorstep.

"I want you to know that I didn't call the girls last night either." Nettie paused for some reason. "Isabelle finally read Albert's autograph."

Good! Nettie hadn't torn it out. But . . . he wasn't sure that he liked her tone.

"What do you think?" He cleared his raspy voice. "How'd she handle it?"

"Well . . . she was shook up, I s'pose. She came down all puffy cheeked and called Wilhoit. She didn't get to speak with Albert, though. Then she went to bed early. When Carolyn went up to check on her, she'd been crying. She wouldn't tell Carolyn a thing.

"What do you think, John? Why would she cry?"

He inhaled twice before he caught his breath.

"If you want, I could make a few phone calls and get the other girls' opinions," Nettie said.

"No. This is something we just keep in prayer. And, in the meantime, I'm proud of you."

"Thank you, John. I didn't want you singling me out in service again. I almost swallowed my peppermint the last time you did."

John almost smiled.

"So she cried?" He hadn't expected that.

"She cried buckets. And, she wouldn't share a word with Carolyn. Almost hurt her feelings a little bit. Said she just wanted to be alone."

"But . . . why would she cry?" He worked the dime around in little circles.

"Well . . . the only thing Carolyn and I can figure is, she has you. And, now, she knows she has Albert, too… if she wants him. Maybe she didn't know that before. And, she can't have both of you. That's probably why she was crying."

Sounded like Carolyn and Nettie had figured out a lot between just the two of them. "I think you're right." He stared at the empty chair to the right of the door.

Isabelle had to give up one of them and probably before Christmas.

He hoped it wasn't him.

* * *

Isabelle followed the girls down the basement stairs for their morning break.

Darlene poured a glass of apple juice. "We're going to Molalla during our lunch break, and Mrs. Hargett said we can take one more choir girl." She locked eyes with Isabelle. "I already talked to Mr. Hoffmeister, and he said that Carolyn and Evelyn can work on their duet in the extra hour that we're gone."

Isabelle's heart stopped. She could stop in at Melton's Mercantile, get a new slip, and see Ruby, Al's sister-in-law. Through the years, she'd been Isabelle's fashion consultant and had often helped her to understand Albert when no one else could.

"Mrs. Hargett's going for an eye appointment, and I want to look for a new pair of heels and—"

"I'll go," Isabelle said.

Carolyn's head spun, and she stared at her.

"I have family in Molalla—my sister and her husband."

"Oh, I didn't know," Carolyn said.

"Then it's a date." Darlene smiled.

Evelyn glanced at her, too.

It was all too obvious that the girls thought she was going to see Albert. She wasn't. She was merely going to Molalla to talk to Ruby about him.

* * *

Opal Hargett drove a black Buick station wagon with lots of chrome. Isabelle sat in the back seat while Darlene sat up front with her host mother.

"Isabelle, I hope you've enjoyed your stay in Silverton," Mrs. Hargett said.

"Oh, I have, very much." She nodded, meeting the older woman's gaze in the rearview mirror.

On the way out of town, scattered oak trees and stands of Douglas fir dotted the rolling farmland. In only a few days, she'd be heading home.

She wondered what Janet would think of the hidden autograph Al had written in her book.

Darlene filed her nails, humming.

"Isabelle, what are your plans for after the choir?" Opal asked.

"I'm not sure. I've thought about getting a job at Melton's Mercantile. I know Ruby—one of the salesgirls there. She used to be a Melton."

"Oh, I thought you might want to pursue your singing. Heaven knows you have the voice for it."

"We'll see what happens." She was trying not to get her hopes up too high. "Thank you, Mrs. Hargett. What about you, Darlene? What are your plans?" Isabelle leaned forward in the seat.

"To be discovered—either by Hollywood or a husband." She giggled and glanced across the cab at Opal.

In the rearview mirror, Mrs. Hargett rolled her eyes.

Isabelle stifled a laugh.

Even though Nettie Cooper had gone through her suitcase, wasn't much of a cook, and was a gossip, Isabelle was glad she'd been her host mother.

"What do you want for Christmas, Isabelle?" Darlene asked.

"I don't know." She studied the passing countryside. "I usually figure it out when I'm at Melton's Mercantile. What about you?"

"A plane ticket to Los Angeles."

They took a right off highway 213 at the Molalla turnoff. A mile or two passed before the Molalla Ford dealership came into view, heralding the start of downtown.

While they drove past, Isabelle scanned the front showroom windows and spotted a tall figure inside which may have been Al. It was difficult to tell in passing.

She sat back in the seat and saw Darlene eyeing her in the side-view mirror.

Mrs. Hargett dropped them off on the corner of Main and Molalla Avenue near Melton's Mercantile.

"I'll pick you girls up right here in an hour." She glanced at her wristwatch. "Four o'clock."

"Thank you, Mrs. Hargett." Adding a wave, Isabelle stepped out onto the concrete sidewalk.

"Thank you." Darlene swung closed her door.

Then they made their way through the double doors. Silver tinsel outlined the glass counters, and large colorful wrapped packages adorned the top of rounders.

"I'm going to go look at shoes," Darlene said.

"I'll go see Ruby. She works here."

"I know. That's what you already said." Darlene started ahead of her down the main aisle.

Ignoring the sour note in her gut, Isabelle followed her before taking a left at the first fork.

Near the aisle, Ruby hung western shirts on a nearby rounder. Pregnant with her second child, her belly looked like she'd tucked a beach ball under her blouse. With her short dark hair and perfect complexion, she was as pretty as ever.

"Ruby." Isabelle gave her a little warning.

At the sight of her, Ruby tipped her head back and giggled. She stepped from linoleum to carpet and, they hugged.

"What are you doing here?" Ruby beamed.

"I hitched a ride with one of the host mothers."

"Let me look at you." Ruby had her step back. "You need eyeliner."

"I didn't want to mess with it today." It was her turn to study Ruby. Her cheeks were a little fuller, her figure a little rounder. She looked happy. "How are you feeling?"

"My mom's watching David during the day. The extra money's nice, but I don't know if it's worth being on my feet for four hours straight." She patted the top of her tummy. "What's going on with you and Al?"

Isabelle shook her head. "Not much."

"I heard what he told you when you left." Ruby rolled her eyes. "About having a ring on another's girl hand by the time you get back. Sounds like it might be the other way around." Ruby buttoned up a shirt and hung it on the rounder. "Al said something about you and a young pastor."

"The last time I saw Al, he'd just had a date with Sue Chavers."

"Is that what he said?" Ruby regarded her.

"Yeah." Isabelle glanced around thankful that buxom Sue wasn't anywhere in the vicinity. "He said no one told him that she has a voice like Minnie Mouse."

Ruby made another eye roll. "Sue Chavers hasn't worked here for three months. You know why?"

"No." She swallowed and tried to prepare herself.

"She got married and moved to Sidney, Nebraska."

Al.

She tried to suppress a giggle but felt her mouth twitch. She glanced toward the front windows, overlooking Main Street and then back to Ruby's curious gaze.

"He also um . . . admitted to being interested in a girl named Janet."

"Janet who?" Ruby's gaze narrowed.

"From Molalla Jeweler's."

"Al . . . bert Gleinbroch!" Ruby hissed. "How long are you in town for?"

"'Bout an hour. Another choir girl's here buying shoes."

"Before you run over and see Al—

"I'm not running over to see Al."

Ruby shook her head. "You need to do me a favor and go to Molalla Jewelers. It's just across the street."

"There's something he's not telling you."

What had he done now? "Just tell me before I imagine the worst."

"I can't. All I can tell you is to go across the street and find out for yourself."

Isabelle huffed.

In the women's department, she found a half-slip and carried it to the front counter where she paid for it. And, then without telling Darlene, she exited Melton's Mercantile.

She waited for a logging truck to pass and then an old beater Ford before she made her way across the street to Molalla Jewelers, a brick building on the corner. The bell on the door announced her arrival in the brightly lit store.

Three feet inside, she stopped, her pulse pounding in her ears.

An older gentleman sat near the cash register.

"How many I help you?" A pear-shaped middle-aged woman turned from feather dusting a row of wristwatches. Then, dusting off her hands, she strode toward Isabelle. Her hair was chestnut colored and her diamond stud earrings large.

"Um . . ." Isabelle gleaned one more look of the place. It wasn't hard to imagine Albert falling in love here.

She'd pretend to act interested in diamond or rubies or something until Janet returned.

"I'm just getting ideas."

"Rings, necklaces, pendants . . . pearls?" The woman's glanced at Isabelle's left hand.

"Rings."

The woman smiled. And, because she was wearing a dress that was tight from her hips to the back of her knees, she took baby steps and rounded the side of the counter to the left of the door.

"Engagement rings, wedding bands, or just a lovely ring to wear?"

"Engagement rings. I hope that doesn't sound presumptuous." She had a hard time spitting out the word, on account of nerves.

"Take a seat," the woman said. "And, no, you don't sound presumptuous. We see young people in here dreaming and getting ideas all the time."

The place looked pretty empty to her, at least at the moment.

Isabelle took a seat in the padded chair, facing the counter.

The woman pulled small black velvet boxes from beneath the counter and set them on top of the glass.

Her name tag read: *Janet.*

Isabelle read it again. J-a-n-e-t. She hadn't been mistaken.

"Is there another Janet who works here?"

"No." The woman clicked open one of the boxes.

"Are you absolutely positive?"

"Yes." The woman glanced up at her. "My husband and I

have owned the store since…" And, while she peered over at the man at the register, Isabelle looked over her shoulder toward Molalla Ford.

Albert!

"Fifty . . . three," he said.

"Twelve years." Janet nodded.

The woman folded her arms on top of the counter and leaned slightly toward her. "Are you Isabelle?"

"How'd you know?"

The woman smiled. "Why do you ask if there's another Janet who works here?"

"Albert Gleinbroch purchased a ring here." Isabelle sat up a little taller, her hands in her lap. "He'd said he'd fallen in love with the girl who'd sold it to him—said her name was Janet."

The woman's expression dimmed then she glanced briefly at her husband.

"Didn't Albert propose at Thanksgiving?"

"No." A mist filled her eyes.

"Oh dear. . . Your choir trip must've thrown off his plans. He wasn't himself the day he picked up the ring."

What did she mean—his plans?

"Did you see him more than once?" Her voice trembled just a little.

Janet nodded. "He picked out the ring in January and paid an installment at the beginning of each month in cash."

Almost a full year of dreaming.

A gush of tears warmed her eyes.

"He'd hoped to be married at Christmas out at Wilhoit."

Albert.

She'd always just imagined him racing in and taking all of one minute to select a ring, slapping money down on the counter, and running out.

For almost a year, he'd told Janet a little of his hopes and dreams. More than he'd ever shared with her.

Oh, Albert.

"He thought you'd like a small wedding out at Wilhoit with your family. And, he wanted your elderly uncle to officiate."

It was a beautiful dream.

"Al . . ." She breathed. Five weeks ago, she would have loved that.

She covered her mouth with one hand.

She still loved it now.

"He was afraid it all might come as too big of a surprise." Janet lowered her chin and smiled softly. "I tried to tell him that he should feel a little more certain about your feelings before he invested such a... chunk of himself."

She could almost hear Janet say... *The diamond might not be big enough.*

Al had been fishing. She understood that now. There had been her chance—another missed opportunity—for her to tell him how much she'd always adored him.

Didn't he know?

"I've made such a mess of things," she whispered.

Janet shook her head. "What do you mean?"

Isabelle glanced down at her wristwatch. It was 3:45. She had fifteen minutes before Mrs. Hargett planned to pick them up at Melton's.

"Would you like to use our telephone?"

"No, thank you." Isabelle patted the surface of the glass counter before thinking about smudges. "Thank you for your time." Then, rising to her feet, she made her way for the heavy-plated glass door and outside into the crisp Christmas air.

She waited for an opening and crossed the street.

Why hadn't Al just told her? Told her the truth?

She wiped at tears and, past the front windows of Melton's Mercantile.

She didn't have time to see him. What was she thinking? Besides, he was at work. She shouldn't interrupt him there. Not with his new job.

Backtracking a few steps, she planted herself down on a bench beneath the department store's curlicue signage. Holding her purse in her lap, she stared out over Main Street and the sporadic flow of vehicles.

Albert loved her.

The day she'd left, he'd done everything but tell her in words.

She clicked open her purse for a handkerchief and quickly dabbed it against her cheeks. Her hankie carried the scent of her Aunt Elsie's White Shoulders perfume.

She had to see him. She got up and started half walking, half running. She made it to the cusp of the first side street when a car honked behind her.

Swallowing tears, she turned.

Mrs. Hargett's black station wagon rolled up behind her. Darlene waved through the passenger window before she rolled it down.

"Mrs. Hargett got done early. Sorry."

Maybe they could wait. Isabelle sniffled and hurried over and opened her door. "Mrs. Hargett, is it all—"

"I know I told you, girls, I'd give you an hour," Mrs. Hargett waved a hand, "but I forgot about my my roast in the oven."

Climbing into the back seat, Isabelle pulled the door closed behind her. She set her purse and bag down beside her and suffocated a sniffle.

"Darlene, did you find some shoes?" she asked.

"Yes, a nice red pair that will go with our sweaters."

"They're shocking!" Mrs. Hargett said.

Darlene ruffled through her bag and held up one tall, lipstick red stiletto.

They were shocking.

When they neared Molalla Ford, Isabelle peered over her shoulder. Through the showroom glass, there was no sign of Al's tall, broad-shouldered frame.

"Where were you heading?" Darlene asked.

"Oh, um . . ." She peered out her side window and didn't even try to answer her.

"You just disappeared. Where'd you go?" Darlene flipped down the visor and studied her in the little mirror.

"Just across the street."

"Molalla Jewelers?" Somehow, she knew.

"Yes." Isabelle stared out her side of the car as Mrs. Hargett turned onto Highway 213 heading back to Silverton. She'd have to wait until Monday to tell Al in person how much she loved him. She could make it a few more days.

CHAPTER 28

Ted had mentioned during his coffee break that Isabelle had tagged along with Darlene to Molalla. But, she was back now. The lyrics to "O Holy Night" and the echo of her sweet voice slipped through John's open office door. He couldn't just sit at his desk, not today. Not after his conversation with Nettie. Quietly, he closed his door behind him and walked through the foyer to the sanctuary.

Of the choir, only Ted and Isabelle were left.

Virginia, who often listened in the late afternoons, was seated in the middle row on the left side of the sanctuary, her silvery gray curls visible above the collar of her wool coat. She'd left space between herself and the aisle, almost like she'd been expecting him. John gripped the curve of the pew in front and sat down beside her.

"It's going to be very quiet after the girls leave," she whispered, leaning toward him.

"Too quiet." He didn't want to think about it.

Isabelle, in her red turtleneck with her dark hair loose about her shoulders, appeared younger than her twenty years.

"Do you need a ride home?" he whispered. It was Thursday.

She shook her head. "Dennis didn't go fishing."

During the final chorus, Isabelle held her hands knotted in front of her like she was trying to prepare herself for something. Her gaze locked briefly on his and then it drifted to the arched windows and the dusk-riddled sky.

Her voice filled every cavern in his heart.

"I thought I'd walk Isabelle home. Do you think that'll make the front page of the bulletin?"

"No. But, don't ask her to marry you. Begin with a walk."

He nodded. It was good advice.

* * *

"John . . ." Ted waved at him just as Isabelle started down the aisle. "You don't happen to know if anyone has a movie camera?"

"I do."

"Good." The elderly man approached, grinning. "I need to film the girls on Sunday. Lawrence Welk liked the tape that we sent. Now, he's requested that we send a film of them, too. My buddy Burt Cohen is going to hand deliver it."

"Wow! Ted, that's great." John glanced toward the foyer but couldn't see Isabelle from the angle he was at. "Wesley Hargett mentioned something the other day about the family's new movie camera."

"Good. I'll give them a call."

Lawrence Welk. John shook his head and strode toward the foyer. Standing near the coat rack, Isabelle buttoned up her coat.

"Hey," he paused a few feet shy of her. "Virginia doesn't need a ride today, so I was hoping I could walk you home."

She glanced over at him, surprised. "Dennis didn't go fishing?"

"No, not today." He shrugged on his wool coat.

"Yes, that works. Thank you."

If he wasn't mistaken, she seemed formal, hesitant.

He started down the stairs ahead of her and held open the door. Dusk had fallen, and it would be dark by the time they reached the Coopers. In front of his place, he stopped and set a hand on top of the picket gate. "This is the parsonage house, where I live."

For a moment, she studied the white bungalow in the fading light. "It looks very tidy."

"It's 840 square feet, two bedrooms, a tiny kitchen, a fireplace. Cozy." He remembered Virginia's advice, *to begin with a walk*.

His heart just wanted to run.

They continued toward Water Street in silence. At the end of the block, he glanced toward the Brazier's old place, a block away.

"Have you heard about Bobbie?" She probably had. Carolyn had probably told her. Everyone in the area knew about the dog.

"Bobbie who?" It was like a light that had flickered days earlier in her eyes had dimmed.

Still, he chuckled, happy that he'd be the one to tell her. "I thought for sure Carolyn had told you."

"Told me what?"

Nearly every day for the past five weeks, the girls had walked past the famous landmark. He was surprised and pleased that he'd be the first to share with her Silverton's most famous story.

"I'll tell you." He grinned, reaching for and just missing her hand as she started across Water Street ahead of him.

"This used to be the Reo Café." Shoulders touching, they

peered through the front windows of a small, vacant building. The space had been gutted down to the cement floor and over the years had changed hands several times. "The Brazier family owned it in the 1920s." He led the way to a nearby wooden bench and only a block and a half from church, they sat down.

Begin with a walk.

He wanted to take Isabelle's nearest hand, but she kept it clasped in front of her.

From the light of a nearby streetlight, he could tell that a blush grazed her cheeks.

"Where was I?" He rubbed his brow.

"The Brazier family used to own the café." She glanced over her shoulder toward the storefront.

"Yes. The story is about their dog, Bobbie—a Scotch collie."

"Like Lassie?"

"Yes, just like Lassie. Except Bobbie's a boy." He cleared his throat and then began the story. "In the summer of 1923, the Brazier family loaded up their car and took Bobbie with them to visit their relatives in Indiana." Silverton residents were weaned on the story. "In Indiana, when they stopped to get gas, Bobbie was chased away by a pack of dogs. For two weeks, the family searched for their Bobbie, but didn't find him."

"That's so sad," she breathed.

She thought it was the end of the story.

A man waved from inside the cab of a green truck that rolled by.

John waved back. Even though they were only seated next to each other on the bench, church gossip was inevitable now.

"Who was that?" Isabelle asked.

"Charlie Waggoner on his way home from work. His

wife's the one who painted the picture in my office." John peered over at her and smiled. He could already hear what Charlie would tell his wife, Beth.

"Oh."

"That's not all there is to the story, Isabelle. There's more." He studied her curious ebony eyes for a moment before continuing. "Heartbroken, the Braziers drove home from Indiana without Bobbie."

"Six months later, their daughter was walking with a friend here in town. She saw a skinny, abandoned looking dog and she pointed it out to her companion. "Oh! Look! Isn't that Bobbie?" she said. And, as soon as the girl said his name, the dog ran over to her.

"Six months, 2,500 miles later . . . Bobbie had found his way back to his family." He paused and smiled softly at her.

"That's not true. You just made that *all* up."

He chuckled softly, surprised by her vehemence. "It is true."

"It can't possibly be." Drawing in a breath, she peered across the street. "Darlene told you. Didn't she?" Tears filled her ebony gaze.

"Told me what, Isabelle?"

"Oh, you're good." Her face scrunched tightly.

"I think you're giving my storytelling a little too much credit." Did she think he'd come up with such a story to make her face her feelings for Albert? And, what did Darlene have to tell him... that Isabelle couldn't tell him? He sighed and gave her a couple of minutes to collect herself.

"Ask any resident here. Ask her," he nodded to an older woman passing nearby, a wrapped package in her arms.

Eyes closed, Isabelle shook her head.

"Bobbie's the most famous dog or person to ever live in Silverton. The story made the newspapers all over the world. Why would I make it up? The family received letters from people all over the world." He tucked a strand of hair behind her nearest ear. "What's going on?" he whispered.

She shook her head.

"I didn't mean to make you cry. I was pleased that I got to be the one to tell you." He chuckled and set an arm along the top of the bench behind her. "I guess part of living in this small town is you just assume everyone knows our story."

"John . . ." Turning, she met his gaze.

There'd been a dear-John note in her voice.

"When I went to Molalla today," she peered up at the lamplights and swallowed, "I didn't see Albert, but I saw his sister-in-law."

The news, her tone . . . it wasn't good.

"The day I left, he had a little black box. I never saw what was inside. I always thought that he bought the ring on the day I left to come here. That he must have hurried in on his lunch hour. But, no..." A tear slipped down her cheek. She brushed it aside. "I found out today, that every month for the last year, he's made payments at Molalla Jewelers." Her lashes, clumped with tears, fluttered.

He managed a soft smile and tried to be sensitive, even though his memory just wanted to return to Sunday and their visit with his grandparents and how for one evening, Isabelle had been his girl.

"You probably had to push your feelings for him aside just to come here." He'd mulled over that thought quite a bit these last five weeks.

"There you go again, saying just the right thing." She peered sadly across the street.

Had Lilly been right? *You're hoping to get this romance of yours all wrapped up by Christmas. When it's going to take her the rest of her life to forget him.*

Maybe Isabelle wouldn't try to forget him. Maybe she would end up marrying the man.

CHAPTER 29

"So, the first thing I do is take the tire off?" Isabelle held the receiver to her ear and scanned through her notes from Al for replacing both the starter and solenoid.

"No, the first thing you do is disconnect the battery. You don't want to electrocute yourself."

"I don't?" She smiled, glad that no one else was in the kitchen to hear her flirtatious tone.

"What's going on with the . . . pastor?"

"Not much." Her smile faded for a moment and then she thought about all Janet had told her. Al loved her... a lot. For a moment, she thought of getting married in front of the fireplace back home—just a small little wedding with their families present.

"I wish you could come help." She wanted to tell Al in person that she'd read his autograph and that she'd spoken with Janet. But, she might have to wait until Monday.

"Now that you bought both the starter and solenoid, it should be a piece of cake. Just have to pop it back up into the bell housing and tighten the bolts."

"Easy for you to say."

"Nothing's particularly hard, Izz, if you divide it into small parts."

"That sounds so profound."

"Henry Ford said it, I just repeated it."

"The guy at the auto parts store said that I'd probably need a man's help."

"You don't need a man for this, Izz. But, he might need you."

The back of her knees almost buckled.

"Does that mean you're coming?" Her voice wavered.

"I have a few things I need to finish around here. I'll do my best."

She smiled. That pretty much meant he'd be here.

* * *

"Hello," Nettie pressed the receiver to her ear.

"Nettie, it's Harriet. I have some good news."

"Oh." Harriet rarely called her. It must be good.

"John and Isabelle have made their relationship a little more public," Harriet said. "Yesterday afternoon when Charlie Waggoner was on his way home from work, he saw them sitting close together on a bench right on Water Street. Beth called here just a little while ago."

"Oh. That's the first I've heard." Nettie pulled aside the curtain and glanced toward their detached garage.

"Our prayers might very well have been answered," Harriet said.

"Not all of them. Poor Isabelle is alone in the garage, right now, as we speak, hacking away on Hilda. She doesn't want to be late for her duet again tomorrow, not that I blame her. Carolyn usually helps her, but Pete, her fiancé, is in town and took her out to Chinese food."

"You should call John this minute and let him know that

Isabelle's working on *your* car all by her lonesome. I'm sure he'd be more than happy to help."

"I'll call him right after I get off of the phone with you." Nettie pulled her little Silverton directory out of the nearby row. "You know, Ted's going to film the girls tomorrow for Lawrence Welk. Pray that we're on time. We'd feel plum terrible if the girls' duet ended up being Darlene's solo."

* * *

ALBERT HAD LIED... again! Putting in a new starter and solenoid unit was not a piece of cake—at least, not for a woman of her size. It had taken every last ounce of her strength and determination to get it up into the bell housing. Feeling around on the ground beside her, she found the wrench and started in on tightening the bolts.

Someone tapped on the hood of the car.

She peered toward her feet. On the passenger side of the vehicle, she could see a pair of men's shoes and the cuffs of his slacks. Was it Al?

"Isabelle, it's John." His knees cracked as he crouched down. "Nettie called and thought you might appreciate a little company."

Oh, Nettie! She winced. "Um... wait a sec... I'm almost done."

With her luck, Al could show up any minute and think the worst.

In the tight space beneath the vehicle, she stalled for a moment and removed the folded paper from her chest pocket. She shone the flashlight on her scribblings. *Tighten all the bolts* was indeed the last step.

"Nettie said you called Albert again and he walked you through how to fix it."

"Yes. I ended up installing a new starter and solenoid. It's supposed to be easier than replacing the solenoid all by itself."

"Wow! Well, it sure looks like you know what you're doing," he said, probably in reference to the tire laid down in front of the frame, and the jacked-up chassis.

"Al walked me through every step."

"How much longer before you're finished under there?"

Taking off the yellow glasses, she slid them into the chest pocket of Mr. Cooper's old wool coat. "I'm done. If you would be so kind to pull the towel slowly toward you."

"Oh, okay. That's a nice little trick," he said tugging her to daylight.

Heaven only knew what she looked like in the old Russian-looking fur hat, but the way John stayed crouched, grinning at her, he didn't seem to mind. Even though she'd already told him her feelings for Al, he looked like he needed to hear it all over again.

"When I spoke with Al on the phone . . ." She sat up and because she knew she looked like a goofball, took off the hat, and ran a hand through her loose hair.

"Izz . . ."

It wasn't John speaking. Her heart hammered in her chest. Was Albert finally here?

"Isabelle . . ." Al's voice echoed through the garage.

John rose and looked over the hood.

"Al?" Setting a hand on the side of the car, she clambered to her feet. "I just finished." Even though his timing was awkward, she smiled at the sight of him standing near the doorway. Wearing jeans, a thick coat and a pair of boots,

he looked like the Marlboro Man on the billboards, but even better.

"Sorry that it took me so long." He glanced at John.

"I was just about to start it and see if it works."

He nodded. "Did you reconnect the battery?"

"No, not yet."

"That always helps." He strode to the front of the car.

"Let me do it." She rounded the side of the vehicle to join him.

"Sure thing."

While she reconnected and tightened the battery cables, Al and John stood one on each side of her, overlooking her work. She brushed past Al on her way to the driver's side.

A few feet away, John turned a crate upright, sat down on it and folded his arms in front of him like he didn't plan on going anywhere.

She slid behind the steering wheel and said a prayer. Then, closing her eyes, she said one for Hilda, too. She pumped the gas pedal a couple of times and turned the key.

Hilda started right up or, as Al would say, the engine turned on a dime.

Al dropped the hood.

While the engine purred, she sat back in the seat and closed her eyes, grinning. Then her mind returned to her present circumstances.

Lord, please help me.

Everybody thinks I'm the Heaven Sent, but I'm not.

I'm just Al's.

She turned off the engine and glanced at Al. "Was it just a fluke? Will it still start tomorrow?"

"That was the sound of a happy engine."

"Good job, Isabelle," John gave her a weak smile. Then, he looked at Al. "I just got here a little while ago myself."

Gripping the steering wheel with both hands, she tried to get her wits about her. She'd fixed Hilda. Now she just needed to fix her love life.

Al rounded the side of the car and stopped about six feet away—the same distance as John. Feet planted shoulder width apart; he folded his arms in front of him.

While they waited on her, the tension in the garage increased.

John wasn't going anywhere. Even though she'd already tried to tell him, he was as thick skulled as Albert.

All she wanted to do was curl down in the seat and lock the door.

"Did ya tell him yet?" Al leaned his head towards John. "Did ya tell him about the dent in my truck?"

"Not." Her voice sounded like Minnie Mouse. "I didn't tell him about your awful proposal either." Oh, Al. Was he going to tell John everything?

"Five weeks ago . . ." Al said, looking at John.

He was.

She cringed.

"Izz was so upset with me . . ." Al tipped his head toward her. "You see, I'd parked across Wilhoit Road and got her hopes up a little, I guess. She was sold out on coming here, and I was being selfish. I was hoping that she loved me so much that she wouldn't…"

During his long pause, she met his gaze.

"I was hoping you *couldn't* leave me. I didn't tell you that." A mist glazed his eyes.

Tears hung heavy in her own, daring her to blink.

"I had a ring in my pocket. But, when I bent my knee to the road, the first thing she did was look over my shoulder toward Silverton. I knew it wasn't a good sign." His voice plummeted. "And, I said some things, Izz, that I'm sorry for."

Al had just said the word. He never said *sorry*.

"We had a little fight. But, I can't stop thinking…" he shook his head, "that you must love me. And, that I got your hopes up. Otherwise, you wouldn't have done what you did." He swallowed then looked over again at John. "She threw a rock at my truck, dented it in the rear fender."

John's eyes widened. Then, he nodded and crossed his arms.

"I've taken it in twice to Shorty's Auto Repair in Molalla. But, I can't bring myself to have it fixed.

"You see . . ." Al gazed softly at her. "I've had this crazy notion that you threw that rock 'cause you love me."

Al was broken. Broken as she'd ever seen him. Ever wanted to see him.

"And, it's funny . . ." He wasn't done. "How I keep hearing from everybody—that you've loved me ever since you were eight...years...old."

"She's told me that, too," John said.

She turned slowly and, over her shoulder, noted John's solemn expression.

One corner of his mouth lifted as he tried to smile at her.

"But, of course, she never told me." Al's voice was lighter now. "I had to hear it from everybody else."

Aunt Elsie must have slipped from sworn secrecy. Maybe Mae had, too.

Albert. Oh, Albert.

John still sat, arms folded in front of him. Like he hadn't been wounded deeply enough yet, to leave the fight.

"After I gave you instructions on the phone, I ended up calling back. I forgot to remind you one more time about disconnecting the battery so you wouldn't electrocute yourself. And, I gave the message to Mrs. Cooper." Al swallowed, taking his time. "That's when she told me, too, Izz, that you've loved me ever since you were eight. How you've told everybody around here. I felt it was a sign."

Al had always been a fourth-quarter all-star. When everyone else was running down the court battered, bruised and winded, it was Albert's Gleinbroch's time to shine.

"I don't want to lose you, Izz. Elsie kept telling me not to hold you back. That you needed time on your own. A chance to follow your dream. Lord knows He gave you the voice for it."

Her throat burned with tears.

"But, I have to live with not telling you how I feel. And, I have to try to make up for that awful proposal. Izz, the hardest thing I've ever done in my life was letting you go."

A tear slipped down her cheek now, right in front of John.

"Is it true?" Al sucked in a breath. "That you were crying out front of Melton's? Ruby said she saw you—sobbing and looking west."

"I wasn't sobbing."

"What were you crying about then?"

"I was . . ." She pinched the bridge of her nose, and then she covered her mouth with one hand, trying to contain all these years of loving Al. She inhaled. "I was crying… because you told Janet more than you'd ever told me."

Through a blur of tears, she saw John rise to his feet, cross the garage, and pat Albert's shoulder. Then he made his way out the door.

"I had it all planned, Izz." Albert walked toward her and bent one knee to the concrete in the expanse of the driver's side door.

She sniffled and smiled at the same time.

He took her hand. "Originally, I'd planned to propose at Thanksgiving. You know, that was before you signed up for the choir. I was such a fool." He gazed softly into her eyes. "I didn't want you to go. I was so selfish, 'cause I was so worried."

She leaned over to hug him, and, burying her cheek in the curve of his neck, she breathed him in. His shirt smelled like the firewood used to heat the old hotel and like a splash of his Old Spice Cologne. Al smelled like home.

"I've made such a mess of things here." Tightening her arms around his neck, she stifled a sob.

"Did he already propose?"

"No." She shook her head.

"Well, don't throw any rocks at his truck. He'll get over you quicker that way." He kissed the top of her forehead and just held her while she cried.

CHAPTER 30

"About time," Darlene said.

Isabelle stood beside her, savoring her view of the congregation. This morning, Hilda had started on a dime and got the Coopers to the church on time.

Come on, Al. Where are you? You told me you'd be here. She scanned the back of the sanctuary for her sweetheart.

She needed his presence to help her face Silverton this morning.

He stepped through the double doors. Wearing his nice suit and tie, Al shook a greeter's hand and took a seat near the back. When he looked toward the podium, their eyes met.

"*Pitter patter. Pitter patter,*" Darlene whispered ever so softly.

Isabelle almost elbowed her then she realized Darlene's pitter-pattering was about John. He walked up the center aisle.

He was too nice for Darlene.

Please, Lord, send John someone special. Someone who loves

Jesus, who loves others, and who loves him. Someone whose heart isn't already taken. Isabelle's gaze returned to Al's.

She'd learned that much in Silverton.

The time on her wristwatch read ten o'clock straight up.

The Coopers were seated.

John was now seated.

Everyone was ready, except for Mr. Hoffmeister who was sitting in the front row. On his left, Wesley Hargett showed him how to operate the family's new Kodak movie camera.

Isabelle's gaze drifted to John. He smiled slightly and blinked.

He was going to be okay. *Thank you, Lord.*

She flinched as Darlene pinched her in the side, right between the ribs.

Isabelle snaked her right hand beneath her left elbow and pinched her equally good right below her Cross Your Heart bra.

"That's enough, girls," Mr. Hoffmeister said from the front row.

Chuckles rippled through the packed sanctuary.

Isabelle's gaze settled on Lilly's in the second row.

Pointing to and lifting both sides of her mouth, Lilly reminded her that it wasn't every day you were filmed for the Lawrence Welk Show in front of a live audience.

She breathed in deeply and smiled.

"This is my big chance. Don't blow it for me." Darlene eyed the congregation.

The girl was as abrasive as steel wool.

"Then, you shouldn't have worn those shoes," Isabelle said.

"What do you mean?"

Didn't she know? Everybody knew. "Lawrence Welk is very conservative. Remember what happened to the first Champagne Lady—Alice Lon?"

"No-oo. What?"

"She showed a little bit too much leg in a show, and he fired her. She'd been with him for years."

Darlene gulped. "We'll just have to film again tonight."

"We can't. Mr. Cohen's leaving this afternoon." The man was going to hand deliver the film to Lawrence Welk.

"Mr. Hoffmeister," Darlene whispered.

He didn't look up.

"Mr. Hoffmeister . . ." she said louder, "don't film my shoes!"

He peered down at her bright red stiletto heels and blinked. Then, his bushy brows lifted above his glasses.

"You should have told me this earlier." Darlene pinched her.

Reality began to sink in. Los Angeles was a thousand miles away, not twenty.

If they made it big-time, she might spend the rest of her life in L.A. being bossed around by Darlene Berry. When everything she wanted was... Isabelle's gaze drifted to the back row.

Darlene pinched her again. "Pay attention."

Wesley rose and returned to sit with his family in the fourth row. People who'd been gabbing turned in their seats to face the front. The sanctuary quieted to *a hushing silence* that you could feel. Word had obviously got around that this morning their duet was being filmed for the Lawrence Welk Show in front of a live audience just like the man had requested.

Adrenaline surged in Isabelle's limbs.

Mr. Hoffmeister gave them a thumbs up. Then he lifted the pint-sized camera, pressed down on a button, and a red light came on.

"Smile." Darlene leaned toward her, smiling through her pearly whites.

The camera was rolling.

Lawrence Welk would hear this, see this.

Isabelle chewed on her lower lip and smiled.

Then, as rehearsed, Darlene clasped her nearest arm in Isabelle's so they'd both only have to worry about one. Holding her right hand palm up and shoulder high, she lifted her gaze to the bow of the boat-shaped windows.

Help me, Lord, help me to sing for you. Not Darlene. Not Lawrence Welk. For You.

She stilled her soul and remembered John's words: *Two thousand years ago, the Light of the World left heaven and the glory of His Father's side to be born a baby.*

Then, she breathed in and sang.

"Sil-ent night. Ho-ly night."

Her gaze drifted to Al's.

"All is calm, all is bright."

Isabelle's gaze drifted to the fourth pew and Frank Hugg. Tears already glistened in the elderly man's eyes.

"Round yon Virgin, Mother and Child."

The retired pastor and his wife had been praying for her every Sunday since she was eight years old.

"Holy infant so tender and mild."

Her gaze drifted to Lilly's in the second pew.

"Sleep in heavenly peace."

Their duet was flowing. As they continued singing, Frank dabbed a handkerchief to his cheek.

Today was their last Sunday in Silverton. The moment was bittersweet.

"Christ the Savior is born."

Nettie's beaming smile couldn't have owned her more.

"Silent night. Holy night!"

Her gaze settled on Harriet, and the elderly woman's gentle smile reassured her that she was forgiven.

"Son of God, love's pure light."

Isabelle's right arm felt all stiff and wonky. Darlene, the more expressive of the two, embraced all of America with her sweeping left arm.

"Radiant beams from thy holy face."

Isabelle didn't want to go to Hollywood or Los Angeles or wherever The Lawrence Welk Show was filmed. It was more Darlene's cup of tea. She was good with her arms.

"With the dawn of redeeming grace."

"Jesus, Lord at Thy birth." The end was near. Isabelle caressed the final notes.

"Jesus, Lord at Thy birth." She lowered her right hand palm up, to her side.

Their audience clapped.

Mr. Hoffmeister lowered the camera to his lap and fumbled with the top buttons before turning it off.

"Oh, no!" Darlene moaned. "He just got my shoes."

CHAPTER 31

Monday morning, when John unlocked the church, he assumed he was the first person in the drafty old building; but, when he flicked on the lights in his office, he saw that someone else had already been there.

A plate of frosted Christmas cookies sat atop his desk, a little card taped to the Saran Wrap.

Pastor Hugg,
You are a blessing to all of us.
Merry Christmas.

They hadn't left a name.

He fingered the card, thoughtfully. When he'd locked up last night, the plate hadn't been here.

Virginia had a key. A number of people in the church family had keys, but who would have visited so early?

His books, stacked in a pile only yesterday, now lined the shelves in a tidy row—and were proof that it had been his grandmother who'd visited. Extra energy was in the air and a trace of sweet floral perfume. It was the start of the Christmas week, and the ladies were making their rounds today, quite possibly all seven of them.

His mind wanted to dwell on happy times, but his heart was heavy.

He sat down in his swivel chair and sighed. "You were there for me, Lord, during Grandpa's stroke," he whispered. "And, You were—"

The phone rang on the desk beside him.

To his knowledge, he was still the only person in the building.

He cleared his throat and lifted the receiver to his ear. "Calvary Christian Church, this is John speaking."

"John Hugg," Lilly's voice wavered on the other end of the line.

He glanced at his wristwatch. It was eight o'clock. Was she at home or work?

"Where are you, Lilly?"

"Your church people broke into my home when I was asleep." Her voice broke.

"What do you mean? Is something missing?"

"No-oo. They left stuff. That's how I know it was them." She sniffled. "It must have been this morning or the middle of the night. I can't believe I slept through it. But, everything is full. All my cupboards and drawers. The fridge and even the freezer compartment are stuffed to the gills."

He heard the tears now. She was so thrilled that she was crying.

Lord Jesus, thank you.

"You put them up to this. Didn't you?"

"No, I didn't put anyone up to anything."

"Yes, you did. It's just like you."

"Lilly, I didn't. I didn't tell anyone. Except for…" He tried to remember if he'd told—

"Not even God?"

"I've prayed for you, yes, but . . ."

"Was it the old lady then?"

"Do you mean Virginia?"

"Yes. It had to be her." Her voice dribbled. "It had to be. My place smells like old ladies—like rosewood perfume."

"Many people love you, Lilly."

"Name some." She sniffled, and he heard the brush of her hand across her cheek.

"Well, there's Joann Goff, my grandmother . . ." He had to be careful and not name all seven of the women who were probably behind it. "And, Nettie Cooper cares a great deal for you."

"I knew it was the old ladies."

"It could also have been Carolyn, the Coopers, my family…"

"Do you think they did it?"

"My family?"

"No, the old ladies group—the Seven Blocks of Granite. Tommy used to talk about them. I think they've been behind it, all along. Don't you?"

He suppressed a smile. Very few things slipped past the Granite Girls. "Yes, it could very well have been Virginia."

"I know they're trying to remain anonymous." She sucked in a breath. "But I recognize Harriet's handwriting on the lid of her canned pears. And there are three jars of Rose's famous dilly beans. And… there's even a Swanson turkey dinner in my freezer.

"It was Virginia," Lilly's voice broke. "Because everything I looked at in the store with her that day and didn't buy, is here. The saltines, the Worcestershire sauce, the VO5 hairspray.

"John," Lilly sniffled, "can you give me your grandmother's number?"

"Yes." He smiled. "Do you have a pen?"

"Yes. They even left me one of those."

He chuckled and gave her the number.

"I'm going to call Harriet and tell her that when I grow up," Lilly inhaled and sighed, "I want to be just like the old ladies and give back all this love. You see, it's not just food that's in my cupboards. Love and prayers are in there, too. I can feel them."

Thank you, Lord, for everything.

"Merry Christmas, Lilly."

She inhaled a shaky breath. "Merry Christmas, John."

He hung up and pinched the bridge of his nose. "You work all things together for good." He reminded the Lord and himself.

He paused, recalling Isabelle's only visit to his office. How she'd been a little nervous when she'd stood in front of his desk. What had she said?

. . . the big shoes you're so worried about filling, I think you already have.

Maybe she was right. Maybe the time had come.

He rose from his chair and moved the painting that for over fifteen years had hung on the wall behind his grandfather's desk.

He found a hammer and nail from the closet in the hallway. Then, he eyeballed the space where Isabelle thought it should hang, found a stud, and hammered in a sturdy nail. Upon it, he hung the lovely painting of the little white church in spring with the thousands of daffodils abloom in the front beds.

He sat down in the chair nearest the door and eyed the picture's new placement. It looked perfect there. Then, he gazed thoughtfully around *his* office.

CHAPTER 32

The telephone rang in Nettie's kitchen nook.
"Hello," she said into the mouthpiece.
"Praise the Lord!" Opal exclaimed.
"What's happened?"
"Darlene just left. Praise the Lord!"
Surely that wasn't all she was going on about.
"Having her stay in our home was like forty days of temptation for a young man. You just don't know how she behaved. But... praise the Lord! Wesley grew in his faith. And, I made sure that Darlene memorized scripture each and every day. I'll admit it's going to be quiet around here without her. But, praise the Lord!"
"I agree. It's going to be quiet around here, too, without our choir girls." Nettie paused for a moment and heard only Russell's snores in the front room. "Carolyn's fiancé already came and picked her up. And, Isabelle's upstairs packing."
"Now that Darlene's no longer here, I must admit that she gave me the sweetest hug before she left. She said that she did the Christmas choir for her parents to get a little more

Jesus in her before she heads to Hollywood to live with her uncle's family." Opal sniffled.

"I sure hope we get to do this again next year." Nettie pulled a Kleenex from the pocket of her housecoat and dabbed at her eyes. "We had so much fun—Carolyn and Isabelle and, John Hugg here all the time, trying not to stare at her with moonlight in his eyes."

"Mrs. Cooper . . ." Isabelle strolled into the kitchen and spotted her. "My sister's here." Wearing her long wool coat and heels, Isabelle looked like she was going to church.

"Opal, stay on the line." Retaining her grip on the receiver, Nettie reached out both arms and wrapped them around Isabelle's shoulders, pulling the dear girl close.

"Forgive me for my cooking. I'm sure no one warned you. Russell told me years ago that he'd rather have a clean kitchen and a TV dinner than a dirty kitchen and a terrible dinner. And, I took him to heart."

"I wouldn't have traded you or your cooking for the world," Isabelle said, loud enough for Opal to hear.

Then, Isabelle took a step back. "Thank you for everything. I'm going to miss you all."

"Well, you better not stay away too long." Covering the mouthpiece now, Nettie followed her to the doorway into the living room. "Have you read my autograph yet?"

"No, but I'll read it in the car."

"Wake Russell. He'll want to give you a hug, too."

"Stay on the line, Opal," Nettie whispered into the receiver.

Then she watched as Isabelle tapped softly on Russell's shoulder. His arms jumped a bit off of the armrest.

"Do you need me to start the car?" he asked, groggily.

"No, my sister's here to pick me up." She leaned down, speaking louder than she probably needed to for him. "Thank you for everything."

"Don't stay away too long. We all like you here," her sweet Russell said.

"Thank you." Isabelle nodded, tears surfacing in her gaze.

"We'll miss you." Nettie waved.

"I'll miss you, too." And, then their choir girl walked toward the entry, picked up her suitcase, and waved before pulling the door closed behind her.

"Oh, Opal, that was so hard." Nettie patted a hand to her heart. "Did you hear what she said to me?"

"Yes, I did, Nettie."

"I can't believe our girls are already gone."

"Between now and next Christmas, we're going to pray for the Good Lord to send us two nice, Christian choir girls. One for my Wesley and one for John!"

"Oh, I agree, Opal, that should be our prayer."

* * *

WHILE MAE DROVE NORTH on Water Street, Isabelle pulled her autograph book out of her coat pocket. Just like had Aunt Elsie had written, the little book had captured many memories for her of her stay in Silverton.

"How's everyone?" Isabelle asked while she turned the pages.

"Good. Trevor's watching the kids for me while he works. Jack's helping, too." Mae laughed softly.

"Oh." A new autograph was on the page after Carolyn's.

Isabelle,

Remember me you must

Whenever you bite into a Swanson crust.

We loved having you as our choir girl.

I hope you never forget your stay in Silverton.

She never would.

Isabelle fingered the page, thoughtfully.

Nettie Cooper - 1965

"What are you reading?" Mae asked.

"Mrs. Cooper's autograph. She was the last person to sign my book."

"Oh, how are you and Albert?"

Isabelle smiled and heaved a heavy sigh. "Silverton agreed with me in a lot of ways, you know. But..." She thought on Albert, and the ache in her chest went bone deep. "If I hadn't gone, there're so many things I would have missed out on. So many people." She gripped the little book in her lap and wished now that she'd had Darlene and Evelyn sign her book, and Lilly, too. And, she was so glad that John had written what he had.

She could leave her autograph book out in the open at Wilhoit, and his sentiments would never hurt Albert.

"You're going home now." Mae's soft voice reminded her.

"I know." Smiling, she stared out her side of the old truck at the Douglas fir trees lining the road. "Did Al tell you that he wrote two autographs in my book?"

"No-oo." Her sister laughed.

"Yep. He did. The second one was far better than the first. Seems he loves me. Loves me a lot." She sighed and twirling a strand of her loose hair around one finger gazed out the side window. She'd be home for dinner, and they could sit in front of the fire like old times.

Mae took the shortcut home through Scotts Mills, through the back hills and the old logging roads of the area. At the fork at Leabo Road, she made a right onto Wilhoit Road.

A half mile later, she shifted into a lower gear, giggling for some reason.

"Looks like Al has something to tell you in person."

"What are you talking about?" Isabelle followed her gaze

to Albert's black Ford truck parked sideways in the middle of the two-lane country road.

She shook her head. The two must have coordinated their plans a bit for him to welcome her home on his lunch hour.

She peered across the cab at her sister, curbing a smile.

Mae brought the old Model A to a jerky stop.

Thirty feet away, Al was just sitting in his truck.

Fortunately, the old dead-end road leading to the resort didn't get much traffic this time of year.

Albert's door swung open. With tears in her eyes, she watched him get out—all six-feet and four-inches of him.

"Prepare your heart, Izz," Mae said.

"Do you know something I don't?" she said for old time's sake.

"He parked across the road, didn't he?"

"Yes. I can say that much for him."

Arms tingly, she lowered one high heel to the paved road and then the other before closing the truck door behind her.

Al stood waiting in a nice pair of trousers, a white button-up shirt and a new striped tie that Ruby had probably helped him pick out for the occasion. He riffled a hand through his dark hair. He was better looking than Clark Gable and James Dean.

She wasn't exaggerating.

"Hey, Al." She halted a few feet away. "Kind of makes it feel all serious, you parked across the road, like that." She held her breath.

Then, her gaze traveled from his truck to his darkly lashed blue eyes.

"That coat sure looks *great* on you." He grinned. Then he lowered one knee to the asphalt, and holding out a little black velvet box, gazed up at her.

She didn't wait for his proposal.

She just flung her arms around him and buried her face in his neck.

She didn't need words anymore.

She just needed Al.

The end.

CHRISTMAS CHOIR SERIES

There is the potential for at least two more romances in the *Christmas Choir Girl Series.* I'd love to hear your feedback. I have several series going on, and it helps me a great deal when readers reach out and let me know which books/series they enjoy the most.

My email is christianromances@gmail.com

My website is www.christianromances.com

If you'd like to leave a review
for Heaven Sent on Amazon.
It would be greatly appreciated!

Acknowledgements and two recipes follow:

HARRIET'S BANANA CREAM DESSERT

I usually refrigerate it for at least 12 hours before serving.

Crust:
  10 Tablespoons melted butter
  1/2 cup chopped pecans or walnuts
  1 ¼ cup flour
  Preheat oven to 325' F.

Mix the crust ingredients in the glass 9 x 13 glass pan. Then, I press the buttery-ball mixture with a sheet of waxed paper (otherwise, it's sticky) until the bottom of pan is covered. Bake in for 20 minutes or until lightly browned. Cool completely.

Topping:
  1 - 8-ounce package cream cheese, softened to room temperature
  1 cup powdered sugar
  8 to 9-ounce container Cool Whip
  2 x 4-serving-size packages vanilla instant pudding
  3 cups milk

HARRIET'S BANANA CREAM DESSERT

    1 teaspoon vanilla
    Bananas, sliced

Beat together cream cheese and powdered sugar and fold in Cool Whip until thoroughly mixed. Spread over cooled crust. Beat pudding mix, milk and vanilla until thickened. Pour over Cool Whip layer. Chill at least four hours or overnight.

Right before serving, slice bananas over the top.

HEAVEN SENT MOLASSES COOKIES

2/3 cup oil
 1 cup sugar
 1 egg
 ¼ cup molasses
 2 cups flour
 2 teaspoons baking soda
 ½ teaspoon salt
 2 teaspoons ginger
 1 teaspoon cinnamon
 ½ teaspoon cloves
 Extra sugar in a saucer for rolling

Preheat oven to 350' F.

Mix oil, sugar, and egg and beat well. Stir in molasses. In a separate bowl, mix the dry ingredients with a whisk and then add to the rest of the ingredients. Mix well. Roll walnut-sized balls in sugar sand place on sprayed cookie sheet. Bake 8 to 10 minutes until golden brown on the bottom. Don't overbake or they'll be crisp. These cookies are ideally chewy.

HEAVEN SENT MOLASSES COOKIES

Freeze the dough: Shape the dough into balls, roll in sugar, and freeze on a baking sheet. Then pop into storage containers and bake when company drops by.

OTHER ROMANCES BY SHERRI

Ethel King Series:
<u>*Sticky Notes – Book One*</u> <u>audio</u>
The Sticky Buns Challenge <u>audio</u>

Counterfeit Princess Series - *for ages 10 to 107*
<u>*The Piano Girl*</u> <u>audio</u>
<u>*The Viola Girl*</u> <u>audio</u>

Standalone Romances:
<u>*Fried Chicken and Gravy*</u> <u>audio</u>
<u>*A Wife and a River*</u> <u>audio</u>
Heaven Sent - audio in the works

FINAL ACKNOWLEDGEMENTS

There are numerous people I need to thank for their help with this novel.

My three main editors: Patty Slack, my line editor/story editor. You helped me meet a tough deadline, pointed so many things - and did a fantastic job, again; Kristi Weber, for your quick turn around and for rewriting my wrongs; and Jean Hall, for your help with descriptions and your encouragement. And, lastly, my daughter Cori Murray for her brutal honesty that was so helpful in the rewrite.

[Click here to contact Patty Slack, Editor](#)

I've worked on this book for many years. I considered it finished at one point, but set it off to the side to simmer for a while. Then a couple of summers ago, I bought two little autograph books at an estate sale. They weren't in very good shape, but I was so intrigued that I plunked down ten dollars for them. The autographs were dated 1941. I went home and read them and was inspired to rewrite *Heaven Sent* again to include some of the autographs that were written inside. John and Ted's autographs are not my own work. I wanted to thank the dear men and ladies who wrote them.

FINAL ACKNOWLEDGEMENTS

-I'd also like to thank Judy Lowery and Fred Parkinson from the Silverton Historical Society—for their help and the fun we had that day exploring old newspapers and advertisements from the 1960's.

-The article in liberaluniversity.org regarding Bobbie – The Wonder Dog of Oregon.

-The article on ourtownlive.com regarding the history of Roth's Grocery Stores in Oregon.

-My dear friend, Annette Bartausky, who inspired Nettie's melted wig scene, a true story that happened to her mother. The wording is almost Nettie's word for word.

-My good friend, Carol Chapman, for her help with choir-girl terms.

-Trifive.com was helpful in researching automotive repair and Don's post from Acardon's Garage for the Bel Air solenoid information.

-My Uncle Norris who wrote "Prayer changes things" in a letter to me when I was in my mid-twenties and going through a difficult time. He was so right.

Heaven Sent

Copyright © 2017 by Sherri Schoenborn Murray

Christian Romances

This is a work of fiction, all characters, places and incidents are used fictitiously. Any resemblance to actual persons, either living or dead is entirely coincidental.

All rights are reserved. No part of this publication can be reproduced or transmitted in any form or by any means, including photocopying, recording, or other electronic or mechanical methods, without the prior written permission of the publisher, except in brief quotations that are embodied in reviews and specific noncommercial uses permitted by copyright law. For permission of said requests, please contact the author through her website:

❦ Created with Vellum

Made in the USA
Middletown, DE
01 December 2017